Undeniable

By

Amy Marie

Self-publishing
AuthorAmyMarie@yahoo.com

Cover Design: Sara Eirew Photographer

Editing by Kathy Krick

Formatting: Angel's Indie Formatting

Dedication

To my son. My buggy-boo. My main man and the one who melts my heart every single day with his puppy dog brown eyes and cute smile.

Always remember you promised to cuddle me when you're big like Batman.

Prologue

Hadley

Seven Years Ago

I walk down the crowded hallways of Wheeling High School the first day of my senior year trying to decide if I look different. I mean I feel different, but I'm wondering if everyone who passes me can tell something has changed.

I try to go unnoticed, looking down at my schedule, in love with the fact that I have my favorite subject–art–during first period.

I'm startled as an ear piercing scream fills the halls, and I don't have to look up to find that it belongs to my best friend, Emie. The sound of excitement gets closer, and her purple sparkly flip flops come into my downward view.

"Did you dye the tips of your hair pink?" She shrieks not moving an inch and blocking me from making my way to class.

I finally glance up and notice a look of disgust across her face.

"There is nothing wrong with my hair, Emie. You're just a prude," I comment taking in her appearance.

When they say opposites attract they were talking about Emie and me. She is shorter than me, curly blonde hair that flows down to the middle of her back, bright blue eyes that pierce you with any stare, and her clothes could land her in a commercial for The Gap. She is captain of the cheerleading squad and student council president. She is the opposite end of the spectrum from me. At five feet seven, I'm on the taller side, medium length brown hair, with bright pink tips, as Emie so nicely pointed out, no makeup over my green eyes, and I usually have paint on some part of my clothes that were purchased from Wal-Mart.

"I'm not a prude," she says insulted. "I gave it up to Todd Mitchell over the summer. You, my friend, still have yet to lose your V card."

I inwardly smile thinking about last night and how amazing it was. Shaking away the thoughts, I continue the trek to my first class. "Where are you off to?" I ask.

She sighs twirling a strand of hair between her fingers. "Gym. Can you believe that? Who wants to get all sweaty first thing in the morning?"

I inwardly giggle thinking of how I wouldn't have minded getting a little sweaty this morning.

We walk together down the hall, and I try not to acknowledge Ryder Blake as he walks towards us.

"Oh my God, Had. Did you see how sexy Ryder looks today? He gained some hot muscle over the summer." Emie quietly gushes over the most popular guy in our class.

At over six feet tall and pulled in all the right

directions black hair, with the bluest eyes you have ever seen, he makes the rest of the guys in our class look like boys. He is on the varsity football team but tends to get into trouble. Because he is the quarterback, and he helps our crappy team win most of their games, teachers tend to look the other way when he does whatever the hell he wants.

He walks past us, eyeing my body up and down, before a sideways smirk crosses his lips. His jeans fit snugly to his body, and his long fingers grasp the black straps of his backpack over his hunter green shirt. I try not to smile.

"He's alright," I answer her, shrugging. "Nothing to write home about."

"Ugh, Hadley," she says annoyed. "You really are blind, you know that?"

I leave her at the door to the locker room and walk the rest of the way to art.

I feel at home as I enter the art room. I've spent a lot of time in here over the past three years. I had the chance to go to Chicago High School of the Arts this year but decided I wanted to stay here. I'd like to say it was because the program here was good, but I knew better than that.

The large rectangular shaped wooden desks are positioned in the same places as last year, and I stop mid-stride when I find Ryder sitting at one of them talking to the teacher, Mrs. Cray.

When he notices me standing there his eyebrow quirks up.

"Hadley!" Cray greets me. "I was just asking Ryder here to pull some supplies out of the storage closet. Do you mind helping?"

I place my bag on a table at the opposite side of the room and nod my head unable to find my voice.

Ryder passes by me invading my personal space, and my heart rate immediately picks up. Regardless of what I said to Emie, he is smoking hot. You'd have to be dead not to notice.

Following behind him back down the hall, he opens the door to the closet lifting his arm for me to cross under. The door slams shut, and darkness fills the tiny space.

Ryder's hands find my hips and whirl me around, pushing me up against the door. His soft lips crash into mine like a freight train and I reach up gripping the hair at the nape of his neck between my fingers.

He pulls away, but I can still feel his lips close to mine. "I was hoping I wouldn't have to wait until tonight to touch you again," he whispers kissing me again. "Are you sore?"

My focus goes to the arousal starting to pool between my legs feeling a slight discomfort. "A little bit," I answer.

"It'll get better." He comforts me. "That was just the first time. Next time will be easier."

"When can we tell people we're together?" I ask breathlessly.

He kisses my nose and drags his mouth down to my lips. "Soon, I promise."

His hand slips up my tank top finding my cotton covered breast. He pulls the left cup down and takes my nipple between his thumb and pointer finger. It feels incredible and thoughts of last night rise to the surface of my thoughts again.

"Ryder," I quietly moan out.

"I'll always treasure what you gave me yesterday, Hadley. I promise. I love you," he tells me causing all sorts of fluttering in my chest.

"I love you too Ryder," I breathlessly tell him.

The alarm screams promptly at six a.m. I lean over reaching for the dream interrupter and hit the snooze button.

The sheets feel warm as I roll onto my back, staring up at the plain white ceiling, just wanting to fall back asleep. My ears perk up as I listen to Braden, my boyfriend of two years, move around in my bathroom. It's not hard to hear everything since my studio apartment is the size of a normal living room. It's all I can afford, and it's really all I need. Braden doesn't understand. He has asked me to move into his condo but I like having my space. Somewhere to call my own. Somewhere that is mine.

At least that is what I tell myself.

"Hey, babe. You awake?" His voice drags my gaze to the edge of my bed, his body glistening with the remnants of his shower. Trickles of water cascade down his torso.

With his dark green eyes watching me and

hands on his hips, I take in his whole body. The towel is wrapped around the bottom of his chiseled abs and I can see his hard bodied chest taking slow, deep breaths. His buff shoulders connect with beautifully chiseled biceps. As his longer than usual dirty blond hair falls onto his forehead, I catch a glimpse of his trademark sideways smirk. It's no wonder women try to throw themselves at him all the time.

"No," I answer back, hoarsely, while bringing the sheets up over my nude body, covering everything but my eyes.

His smile turns seductive. "I can help with that."

He grasps onto the knot in his towel and pulls it apart, letting it drop to the floor. Tension immediately starts to radiate through my body. Lowering to his hand and knees, he crawls up the bed until he is hovering inches above my body. Goose bumps prickle my skin. The sheet is quickly pulled off and his smooth hands bring my knees up around his hips. Without question, he slips inside of me not caring to see if I'm ready for him.

I allow him to use my body as I continue to stare up at the ceiling. Within minutes, his thrusts get faster. His grunts louder, and I feel him swell inside me as he releases. He slides out, kisses me on the nose, and gets up to finish getting ready for work, not bothering to ask if I came.

I didn't.

I turn to my side and close my eyes trying to remember how it used to feel when I would just see him across a room and butterflies would create chaos inside not only my stomach but my heart. Or when he would send me flowers, or make me dinner. We've just fallen into a comfortable routine. I feel as though we've lost that spark. Maybe not so much Braden's spark for me as I for him.

I remember meeting him at a Shell gas station the summer after I graduated college. I had just arrived back into town. He was pumping gas behind me, and we just started chatting about my death trap of a Jeep and we immediately hit it off. The confidence he exuded was a turn on, and no one had made me laugh in such a long time. The boys in college acted like immature drunks but he was all man. I spent four years of college boyfriendless, sexless and lonely. I don't know what it was about Braden that made me push my apprehensiveness about guys aside but a week later I broke my five year dry spell and we became officially exclusive.

I had taken a chance. Something I hadn't done in a long time.

As I lay there, bare and unpleasured, I try to recall when exactly things took a turn. I rack all my memories, but it seems there wasn't a specific point in time it all started to go south. It just happened gradually. Things between us were exciting at the beginning. Laughing, joking, and enjoying each other's company. Barely a moment was spent apart and all I thought about was him.

Now, two years later, we're comfortable yet so far removed from each other it's almost senseless. I'm afraid my heart isn't in it anymore, and if I'm honest with myself, I'm not sure it ever has been, but I stay. I stay because I trust him, and that is something I never thought I could do with a man. Not since high school. Not since my heart was shattered, my trust betrayed and my world caved in. When I was forever changed by the only other man I've been with. The one who broke me into a million pieces so long ago. The reason I have yet to be put back together again. After all this time, Braden hasn't been able to do that...not that he would know it needs to be done.

Since high school, I've kept my heart guarded. I've never gotten out of the waiting to exhale moment in Braden's and my relationship where I felt I could truly be myself. It's hard to walk around and pretend like everything is okay. That you're happy when you're not. When you want to be yourself with the people you love but you don't feel you can. That you have the perfect relationship when you don't and it's not even his fault. It's mine. Despite letting him in, I've kept myself protected for seven years, hiding away, scared to let the true me out, feeling as though people won't accept me for who I am.

The artist.

The risk taker.

I'm startled when Braden's cold nose touches mine, and then he steals a quick kiss. "I'm off to work, baby. Dinner tonight?" he asks slipping his hand down to my breast and flicking his thumb over my nipple, taut from the cold.

My eyes flutter shut, trying to revel in his touch. "I can't. Girls night with Erin and Noe," I answer in a whisper.

His loud sigh doesn't surprise me since he doesn't like when I go to bars without him. "You know I hate when you go out without me."

I sit up in bed, pulling the sheets over my chest

giving him a knowing look. "I'm a big girl, Braden. Why don't you trust me?"

He shakes his head. "I trust you. It's everyone else I don't trust. I don't want some guy hitting on you."

"Well, if you trust me then you know that they can flirt all they want but I'm yours."

He drops his hand and kisses me on the forehead. "Okay, but be safe and call me when you get home," he says annoyed.

I listen to him walk out the door without saying "I love you", bag in hand and ready to take on his morning shift, thankful that I will be able to sleep alone tonight.

~~

"Spill it, Grant!" I say to Noelle over the horrible eighties music playing in the bar.

Noelle Grant is my boss, great friend, and sometimes workout partner. I started working as her assistant for event planning and we hit it off almost immediately. Right now she is going through some major boy drama. She's stuck between, Jace, a guy she just met and Erin's brother Trent.

Oh, to be so troubled.

"What's going on?" Erin asks from across the table, pretending she didn't get a text from me about it hours earlier.

Erin is a terrible actress. I watch as her doe-ish brown eyes give her away and since she and Noelle are best friends, I know she can't get away with it. Even I see right through her.

Her short auburn hair is perfect without a strand out of place and her smile lights up the room. I guess having a man that thrills you does that to a woman. From what I heard, Erin and Walker are a fierce couple. Fiercely in love.

"Noelle threw her bag again today and she passed up a chance to go to Maggiano's with Jace," I say raising an eyebrow at both ladies. "You know we would have let you bail, right?"

Erin shoves her shoulder into Noelle. "Maggiano's? You passed up Maggiano's for us?"

"I didn't want to go with him," Noelle responds and shrugs her shoulders when she realizes her slip up and her eyes go wide.

"You didn't want to go or you didn't want to go with Jace?" Erin pushes to get her to clarify though we both know the answer.

"So, which is it?" I push Noe a bit more when she doesn't answer and take a sip out of my drink.

"With Jace!" she shouts causing me to drop my glass back onto the table. "I don't think it's working out."

"Because of Trent," I state. I know she is having a rough time. Having two men vying for you sounds great until it happens and you don't know what the hell to do.

"I don't want to talk about it and even if I did I wouldn't know where the hell to start," Noelle sighs into her drink.

She is normally a beautiful, confident woman. Her natural blonde hair matches her delicate skin tone and her blue eyes can turn from business to blissful in seconds. She is the total package. Sexy, secure, successful and yet she has that vulnerable side that has two men salivating over her.

I do envy her though. Not the guy trouble because I don't even know what to do with the one guy who I do have, but she speaks her mind. She's herself and never pretends to be anything else.

It seems we are about to drop the subject until a male voice breaks up our all female conversation. "Don't want to talk about what?"

I look up from my drink, ready to fend off any advances by the just-turned-twenty-one year old boys in this place when my eyes find a sexy God of a man. With blond hair and beautiful green eyes that seem to be only for Noelle, I assume I'm met with one of her men of the hour...Jace.

I glance her way and, for the first time since I've met her, Noelle is at a loss for words. Her eyes are wide like a kid who was just caught with their hand in the cookie jar.

"Work," I jump in to answer, shrugging. "She said no work talk tonight."

Breathing a sigh of relief, she composes herself and slides out of the booth into Jace's awaiting arms.

I look away because in their state of relationship, they seem to be more intimate with each other out in public than Braden and I have been lately behind closed doors. I'm almost jealous at the half-hearted hug she gives him.

My eyes shift to the dance floor to watch the drunken people grind on one another, zoning out of the table's conversation. I know it's rude. I've never met him but I already know that he isn't good for

Noelle. From what Erin has told me, Trent, her brother, has longed for Noelle for years now, whereas Jace treats her like a trophy to be won. Trent, I heard, treats her like a queen.

I'm finishing up the last of my drink when I hear a name I haven't spoken or heard out loud in years. "...and this is our friend Ryder."

Time stands still...or travels back years ago to the heat of the summer before my senior year.

My eyes flicker over to see the man Jace just introduced. They bypass someone who looks like he could be Jace's brother straight to the man standing next to them.

No longer a boy.

All. Fucking. Man.

My heart stops.

It can't be.

Butterflies that have long since lost their wings start to wreak havoc furiously inside my stomach as if they just emerged from their cocoon. My body heats up under the carnal stare of the dark ocean of blue eyes and I hate it. I want to hate it.

A flashback of his mouth in the crook of my neck, and his hands grabbing onto me for dear life cause me to involuntarily tilt my head back. I can feel his breath all over me.

I break the trance of his unbelieving stare and lower my eyes to take in his body. It's much thicker than I remember. More muscular yet lean. His biceps flex against the black shirt that shows off the car he used to sneak me around in, reminding me of all the nights they surrounded me.

A smile stretches across his face and heat rises in my cheeks. And then I meet his eyes again. They seem to be looking right through me. Smug, as if though they know me. Like they can see right through the bullshit façade I've been putting up for everyone and it instantly angers me.

He doesn't know me. Not anymore. He lost the right to a long time ago.

Noelle's voice breaks through my angry thoughts. "This is Erin and this is..."

"Hadley," Ryder says, his eyes still searing into me. The way my name falls from his lips seems effortless when I can barely think his without breaking a little bit more. I'm pissed and simultaneously turned on. I'm officially a walking contradiction.

In the loudness of the bar silence fills the space around us.

"You two know each other?" Jace asks seemingly uncomfortable, and his brother snickers.

Neither of us says a word, silently daring the other to speak.

Ryder breaks first quirking a brow up at me. "Do we?"

"No," I answer without hesitation. "I don't know him at all."

Because I don't. What I thought I knew wasn't true. He lied. He schemed, and he lied again. I spent years trying to forget him yet he never left my thoughts.

Our exchange seems to make everyone uneasy. I decide to leave the table, but before I have a chance to jump up Ryder slides in next to me.

My body turns electric. I'm at war with my emotions and my hormones. I hate him, but my reaction to the brush of his leg on mine says otherwise.

"You have no idea how happy I am to see you," he says while sliding his hand over mine in the gentlest of touches.

I push him away as the spark strikes. Whether it's an angry spark or not, I'm unsure.

"Hadley, look at me." He pleads but I continue ignoring him while looking down at my phone, acting as though I'm more interested in my email than I actually am.

"Hadley," Noelle calls out. I look up at her. She seems just as uncomfortable as she sits next to Jace. "Is Braden coming?"

The look in her eyes tells me she is trying to help the situation I'm in.

I've never spoken to her about Ryder. There was no reason to. He was my first love...my first everything but he ruined it with just three sentences. It's amazing how much words can skew your world. Change you for life. I get what she is doing...and I'll play along. "No, but I told him I'd meet him at home later," I lie shooting her a wink.

Ryder stiffens next to me. "Braden?" he questions, but his words are directed towards Noelle.

"Her boyfriend," she says looking at his hand next to mine.

"Braden?" He repeats to me once Noelle and

Jace travel onto the dance floor and the man who I now know as Jace's twin, AJ, moves next to Erin.

I ignore Ryder, taking the first sip of a new drink the server brought me. My finger glides along the edge of the rim as I watch Erin eye Noelle across the room.

I chuckle as I wonder how later is going to play out since Erin gave Trent the inside info on our whereabouts tonight.

"Spark." Ryder's firm tone calls me when I don't respond to him.

I turn my angry gaze towards him. His head jerks back at the ferociousness of my stare. "Don't call me that!"

"Braden. Is he really your boyfriend?"

His question irks me.

"Yes!" I yell pushing on him until he hits the edge of the booth and scrambles to his feet. "I wouldn't lie," I say looking up directly in his eyes. "That's your thing."

I slide out before he can say another word and throw my purse over my shoulder headed for the bathroom. I need to get away from him and fast.

I lock myself in a stall, throwing my head against the metal door as tears prick the sides of my eyes, threatening to spill over. Seeing him here, again, unexpectedly brings the bad memories of the last time I saw him to the surface. The reason why I couldn't trust any man becomes fresh in my mind. I wipe a rogue tear away and straighten my back.

If I was looking for a sign that I needed to try to work through my issues with Braden, I found it clear as day at The Cubby Bear North.

Braden would never break my heart the way Ryder did. It's secure. He is nothing like Ryder, and that is exactly why I should stay with him.

Chapter 2

Ryder

It's been a long time and Hadley still looks just as beautiful as I remember. Her soft skin glows even under the flashing lights of the bar. Her hair, darker and much longer than I remember, falls down over the breasts that I've never forgotten the feeling of underneath my fingertips. Her passionate stare still pierces through me, but I could see the lust behind them...she remembers too. No woman has had this effect on me. Not since Hadley walked, no disappeared, out of my life.

One day, seven years ago, I am getting ready to let my asshole parents know that I'm in love with their nemesis' daughter and the next she is gone. Vanished. Her mom and dad even refused to look my way when I went to her house after my numerous texts went unanswered and Emie, her best friend, didn't have a clue where she went.

I searched for her. I did. I was in love with her. I wanted to spend my life with her. Go to the same college as Hadley and build a foundation with her. She took that from me without as much as a Dear

John letter. Never responded to my emails. I spent a long time trying to figure out why she did it. What I did. No one could give me the answers I was looking for.

Maybe she never did love me.

It took me four years before a girl ever got more than sex from me and even that didn't last long. At the frat house, I took each opportunity I had to get laid but never once was my heart in it. Not like it was with Hadley. I'd just use them to mourn the loss of her. I knew that and I made sure they did too.

Yea, I sound like a pussy, but when someone as fascinating as Hadley Chase comes into your world, loves you unconditionally, knows you better than anyone else, and then takes off nothing is ever the same.

Ever.

I should be pissed at the sight of her but all I feel is relief at finally seeing her again.

I excuse myself from the table and head in the direction of where Hadley squeezed her way through the throngs of people. I find a long hallway that leads to the bathrooms. Assuming she is in there I stop and I lean my head back against the wall and close my eyes.

The image of my first glance at her in almost a decade flashes across the darkness created by the back of my eyelids. How utterly stunning she looked staring off into the distance. That was until Jace introduced me. I watched her body go rigid and her teeth clench. Her green irises dilated in disbelief as they met mine.

All the hurt I felt from her leaving me without a word dissipated and I just needed to touch her. To feel that she was real.

My palms are slick with sweat and my heart is beating so fast that it's creating a thumping that reverberates through my body and pounds in my ears. I feel like that high school kid again, nervous to ask her out or kiss her for the first time. My dick twitches mentally recalling the memory of my hands touching her body. The first time she trusted me fully. The night she gave herself to me.

Her satin skin feels incredible underneath my touch. My hands glide up her smooth legs as she wiggles beneath me, daring my fingers to climb higher. When they do, they're met with warmth. Her hips rise begging for my digits to enter her. I'd give her anything she asks for, silent or aloud. They slip in easily. It's amazing how ready for me she can be with just a few strokes.

Her soft voice whimpers at the invasion and my eyes flick up to hers. They're open. They love to watch what I can do to her body. I up the pace earning myself a loud call of my name.

"Shhh," I tell her quietly. "You need to be quiet. You don't want your parents to catch us."

I've snuck into her room a few times a week all summer. My parents are too busy to notice I'm gone most of the time and I use it to my advantage to spend every moment I can with Hadley.

She silently nods biting her bottom lip...something that turns me on more than her whimpers of pleasure.

"Ryder," she breathlessly whispers my name. "I love you."

"I love you too, Had," I declare, pushing my fingers deeper and faster inside of her.

Her teeth unfasten her lip and she asks, "You'll never hurt me?"

I can see the vulnerability in her eyes silently begging me to give her the answer she wants...needs.

"Never," I promise. "I'd walk through fire before I ever hurt you."

A tear rolls down her cheek and I wipe it away. "Hadley, what's wrong?"

Her hand comes down from my shoulder and stops mine, delaying her impending orgasm. "I want you," she says. "I'm ready."

My body freezes, halting all movement. "Are you sure? We don't have to. I know you want to wait."

She nods as her small hands pull at the button on my jeans, the popping sound filling the night. My zipper follows and she pushes my pants down enough so that my erection is free.

"I want this, Ryder." Her hands wrap around me. "I want my first to be with you and I believe that you'll never hurt me. I know you'll take care of me."

Hadley won't be my first, but I'll be hers, and hopefully her only. "I promise."

I stand up and pull my jeans and boxers all the way down and reach into the pocket, pulling out the condom from my wallet and securing it on me. She slips off her dress and her legs open in anticipation, no reluctance in sight on her face.

I nestle myself between her thighs, placing the head of my dick at her entrance. She tenses for a brief moment before determination takes over. Her hands grab my sides pulling me gently towards her. Her tension returns when I push into her and I still at the now scared look on her face.

"We can stop. We don't have to do this," I plead. "I'll wait...years if I have to."

She smiles up at me. "I want to. Please, Ryder. I want to be yours. Keep going."

Her words fuel me and I do what she asks, stopping every so often so her body gets accustomed to mine. It's nothing like I have ever felt before. I've been with one other girl and she never wrapped around me this tight.

I thrust the rest of the way inside her and tears prick the sides of her eyelids.

"Did I hurt you?" I worry.

"No." She shakes her head side to side. Her beautiful hair spread across the pillow. The strands of pink mixed with the auburn show the personality of a girl who lives her life to the fullest despite her upbringing. "Just uncomfortable. Keep moving."

So I do. I move inside her slowly until she relaxes. I've had my fingers inside her more times than I can count and I can tell when she is close. Her body's response to mine is electric. Even at eighteen, I know this is different. This isn't sex. This is making love. I love her.

Her voice speaks softly into the night. Sounds

of pleasure and love. My name, God's name and a few quiet prayers. I'm holding off so I can give her the pleasure she deserves. Most girls don't come their first time. Hadley will. I'll make sure of that.

She clenches around me, her grip on my arms tightening so hard her nails dig into me.

"I can feel it, Ryder. I'm going to come," she whispers. "My God, this feels incredible. Don't stop."

"I won't," I promise her. "I love you."

She falls over the edge at my words. Promising her love to me too. When she is sated and pleasured, I plunge into her a few more times before I come.

I fall on my side, dragging my finger along the curves of her unmoving body.

"Are you okay?" I ask.

Her head turns towards me, her smile lighting up the room. "Never been better."

We lay there trying not to fall asleep. A few minutes later she starts to giggle softly.

"What's so funny?" I ask hoping she isn't laughing at what we've just done.

She jumps up and straddles me. "We need to do that again," she says laughing again and securing my wrists above my head.

I drag my hands out of her grasp and grab her hips, grinding her against me and wink. "If I have to," I joke.

"Why are you just standing there?" Hadley's

harsh voice, very much different than in my memory, startles me.

An embarrassing tug of my jeans alerts me to my rock hard cock and an annoyed huff from across the hallway lets me know she can see it.

"Looks like nothing has changed." Hadley's sharp tongue states but her voice falters giving her vulnerability away.

I reach down and adjust myself as I watch her walk past me, wanting nothing more than to spank her tight ass. I grab her arm and whip her around so we are face to face.

"Oh, I've changed, Hadley...and I can show you how if you'd like," I say pushing up against her.

Her breathing deepens as she attempts to tug her hand out of my grip. "Let. Me. Go," she says accentuating each word.

"No. Not when I just found you again." I intently promise.

She scoffs. "I don't belong to you anymore, Ryder."

"You know," I say lifting my hand to caress the side of her cheek. She flinches but doesn't move. "Since you vanished into thin air we technically never broke up. So, you still belong to me. Have you been cheating on me with this Braden asshole?"

I'm trying to lighten the mood but her eyes go wide. She's seething as she swats my hand away. "Oh, yea? And how many girls have you fucked since high school? Go back to them."

"I don't want them. I want you," I say shocked at my own admission. I've just found her and already I want to commit myself to her?

She looks between my hand wrapped around her arm and my eyes. Resolve shines through. "What's that you said?" She taps her finger against her lips. "Oh yea. I've been there and done that."

She pulls out of my grasp, shooting daggers with her eyes, and walks away from me, again.

I'm confused by her words. I've never said that. Stomping my way through the crowd, I'm determined to find her and demand she explain what she just said but I'm stopped by AJ.

"We gotta go, man." His hand is over my chest, keeping me from moving any further. I glare at him before he immediately removes it.

AJ is my best friend. He and Jace lived down the street from me but in another school district, and he is well aware of all the bullshit that Hadley put me through. It took me almost ten months after she left to tell him what happened. After a drunken summer night, I spilled my guts. Told him about our summer together and how much I loved her. He was upset I had hidden it from him but Hadley and I had our reasons and we were working through them.

"No, I need to find Hadley." I shove him to the side. "I won't lose her again."

"Well, Jace wants to leave. I guess that fuck stick Trent showed up and his girl went all doe eyed. Plus, I might know where you can find her on most days. I heard Hadley works with Noelle."

I raise a brow at him. "You serious? She works as a wedding planner?"

I don't see Hadley as the type to plan

someone's wedding. I remember how she loved art and someday wanted to paint murals on the sides of buildings. Her dream was to paint the ocean on a tall brick building in the city. 'A sea of blue in the middle of the concrete jungle,' she had said.

"Yea, man. But we gotta go before he leaves without us."

I look behind him into the crowd and see that the table we were sitting at is now completely empty. If she works with Noelle then I don't need to chase after her. She'll see me soon enough.

Chapter 3

Hadley

"I don't know why you drag me out every Friday morning to run with you. I can't keep up!" My best friend since high school, Emie, wheezes through the shade of tall trees on our weekly run.

I stop, placing my hands on my hips and look at the relief written all over her face as I do. "Your personal trainer needs to work you harder," I chastise.

The woman has more money than sense, thanks to her parents, and can afford to have a personal trainer. Being rich was passed down to her and it's evident in her brand new Nike shoes she purchases every month and her matching workout outfits that she never wears more than once. Her hair color doesn't come from a five dollar box at Wal-Mart like mine but from the skilled hands of a beautician every four weeks. Its blonde curls are wrapped up in a tight ponytail.

A devious smile crosses her lip glossed lips. "Oh, he works me hard." Her long eyelashes flutter in a wink. “Morning, noon, and night.”

I slap her lightly on her arm. “I don’t doubt it. I just don’t understand how he can give you sessions four times a week and you can barely run three miles.”

The same smirk appears again. “I can’t help it if his sexy blue eyes and black hair distract me and we end up using the work bench for something else.” She giggles.

I start to jog again, much to her dismay, and try to envision what her trainer must look like. The image that appears looks a lot like the man I was reunited with last night.

Ryder Blake.

My heart rate picks up a little more at just the thought of his name. Last night, despite my anger towards him and what he had done, I could still see through his eyes the same boy I fell in love with all those years ago. I had dreamed of them last night...looking into mine as we made love the first time. I woke up in a puddle of sweat with my chest heaving up and down. Thankfully, Braden slept at his own place or he would have bothered me to tell him why I woke up in such a state.

I’ve never told Braden about Ryder. Mostly because I know how jealous Braden can get. When we’re out in public he makes it known that I am his. It’s not affection but possession. If a man stares he says something. At first I loved it, feeling as though he wanted the world to know I am his but that soon faded away, like a lot of other things, and now I find it an annoyance.

If I’m really being honest with myself, though,

I would say I haven't told Braden because I don't want to relive the hurt I felt from Ryder's words. How a voice can make your chest feel constricted and the air within your lungs whoosh out with no warning. Even though Emie now knows the whole story I had been reluctant to tell her.

She was the only confidant I had after I left. Emie was the only one besides my parents who knew where I went so I had to tell her about Ryder and me. She was team Hadley, of course, and never spoke a word about it to anyone…she did make me aware of his dating life after I left and apparently he didn't wait more than a week to find a new conquest.

"So," I nervously start, knowing how mad she is going to be right along with me. "I saw Ryder last night."

I close my eyes for a brief moment as I run, waiting for a reaction. When I don't hear it, I open them to find empty space along side of me. I turn my head back and see her stopped a hundred feet back.

Her screech fills the forest preserve. "Are you kidding?!" She closes the distance between us faster than I've ever seen her run. Her hands grasp my upper arms with a shake. "Where? What did he say? What did you say?"

She seems to be going into hysterics. I pull from her hold and reach for her face. "Em, stay with me. It's fine. I didn't even give him the time of day. Relax."

A puff of air blows across my face as she breathes out. "Okay. I just know how much he hurt you and I will personally kick his ass if he so much as looks your way again."

This makes me laugh. I can't imagine little Emie beating up an over six feet tall Ryder. Maybe she would send her trainer.

"You need to stay away from him, Hadley. Don't even talk to him," she commands.

I just nod my head unsure why she is being so adamant about it. I think I've grown up enough to take care of myself.

We finish up our jog and jump in the car. She has barely spoken a word since I told her about Ryder and I smile knowing she just wants to protect me from getting hurt again.

Before we hit the end of the road leading out of the trees, I spot some teenagers splashing in the river. I start to tense, worrying for their safety. They don't know if they will be swept away. And then I cringe at where my thoughts have taken me. I used to be like them. Carefree, doing what I wanted, taking chances and loving life. I used to want to grab the bull by the horns and do some of the crazy things my parents would have freaked out about. Go skydiving. Bungee jumping. Zip lining from the tree tops. But life changes us. We grow up, we get hurt. We reevaluate, and we lose ourselves. I took a chance on Ryder, allowing myself to fall in love with someone who supposedly accepted me for me and I got hurt so bad that the carefree Hadley back then is no longer.

Seeing those kids looking so innocent and full of life makes me jealous. I want to be that way again. To live my life not afraid because right now, I'm pretty damn petrified.

~~

"Do you want to tell me what all that was about last night?" Noelle questions the second she walks through the doors of Events Unlimited.

I peer up from my computer finding her, as usual, flawless. "I could ask you the same thing."

She smirks. "Touché."

"So," I start. "What's up?"

She sets her stuff down and rifles through her messages. "Hard dicks and airplanes." She deadpans.

I push away from my chair smoothing down my casual Friday jean skirt and stand to make her a cup of coffee. I don't have to. She never asks but I do it because I don't want to deal with a non-properly-caffeinated Noelle. After last night...her leaving Trent on the dance floor and Jace leaving her at the bar...I'm not sure what kind of Noe I am going to get.

I make her coffee the way she likes it, placing it on the desk and sit back at my own.

"Ryder is sexy, huh?" Noelle asks over the top of her computer. "I'd do him."

Rubbing my hands around on my temples to ease the onset of a headache I try to push back the jealousy when I envision Noelle and Ryder.

"You have two men to choose from, Noe. You don't need a third." I bite back at her.

She notices immediately. "Hmm, I see a hint of the green-eyed monster. Do you pine for this...this Ryder?" Her hand waves around like talking about him isn't a big deal. She doesn't know what she is asking.

I try my best to ignore her. She is a great friend but can be very nosy. I should go rearrange the stuff on her desk so the little neat freak has something else to focus on.

An hour later the office doors open and even though it's not her job, Noelle stands to greet our next client. My eyes go wide with surprise when I realize it's not them.

In walks a shorter man with a bouquet of red Gerber Daisies that's so big that it covers his entire torso. They are my absolute favorite. This arrangement is nothing short of the most beautiful thing I have ever seen in a crystal vase with a yellow bow wrapped around it. *Very expensive*. The man sets the flowers on the reception desk asking for me and she points my way rolling her eyes. The small looking Asian man huffs and picks them up off reception and brings them over.

He doesn't say a word as I thank him and he walks out. So glad I didn't have to tip him.

"Lucky bitch," Noelle murmurs and retreats back to her chair so I can admire them in peace.

I take the card out of the envelope, blushing as I read it.

<u>You only need a little spark to start a forest fire. Call me.</u>

"Who are they from?" Noelle asks tapping her pen down onto her calendar.

I throw the card with his cell phone number

watching it float in the air down to my desk and lean back into my chair. "Nobody," I deflect.

Her eyebrows rise. "Ah, does 'nobody' have blond hair or black hair?"

I walk to the back room ignoring her question and lay down on the couch next to the coffee machine. My head falls back, and a view of the popcorn ceiling reminds me of the starry night that seems like it could have been just yesterday.

The heat is thicker than normal for July. The temperature has reached the 110's but that doesn't keep anyone away from the Family Fest that Wheeling holds every year. Emie and I are dressed in our bikinis and have a pair of loose jean shorts over the bottoms. This was her idea. She said we needed a man and showing some skin would help.

"Stop looking embarrassed, Hadley," Emie, obviously annoyed, scolds as I cover up my bare stomach with my arms. "You're never going to lose your virginity acting like that."

I let my arms fall to my side and my eyes roll into the back of my head. Emie is adamant about both of us losing our virginity this summer. She says that we need to have experience throughout our senior year so that when we get to college we will know what we're doing.

I disagree. I want my first time to be in a moment when I can't think of anything else but giving that one person what my mother has taught me to keep sacred.

My mom isn't stupid. She has told me plenty of times that she isn't ignorant to the fact that I most likely will have sex before I get married but has drilled into me that I should be prepared not only physically but mentally.

Just in the distance I spot the spin art tent. It's my favorite. I used to make them all the time with my dad when I was younger. He would turn the wheel on and watch me throw in all kinds of colors. It amazed me how much art could affect me even then. It always makes me happy.

"Let's do that!" I point out with one hand and attempt to grab hers with the other. When it comes up empty, I look around finding her and Todd Mitchell within breathing distance of each other.

Barely acknowledging me, she waves as though she wants me to go away. Annoyed, I stomp away from them and zero in on my destination.

The tent is empty, which makes me happy, so I don't have to wait in line. The man throws a paper plate into the box that has a spinner at the bottom. The plate starts to turn and I spray my favorite color first, red. I swirl it up and down amazed at the lines it makes as it rotates. I do the same with the blue before the man picks it up and hands it to me. I'm not three steps away from the tent when a stone wall hits me, hard, and I fall to the ground.

"Shit!" A guy's voice yells. "I'm so sorry."

He pulls back on my upper arms to lift me up and I turn around and gasp when I find Ryder Blake, my longtime crush, with a black eye and busted open lip.

"Are you okay?" I ask grabbing some tissues from the spin art tent and handing them to him.

"Yea." He chuckles taking them from me. "I'm good. Just talking shit to the BG football players. Next time I'll make sure to have back up."

He laughs again but winces when he touches the tissue to his lip.

"I'm sorry." He repeats running his fingers through his thick black hair with his free hand.

I shake my head. "Don't worry about it. I'm okay."

"I'm actually kinda glad I ran into to you," Ryder says. His blue eyes staring straight into mine, most likely finding the teenage hormone induced lust I feel anytime he is near me.

Embarrassed, I look at my feet as we walk down the small hill towards our cars.

His warm grip covers my arm, turning me towards him, and he lifts my chin up. "Why do you always look down?" he asks as his touch sends electric shockwaves through my body. Ryder does funny things to me. Always has since freshman year. "I love to see your face. Not the top of your head."

Is he serious? This is one of the most popular kids in school and he is FLIRTING with me. This has to be a joke.

I turn my head away deflecting his half-hearted humor. "Don't do that."

His head turns sideways, a curious look crosses his face. "Do what?"

"Flirt with me like you like me," I angrily say crossing my hands over my exposed stomach.

He can't like me. Even if we were both poor

and not just me. If we were both popular and not just him. None of that would matter because our parents despise, no hate, each other.

Ryder steps closer and all thoughts of standing firm go out the window. He lifts his hands up to cup my jaw. I jump at the start of the fireworks show, but Ryder doesn't even flinch. His eyes are trained on me, and I have never felt so vulnerable as I do at this moment.

His thumb brushes across my lips and I watch his tongue slide over his own. "I do like you, Hadley. I've liked you for years."

My head falls helplessly into his hands. "What if I don't like you?" I whisper.

His mouth moves closer to mine. I can't breathe. I can't move.

"Not even a little?" His voice is hoarse...so close he is inhaling the same air I am.

"Maybe a little."

A slow smirk creeps up and he moves within licking distance. "Well, you only need a little spark to start a forest fire."

Instantly his mouth is on mine. His tongue invading my virgin lips. I've never kissed a guy. I worry I'm doing it wrong but he seems to be taking the lead. Pushing and pulling with every breath. I melt into him, fueling the flames, wanting everything he is giving me. His hands never leave my face and the fireworks booming in the background are nothing compared to the ones I'm feeling throughout my body right now.

He pulls away and I step back. My hand flies to my chest trying to calm down the rapid beating.

"Ryder..." I start.

"Where have you been?" A shrill voice belonging to Bridgette Tate, class bitch, asks stepping between the two of us. "Let's go. I have to be home by curfew."

With that he is dragged away, watching me as he goes.

The memory of that night still haunts me. I should have pushed him away and remembering Bridgette makes it worse. She saw right through it. I jump up from the couch and stomp back into the office. I fall back into my desk chair, ignoring Noe's annoying stare and the strong scent of the flowers, and get back to work.

Chapter 4

Ryder

Tying up the laces of my sneakers in the police department locker room, I can feel the nervous energy seeping throughout my body. My fingers shake as I wrap one lace around the other and a bead of sweat seeps down my temple. I can run into a house, weapon drawn, no problem but I can't send flowers to Hadley Chase without freaking the fuck out.

"What's up, man?" James, my new partner's hand comes down hard on my shoulder causing me to jump. "You've seemed edgy all today. Lady troubles?"

He takes it upon himself to sit across from me on the long wooden bench as I pick up my phone and check it for the one hundredth time in as many minutes.

I wasn't a big fan of James when I first started. Being a recent transfer to the station, I had to play nice with all the other officers and initially he just rubbed me the wrong way. My first day, three weeks ago, he was the one to–as he calls it–take me under his wing. He seemed like an egomaniac and thought he was God's gift. I've just learned to tolerate him.

"I'm good," I tell him waving him off.

A chuckle fills the locker room. "Bullshit. Your eyes haven't left that phone. Every day for three weeks you've been ready to take on a new city PD and today you seem more interested in a text than that woman throwing shit off the balcony of her cheating boyfriend's apartment."

He's right. My head isn't in it today.

I drop my phone down, knowing she must have received the flowers by now and just decided not to call me, and drag my hands down my face. "Not a girl. Not anymore. A woman," I tell him as I stand and slam the door to my locker shut.

"You've been waiting for her to call you all day?" He shoves my shoulder. "Call her. Don't be a pussy."

I sigh. "I can't. I don't have her number. I have her work number but doesn't that seem a bit stalkerish?"

The clatter of his stuff being taken out of his locker halts with my words. He shakes his head. "You don't have her number? How is that possible?"

I throw my head back in defeat. I might as well tell him since I'm pretty sure we're going to be partners for a while. "A girl from high school. THE girl. The one I thought I would marry. She vanished and left me cold. No word and her parents, man, they hated me, hated my family. They wouldn't tell me where she went. Then last night I saw her. She was delivered to me on a silver platter and she couldn't even stand the sight of me."

"How can some teenage girl just disappear?" he questions.

"I don't know. It's not like anyone had a reason to let me know she was leaving. No one knew about us since our families hated each other. We decided to keep it quiet for just a little while and when I finally decided to stand up to them, she was gone. Dropped out of school and didn't tell anyone where she was going except her parents."

My eyes slam shut remembering how it felt when I realized she was gone. It was like a knife to the heart. She was the air in my lungs, and after she left I couldn't breathe anymore. I'm still gasping.

"Anyways, I sent her flowers this morning with my number that she has yet to use." My head pounds against the metal of the locker. I don't know what I did for her to hate me this much. "Plus," I add. "She has a boyfriend."

"Do you want my advice?" James asks and I look up nodding. Why not? It can't hurt. "You know where she works. Go see her, and as far as a boyfriend...well she isn't married..." His words trail off.

He's right. He's fucking right. I don't know when the hell I ever backed down from a challenge.

Collecting the rest of my shit I pat James on the back. "Thanks, man. You're right."

"So what's the name of the girl that has you all strung up?" he asks to my back as I head to the exit.

"Hadley," I say pushing the door open.

Jumping in my car, I roll the windows down and see James running out towards me, a weird look across his face. “What did you say her name was?”

“Hadley, but you might as well call her Mine.” And with that I speed off towards the only love that I have ever experienced.

~~

The door opens, and I walk into Events Unlimited. It’s not at all what I expected. There are no offices, but only four desks strategically placed so that they are all facing each other but not so close that you don’t have privacy. No one is at reception and I just decide to walk all the way in. I find the large bouquet of flowers on top of a desk that must be Hadley’s.

I slowly walk towards it and stand behind the chair finding her computer still on. The windows are minimized and I find a picture of her and Emie as her screensaver. I’d forgotten all about Emie. She was such a crazy bitch in high school.

“What the hell are you doing here?” An angelic voice, though it sounds like an angry angel right now, asks.

I pull a flower from the vase before turning around and finding a vision that has me going from half-staffed to instantly hard at hearing her voice. Her dark hair is curled and pulled partially up showcasing her blushing cheeks and beautiful eyes. My heart pulls remembering how they looked the night I kissed her for the first time, and it makes me smile.

“Stop smiling!” she yells her hands going to her

hips.

I'd love my hands on those hips again. I step closer to her and she stands her ground, her mask of anger fading a little. "I didn't hear from you," I say, my voice low as my feet close the distance. "Do you like my flowers?"

I point the one in my hand to the large vase of them and turn back to her. She hasn't moved a muscle except her hands have dropped and are balled into fists. Her chest moves up and down with each slow and deep breath. Her nipples are perked up, pushing through the fabric of her green V-neck shirt.

I lift my hand but she slaps at it. Even the harsh contact is a turn on. The air has shifted and all I want is to touch her. I extend my arm holding the daisy towards her.

Her eyes watch it get closer. "Don't touch me, Ryder," she weakly commands, coming out barely a whisper. Her skin above her cleavage prickles. I can still affect her.

Continuing my torturous journey, the flower finally touches the skin of her wrist above her fisted hand and I draw it, slowly, up her arm, leaving a trail of goose bumps. She doesn't try to push it off. When I reach her shoulder, I find her eyes closed.

So beautiful.

I lightly drag it over her collarbone and across her exposed neck. I step closer, her breath hitches, and her head falls back slightly. If I wasn't looking, I wouldn't have seen it. But I did.

"I'm not touching you, Hadley. Not unless you tell me it's okay," I tell her as I step nearer.

Her eyes slowly open, lashes fluttering with the light, and train on mine. “Ryder,” she starts. “Please.”

I move in closer, if that’s possible, and her pupils dilate. I can see the black take over the green and I can’t help but groan. I remember her tells– her pupils dilated, her breaths increased and her fingers spread out every time I turned her on.

I lower my head, bringing my lips closer to her ear. “Please what?” I whisper drawing out the air that blows across her neck.

Her hands hit the wall I didn’t realize I backed her up against and she fastens her bottom lip between her teeth, looking up at me, her eyes begging me to stop.

My free hand moves to the wall, trapping her. “I won’t touch you, Hadley, but I’ll keep pursuing you, boyfriend or not, until you tell me to stop.”

She dips down, escaping me and puts a distance between us. “Ryder.”

“Hadley.”

“Ryder.”

“Hadley.”

She rolls her eyes, snapping out of the haze, and steps towards her desk, gently pushing me aside. As she sits down she starts typing away. “I have to work. You need to go.”

“Tell me to stop, Had. Tell me to go away and I will.”

She doesn’t say a word, she just mindlessly types away on the keyboard.

I grab the back of her chair and without warning I spin her around to face me. Dropping to my knees in front of her, I grab the arms of the chair and pull it towards me. Her eyes go wide in surprise and her knees involuntarily spread, pushing at the denim in her skirt, allowing me to nestle myself between them.

My chest leans in but I don't dare give her the satisfaction of touching her. "Tell me to stop or tell me to touch you. Pick one, Hadley."

"I..." she starts but the phone interrupts her. She picks up the receiver. "Events Unlimited. Hadley speaking."

She eyes me for a moment before pushing back on the chair, rolling herself away. I stand up and listen to her conversation waiting to finish ours.

"Hey!" she says happily. "Nope, I'm just wrapping up...No, someone is still here...yea, I can meet you at my place...I was in the back, Braden, relax...I love you too...Bye."

Turning back to me, I find an apologetic look on her face. "I think you should go."

Looking up at the ceiling, I grab the edges of my hair and pull. "Yea." I blow out a breath as I stand up and start walking towards the door.

There are so many unanswered questions racing through my mind as I near the exit. Why did she leave? Where did she go? Did she even love me?

I've wondered long enough.

"I fucking loved you, Hadley." I spin around to face her. "I loved you and you left me. Abandoned me. I cried. I fucking cried like a chick when you left. How could you be so cold? You didn't even leave a note! Do you know what you did to me?!" I yell.

She stands from her chair and clasps her hands together, taking a deep breath before unleashing on me. "Did to YOU! Do you know what you did to me? What I went through? I loved you too, Ryder. God! I was willing to risk my family HATING me for loving you and you fucked me over. You hurt me with your words and you can never take that back. Never! I ran because I wanted to follow my dream...and not just be a secret side FUCK to the high school football star!"

I point my finger at her. "You were never a side fuck, Hadley! I was making plans for us. Plans that involved marrying you! And following your dream?" I turn to look around the office. "Painting was your dream! You had dreams to teach others. Not planning someone's wedding! Did you lose the fucking balls you used to have, Hadley? Where is the Hadley I knew?"

Her feet stomp on the floor, stopping just in front of me. Her tiny finger pokes into my chest. "The Hadley you knew is GONE! You ruined her. You fucked me and got what you wanted. And don't you ever, I mean EVER, talk about my dreams. They don't involve you. Not anymore! So, leave! Go back to your country club life and leave your EX secret side fuck alone. I'm fucking someone new now!"

My face drops as do my hands. I can't think about her with someone else. "I'm leaving."

She snorts. "Good."

"Are you going to tell me to stop?" I ask.

She just stares at me saying nothing until the phone rings. She turns around to grab it. "Events Unlimited. Had..."

I don't wait around to find out if it's her new fuck.

My feet drag as I walk into my apartment. My shoes are haphazardly launched across the room. I'm not only physically exhausted but even worse, mentally. The last twenty-four hours have taken its toll and all I want to do is lie on the couch and fall asleep to some mindless TV.

Clatter from the kitchen startles me, and I slowly walk in finding Braden cooking dinner, something he hasn't done in a long time.

"Hey, baby. You're home on time," he says, surprise evident from his raised eyebrows.

I walk over and lean on my tiptoes, placing a kiss on his cheek. "On time? Yes. Why are you surprised?"

He walks over to the fridge and pulls out a bottle of my favorite wine and pours me a glass handing it over. He continues his assault on the ground beef in the pan as I lean back against the counter and watch him over the top of my glass.

"No reason." He stops chopping and looks at me expectantly. "How was your day? Anything exciting happen?"

"Fine." I shrug my shoulder, taking another sip. "Yours?"

From the outside looking in, it would seem like we do this all the time, but I can't remember the last time he was cooking in my apartment or asking how my day was. We've been long past those kinds of pleasantries. But this is nice.

His eyes don't leave mine. A look crosses his face like he expects more of an answer and when he doesn't get one he smiles and turns back to the stove. "Mine was fine too. Same shit different day." He chuckles to himself. "Why don't you go relax? I'm almost done."

Not hesitating, I make my way to the living room and sit on the couch, closing my eyes. "I'm starving," I call out.

"Me too," he replies while creating more clatter in the kitchen.

My mind wanders to the day's events. Seeing Ryder in my office was surreal. Never in a million years did I envision him where I work and when he caressed me with that flower, my body started an all out war with my mind. I had to reel it in. I know the physical attraction will never go away, he was my first love, but when I think back to how he was the center of the worst day of my life, all draw to him is lost.

I needed him and he ruined me. I can never take back the time spent with him but I do blame Ryder for a lot of what I call the domino effect that is my life.

He hurt me. I left. I went into protect mode. Don't let anyone in and don't let my true self out. I expressed it in my art but never outwardly. He changed me and not for the good.

Amazing pressure is being applied to the balls of my feet and I open my eyes to find Braden with one in each hand. He's looking down at them, a worried look on his face.

"That feels amazing," I compliment.

Not looking up or responding, he keeps massaging. I leave him be for a minute, not only because it feels good but also because he seems to be lost in thought.

When I can't contain the silence anymore I ask, "Are you okay?"

Lifting his head, he smirks, never letting go of the hold on my feet. "I'm good. I was just thinking."

"About what?"

He doesn't answer. He just pries my legs apart and slides between them. The memory of Ryder doing the same invades my thoughts for a split second until Braden sweet voice speaks, "I love you."

My heart constricts. "I love you too," I say but it's an automatic response. I lift my fingers to his face and rub down the side of cheek. Guilt creeps in. I do love him. So much. I'm just not sure I'm in love with him anymore. Ryder's recent presence has made sure I'm fully aware of that.

"I trust you, Hadley. I want you to know that."

I give a half smile. "I know. I trust you too."

Braden lifts up onto his knees and pushes my jean skirt up. My thighs start to tingle at his touch. His hands creep up higher. “Is this mine, Hadley?” he asks caressing the fabric of my panties between my legs. My toes start to dig into the carpet. I squirm. He hasn’t been this attentive before sex in a long time.

I love it.

“Yes,” I breathe out.

The pressure gets harder between my legs, and he slides the material over, teasingly caressing me up and down.

“I couldn’t hear you,” he commands, dipping his finger into me.

I throw my head back and the invasion. “Yes!” I cry louder.

In an instant my panties are ripped down and off my feet.

“I thought you were hungry,” I whisper.

His arms burrow their way under my thighs and wrap around pulling them towards his waiting mouth. “I’m famished.” He growls just before he licks me up my center. “Starving, Hadley.”

And with that, his mouth moves quickly, sucking, pulling, pushing against me. I can’t help but rub myself all over him, trying to reach a destination that hasn’t been visited in a while. I whimper as my body tenses and the explosion consumes me. I scream out his name and push his face into me, riding it out, almost embarrassed at how fast I came.

I’m sated but have no time to relax before I’m

pulled up and thrown over the back of the couch, my ass pushing towards him. I lean over and use my hands to steady myself. I can hear the zipper of his pants come down as he situates my skirt over my ass.

He's in me, gripping my hips from behind, pushing in and out at a rapid pace. His mouth teases my ear and his hand grasps my shoulder. I can already feel the start of another orgasm. "Louder, Hadley. Tell me this is mine."

My body lurches forward and back. I can barely breathe, let alone talk. Another orgasm is within reach but he stops just short of completion. I let out a frustrated groan.

His breath caresses my ear and he whispers, "I won't ask again. I said louder."

"Yours! It's fucking yours! I'm yours–just make me come, Braden!" I yell. I'm pissed. I'm frustrated and I want a fucking orgasm from a dick and not from a vibrator finishing me off after he has long since come inside me.

He starts his pace again, punishingly slapping his front to my back. The tingling sensation starts all over again and when he reaches a hand forward and slaps my clit I yell out, seeing stars take over my vision as an orgasm to end all orgasms rips through me.

"FUCK!" I scream over and over again riding it out.

Braden doesn't stop. He continues to thrust into me. "Again," he says grabbing a nipple in his hand and pinching it. His mouth coming down onto my shoulder before he takes a bite. "I want you to come again!"

"Braden, I can't..."

"You can and you will," he states, moving his hands so one is on my hip and the other is holding onto the crease between my neck and shoulder. He pulls back gently, lifting me off the back of the couch and fucks me so fast I have no warning before I come again. My body screams out in protest. I haven't come this many times, ever, and the third time is better than the first and second combined. It lasts longer, and I feel as though I might black out.

His speed increases and I'm thankful that this amazing torture is almost over. My body is spent with his newfound aggression.

"Again," he commands.

~~

I look like a mess. The curls I spent most of the morning fixing are tangled and mascara is smeared under my eyes. There is certain glow to me though. The glow of four orgasms. I was thankful that he stopped after the fourth. I think that I would've died if he tried to command another one out of me but that tops the sex we used to have...by far.

The bathroom door opens as I'm ripping the knots out of my hair with a comb. Braden walks in and wraps his hands around me, eyeing me in the mirror.

"Are you sure you are okay?" I ask trying not to hit him with the bristles as I untangle another knot.

"I am now." He smiles, giving me the answer I was hoping for.

I take a long look at him for a few moments, and I grin. Today I see the man I fell in love with, the man who I trust. The man who used to treat me like a princess is coming back to me.

"Me too." I say, earning myself a barrage of kisses along my neck. Turning in his arms I clasp my fingers around his neck. "Let me work through these knots and I'll be right out...then maybe we can eat."

A smile stretches across his face. "I'm pretty full now, but I could always go for seconds." He winks, and it warms my body.

I've missed this.

I kiss the tip of his nose. "Maybe tomorrow, the buffet closed for the night." I giggle.

He sighs exaggeratedly. "Okay, I guess I can settle for spaghetti." He turns but not before he slaps my ass. "Oh, and I'm spending the night again. I'll grab my stuff while you're finishing up."

He leaves me alone and I scrub my face and throw my hair up into a ponytail. After putting on some shorts and a tank top I head for the living room and the sight of my phone stops me.

I pick it up and open a new text, typing in the number that I didn't want to memorize but that is now engrained into my head.

Me: You said I needed to tell you if you should stop or not.

I jump as my phone rings in my hand. I see the same number I just texted pop up and I look out of my glass doors towards the parking lot, spotting Braden talking to one of my many nosy neighbors.

I hesitantly hit accept on the screen.

"Hello," I whisper not that Braden can hear me.

"I want to hear what you choose...not in a text." Ryder's sexy growl comes from the receiver.

My head falls forward. His voice is affecting me in ways that I hate and love at the same time. I glance back outside and see that Braden is now smiling. He's handsome, educated, successful, and he has never given me any reason not to trust him. After tonight, I feel like our slump might be over.

I've decided. "I want you to stop."

"Hads..." Ryder starts.

"No. You told me to choose. I chose. I want you to stop. I love Braden and I trust him. I want you to leave me alone."

The door to my apartment slams shut, and I hit end on the screen.

Braden's head tilts to the side in wonder. "Who was that?"

I look at the phone, deleting my text and dialed call within a few seconds. "Telemarketers," I breathe out, dropping my phone onto the table, and hopefully keeping Ryder out of my life and as far away from Braden as possible.

Chapter 6

Ryder

"What's up your ass?" AJ asks sitting his lazy ass on my couch. I've just walked in after leaving Hadley's office and he was already here.

Cracking open a beer, I lean back in my recliner and flip on my big screen TV. "Shut the hell up."

He stands up and reaches over to slap me upside the back of my head. He may be my best friend but he can be annoying as fuck.

I don't give a shit. I feel like I'm in shambles. The last day has rocked my world and not in the good way. All I want are answers. Or a chance. Or something. Anything from Hadley. The last thing I want is AJ to be hanging around but unfortunately he was already in my house when I got home from Hadley's office.

I love this place. It's the reason I moved back to my hometown. It is what I had in mind when I thought about settling down after screwing around for so long. I had a great job at the Elgin police department but I found this house and fell in love with it. The bonus is being closer to my sister and Mom. I know my mom misses me and my sister is always looking for help with the girls. The down side is that I have to start at the bottom at the new department.

Settling back into the couch, he takes a pull from his beer. “Are you still crying over that Hadley chick?”

I stop flipping through the channels to give him the “don’t fuck with me glare” but he’s immune to it. He’s seen it a time or two.

“Don’t look at me like that, Blake. I saw what happened last night and after hearing what happened at her office I think you should just leave that chick drama alone.” He stands up again because he couldn’t keep still to save his life and glances down at his phone. “Let’s get the hell out of here. It’s Friday and I want to get laid. Unless you’re putting out?”

I whip the remote at him and down the entire can of beer.

Why the hell not. I can’t just sit here at home and think about her like some pathetic loser. I’ll do it in a bar.

~~

I’ve been here all of two hours and drank more than my weight in Heinekens.

“Screw her out of your system, bro!” AJ yells over the loud bar music. It’s pretty packed in here tonight but I barely see anyone around me. “There are hot pieces of ass everywhere!”

I finally look up and take notice of all the

women here. It's ladies night and they are all looking for some poor sucker to buy them all of their drinks.

I order another beer and try to block Hadley out of my thoughts but it's no use. I flip between how fucking sexy she looked last night and today. How much her body has changed into a toned and tight woman and before I can think better of it I imagine her body underneath mine. On top of mine.

As the waitress drops the green bottle in front of me, I feel my phone vibrate in my pocket. I pull it out and see an incoming text that has to be from Hadley.

Unknown: You said I needed to tell you if you should stop or not.

It's like she knew I was thinking about her. Caressing her in my thoughts. But whether she tells me to stop or to come over and take what I want, I need to hear her voice say it.

AJ calls out when I stand up without a word and walk outside. The summer heat instantly brings to sweat to my forehead or maybe it's the fact that I'm going to hear her voice again.

When I dial her number it rings once and she answers quietly, "Hello."

I don't know what it is about her voice. The innocence in it makes my mouth dry, and I have to lick my lips so I can talk. "I want to hear what you choose...not in a text."

It's quiet on the other end, and I'm hoping it's because she doesn't know how to tell me she wants me.

When she finally speaks it makes my stomach drop. "I want you to stop."

I look up to the Heavens hoping I can change her mind. I told her I would stop if she asked me to. I just don't know if I can. "Hads..."

"No. You told me to choose. I chose. I want you to stop. I love Braden and I trust him. I want you to leave me alone."

A beep sounds in my ear notifying me that the call has ended and I rest my back against the brick building. It's like I've been shot. Her words come out so harsh...like she never loved me. Like she never trusted me.

I gave all of me to her. She knew things about me that no one else did. If anyone should have trust issues it should be me. The day I found out she left still haunts me. It's like one minute you are whole and you know everything is going to go right for you for once and the next it's ripped away from you leaving the imprint in your hands.

I drop my cell on my bed for the eighth time as I try to figure out why the hell Hadley won't answer my calls. I've sent too many texts to count, and at this point I am starting to worry. It's Sunday and the last time I saw her was Friday at the football game. I had big plans for us today.

I was going to pick her up and take her back to my house and confront my parents. I don't give a shit if Hadley's dad is married to my dad's high school sweetheart or that they had been sneaking around behind my dad's back for months.

Hadley looks just like her mother did back

then and I almost sympathized with my dad for losing Mrs. Chase to someone else. I wouldn't let that happen to me. Hadley will one day be my wife. I can guarantee that.

Deciding to stop being a damn chicken I run out of the house to my truck and drive the few minutes over to Hadley's house. It practically sits on top of the other houses on her street and looks run down. I've never taken Hadley to my home. I'm almost embarrassed at how massive it is just for four people. I'm not a show off. I don't flaunt money around like my parents do or my friends who also have well off Moms and Dads. Unlike them, I would never look down my nose at someone because they had less than I do. Money doesn't buy you the kinds of things that are necessary in life...like love. And I fucking love Hadley and will spend every day proving to her how much...and after today everyone else will see it too, not that I care what they think.

I park along the street and walk up the short sidewalk to her front door. I rub my sweaty palms on my pants. This is the first time I've gone to her house without sneaking in the window. I ring the bell with no response. I find her bike in the driveway along with both of her parents' cars. Annoyed, I press the bell again two more times and wait. Footsteps grow heavy as someone approaches and then opens the door.

Her dad stands there looking at me half smiling until he realizes who I am.

"What?" He scoffs glancing behind me.

I take a deep breath now nervous to ask for her and scared shitless for when we tell this man that I am dating his daughter. I can see from his eyes that he hates me just because of who my dad is. I don't understand it though. He is the one who stole his best friend's girlfriend.

I know my dad has made his life a living hell. I've overheard him talking with his numerous contacts about keeping his ex-best friend, Hadley's dad, from promotions at work, promotions he deserved. At least that's one good thing about feeling nonexistent in your home. No one hears you coming or going and you listen to things that weren't meant for your ears.

"I'm looking for Hadley," I manage to get out. My voice cracks, sounding like a prepubescent boy going through the change.

I feel as though I can see smoke coming from his ears. He snarls, his face morphing into what I can imagine a murderer looking like just before stabbing his victim. "So, YOU'RE the reason, huh?"

My chest vibrates at his booming voice. I think the entire neighborhood heard him.

"I'm sorry, sir. The reason for what?" My eyebrows scrunch together in confusion.

"AVA!" he screams behind him and Hadley's mother almost instantaneously appears next to him. She looks outside the door, finding me, and her face drops. She's pissed too.

"Go home, Ryder," she tells me after her husband walks away. Slowly, she proceeds to close the door on me.

I put my hand up to keep it from shutting. "Where is Hadley?" I ask pleading. This doesn't seem right. Something is very wrong.

Why do my lungs feel constricted?

"She's gone. She won't be coming back to that school. You need to leave now and don't you dare step foot on this property again."

Taking advantage of her hit to my gut, this time she is able to fully shut the door.

I sink to the ground and shake my head side to side in disbelief.

She can't be gone.

But she was. That was the first of many failed attempts at finding Hadley. She left me and found some douche and now she has given all her love and trust to him.

I head back inside stopping at the bar to order three shots of tequila. Downing one of them I sit back at the table with AJ. He just stares at me as I numbly push the shot over to him. Our small glasses clink and we poor the liquid down our throats. He still says nothing as we sit but points his beer bottle in the direction behind me.

I look across the bar and my eyes are met with a hot blonde. She's dressed fucking sexy in a tight blue tank top and jean skirt with a long black shirt over her outfit that has holes everywhere. She tops the look off with tall black boots that say "screw my brains out."

She catches me staring at her and gives a little finger wave. I drunkenly wave back and raise my eyebrows. Her plump lips curve up into a smile and she nods towards the door.

Hadley's words repeat over and over again in

my head in her soft delicate voice.

I love Braden.

I trust him.

I love Braden.

"Sorry, AJ. I'm out of here." I stand up and walk towards the hot goddess and realize how drunk I am when I trip a little bit.

She giggles and I shake my head in embarrassment.

"Hey!" she says when I reach her.

"Hey yourself."

"You look sad." She pouts and takes her index finger and glides it over my frown.

"I'm not sad. Just looking to forget," I say sticking my tongue out and licking her finger.

She gets a little closer and kisses me lightly on my lips. "I could help you with that."

I haven't taken a girl home I've just met in quite some time but tonight I couldn't give a shit. The alcohol is making sure of that.

"Wanna get out of here?" I ask nipping at her bottom lip.

"Sure. But I'm driving. Give me your keys," she demands and I hand them over. I have no problem letting her drive my car as long as I lose myself while I'm inside her.

We leave the bar and jump in the car. The ride over to my house is silent but I have my hands on her thigh inching my way up. I show her which house is mine. She's a terrible driver but a hell of a lot better than I would be right now.

As she walks into my house, she immediately turns back to me and doesn't hesitate before taking off her holey black top. Her boobs are practically falling out so I decide to help them the rest of the way. Pulling one side of her strap down and then the other I see she's braless and my dick becomes rock hard.

She moans when I lean down, taking her peak between my lips. My free hand grips the other pinching it hard.

I'm a rough kind of guy. If you don't like a little bit of pain with your pleasure than you're not for me...and she seems raring to go.

The next few minutes are a rush of us getting our clothes off and barely making it to the couch that just a few hours ago AJ occupied. She pushes me down and straddles me, her hair whipping me in the face.

"Condom?" she asks, her brown eyes boring into mine, and I bring my hand up showing the one I grabbed. "Ah! Prepared huh?"

I nod and she takes the package from me opening it with her teeth. She rolls it on my dick slowly.

A vision of Hadley doing that the last time we made love so long ago fills my thoughts. Her innocent green eyes look into mine to see how it affects me and her hair falls into her face just before I swept it away.

"Shit! I can't do this," I say dragging my hands down my face.

She is hovering above me, her wet entrance to

my tip. “Are you kidding me? You expect me to stop right now? All I have to do is slam down right now and give you a fucking ride.”

Damn this girl is hot.

My hands grip her waist debating on if I should just push myself into her. She is my usual fuck and run type–the girl who I will screw and then send her on her way without a second glance. But she isn’t what I crave right now. I crave Hadley.

“I can’t. I’m sorry. I’m in love with someone.”

The words stun me further. Seven years later and I can’t help but still be helplessly in love with her. I thought it was neatly tucked away but there it is right in the forefront.

“What the fuck? Am I a homewrecker?” she shrieks jumping up off me scrambling for her clothes.

“Huh? NO! Oh, shit. I’m sorry.” I stand up taking the condom off and looking for my own clothes. “I feel like an asshole. I’m sorry.”

“Wife? Girlfriend? What?” Her hands find her hips looking murderous.

“No. Just a girl who has me twisted up.” I pull my jeans up, zipping and then buttoning them. “Again I am so sorry.”

She saunters over to me, her body swaying as she drops the clothes from her grasp. “I told you I could help you forget.” Her delicate finger runs along my jaw line but instead of being turned on I flinch.

“I’ll just call a cab back to the bar,” she huffs reaching down again to retrieve her clothes. “Since you are obviously too drunk to drive me back."

After she makes the call the awkward silence is stifling.

"I'm Wendy," she says looking my way, extending her hand.

I grab it feeling like a jerk. "Wow! I really am an asshole. I didn't even ask your name. I'm Ryder."

She smiles. "I like that name. Well, Ryder, do you just want to talk?"

I start to open up to her and when the cab arrives, I give him twenty dollars for his trouble and send him along his way...without Wendy.

Chapter 7

Hadley

4 Months Later

November

I wish I could be like the heavily falling snow that I'm currently watching fall to the ground across a sun rising sky. It's pure, true to form and seems to wash away everything. Sort of like a rebirth. Growing up I learned that each snowflake was unique. No two were the same, and I wished to be one, floating through the air and to be my own true individual self.

I soon realized that maybe being a snowflake isn't what I want. That I'm unique, but just like the rest, once I fall among the other flakes we form together into one giant mold losing our individuality.

Braden's voice is pulling me out of my snow driven hypnotic state but I have no idea what he is saying. With my hands wrapped around my mug of warm hot chocolate, I inhale the scent before I turn my attention to him and my cheeks rise from my smile. It's amazing how much of a difference a few months made for us.

Since my run in with Ryder, I have shifted my focus back towards my relationship with Braden and things have been incredible.

The sex? Amazing.

The romance? Better.

The communication? Could use more work. Despite the effort we've been putting in I still feel as though something is off.

I haven't felt so loved and protected in so long that I sometimes wonder if it's all real...or that maybe it will all fade away at the drop of a hat.

He's half smiling at me, waiting for some sort of response to a question I didn't pay attention to.

"I didn't hear you," I tell him giving him a smirk back.

He laughs, used to my daydreams, and it makes the twinkle in his green eyes shine brighter. He seems happier too. A bit more overprotective than he used to be but sometimes it's comforting.

"I said...what are you thinking? You look so peaceful staring out the window."

I glide my fingers through the locks of hair that have fallen over my shoulder. It's the longest it has been since we have met. "Nothing really. Just watching the snow fall."

The couch dips and his warm arms embrace me carefully not to spill the drink in my hand. His lips brush my temple and my eyes flutter closed. "What do you want to do on this lazy Sunday?" he asks as I open them back up.

Taking another quick glance outside I think of the perfect idea, though I'm unsure how he will respond. Braden isn't usually up for things he might consider childish.

I bite my lip at the thought of what my heart really wants to do.

"I think it would be fun to go sledding," I tell him.

When I was a kid there was a hill down the street from my house. My friends and I would go there anytime it would snow to feel the rush of sledding down the freshly fallen pathway. It was exhilarating. My life has been a bit boring lately despite the incline of my relationship with Braden but I'd just love nothing more right now than to feel like a kid again and take a risk...even though back then it didn't seem that way.

"That's silly," he admonishes. "We're not ten years old and you'd probably get hurt."

Him blowing off my idea instantly hurts my feelings and as we watch the news for the next hour I inwardly boil. It's not healthy for a woman to simmer inside but I don't want to start a fight over something as "silly" as going sledding. Do I?

As the news on the TV is starting to come to an end, I think of all the times I've done things for him. I've gone to movies that I didn't want to see. I went bar hopping with *his* friends when I wasn't feeling well. Missing my friend's wedding because he was sick, and I felt I needed to take care of him. I've been dragged to his work party when I was sick because I didn't want him to go alone...because he was going to.

Which reminds me.

"Is there a Christmas Party this year?" I ask

excitedly, almost forgetting about how annoyed I am with him. Every woman, no matter what she says, loves a good formal Christmas party so she can get a pretty dress and do her hair and makeup.

His body stiffens and he clicks the television off, standing up. He doesn't look at me when he answers. "Yea, but we're not going."

My jaw drops when he abruptly walks to the door taking his coat off the back of it and puts it on not bothering to look my way again.

I follow after him, concerned about the sudden change of mood and how a little bit ago he was asking what I wanted to do today. "You always want to go."

"Well," he starts, and finally looks my way. "This year I don't. Plus, they haven't even started to plan it out. I just couldn't care less."

"I'd like to go," I say attempting to stick up for what I want. It doesn't happen often and he isn't used to it.

His eyes flash to mine with a hint of anger behind them. "No."

"Are you leaving?"

He takes a deep breath. "Yes. I'll call you tomorrow."

Before I could push anymore he kisses me chastely on the lips and walks out.

I spin around trying to find the reason he up and left without explanation, coming up empty.

What the hell just happened?

I swear I will never understand Braden. That's

one of the things that haven't changed. His mood shifts.

I grab the blanket off the back of my couch to cozy up and take one more gaze outside. I throw it back down and race to my room.

"Fuck it."

~~

Forty minutes later, I'm staring down the same hill that just a decade ago looked like Mt. Everest to me but now seems like nothing more than an ant hill. Dressed in every warm material imaginable I set my newly purchased red circular sled down and place my padded bottom on top of it. I look around finding nothing but kids and parents. I almost stand back up, embarrassed, but determination sets in and for just one moment in my adult life I want to feel the rush. Just a small, very small, taste of what my life used to be like.

Risks. Taking chances. Not being afraid.

I mean, really, who is scared of a little sledding?

Pulling up my scarf over my mouth, I push off the cold ground and shoot down the hill. The slickness of the sled and my ten years of added weight propel me down faster than I expected. I pull my legs in to crisscross them and hold on tighter to the edge of the disc. The frigid wind whips past me and my eyes involuntarily close.

All tension releases from my body as it loosens up. I feel free like a snowflake. In my own world, not caring about bills, work, or my boyfriend. Not caring about what others think about me or what choices I've made in my life. I open my eyes not caring if I crash...until I see someone standing at the bottom in my direct path.

Then I care.

I try to scream but the scarf muffles my voice and I refuse to let go of my sled.

What the hell was I thinking? This was childish. This was stupid.

I brace myself for impact hoping it doesn't hurt too much and all the while thinking of how I'm going to explain to Braden why he has to pick me up from the hospital. He'll never let me live this down. Calling this childish and stupid. I just wanted one minute of release. Of freedom.

The instant I hit my unsuspecting victim's legs the sled stops and we both propel forward. I hear mutterings of curse words as I land on top of a body that, despite the coat, is rock hard. We land with a thud and my head hits their chest. Not immediately wanting to look at the one I assaulted, I take inventory of my body. Only a slight pinch in my knees and right cheek. Maybe a trip to the ER isn't necessary.

"You okay there, sweetheart?" the hard bodied man asks.

I can't respond because that voice, it's familiar. Too familiar.

It's one I haven't heard in months and one that instantly sets my body on fire despite our past.

Ryder fucking Blake.

My toes curl and my heart rate picks up faster. I can smell his musky scent even in the harsh cold and his heavy breathing is sending shockwaves throughout my body at every single small movement.

I'm scared to look up now. I don't want him to know it's me but there is no way to get out of this one. I can feel his chest bob up and down with his chuckles. "Come on," he starts, pushing my shoulders up as my scarf falls. "Let me see if you're hurt."

I allow him to lift me up off of him, and I prepare to run for it until his grip tightens in realization. People crowd around us but as I struggle to get away, and he holds firm, our eyes meet and I can't help but be powerless.

His mouth opens, his glorious tongue moves across his lips, sending shivers down my spine. "Hadley?"

"Ryder?" I try to say but another female beats me to it.

She runs up alongside of us and looks down, hands on her skinny hips. "You okay, babe?" she asks and a sinking feeling consumes my stomach.

I feel sick.

His eyes never leave mine. I don't know what he is waiting for so I make the move. I break the hold he has on me and stand up.

"I'm sorry," I say under my breath, picking up my sled and walking away, my feet kicking up snow in the process.

I hear louder voices behind me but I don't look back. I keep walking wishing I had parked closer so the embarrassment wouldn't last as long.

Out of all places why here do I literally run into

him? And who was that beautiful blonde woman he was with?

I tug the keys out of my pocket and open the door. Before I can swing it around a gloved hand pushes it closed and my front gets pressed into the cold steel of the car.

My hat is pulled over my ears but I can hear his whispered growl loud and clear. “Haaadley,” he says, elongating my name, taunting me.

I should push him back...but I don’t.

“Leave me, Ryder,” I tell him, hoping I don’t sound weak but knowing that I do. “I told you a while ago not to touch me.”

He laughs, the vibrations shaking me. “I’m not touching you, Hadley. No part of my flesh is touching your flesh. It’s all material that’s making you tremble, Spark.”

Anger surges through me. I shove off the car, whipping around to face him. “How dare you call me that! You are not allowed to call me that ever again.”

He steps forward, his hand reaching out to me. “Looks like your feistiness hasn’t changed.”

I look past him, seeing the blonde making her way over. My body temperature rises with what, I don’t know.

I cross my arms over my chest after pointing towards her. “Go back to your girlfriend.”

Glancing back he shakes his head and then steps dangerously close to me again.

He tilts his head to the side, showcasing his crystal blue eyes. “You’re not jealous are you?”

I let out a loud “ugh” as I shove off him. He backs off and I jump into my car turning the ignition.

Nothing.

Shit. I try again.

Nothing again.

Dammit!

I throw my hands down on the steering wheel just as someone taps on the window. I don’t have to look up to know it’s Ryder.

His Cheshire cat smile irks me.

I roll down my window, the cold air infiltrating my car. The pretty blonde is now standing just behind him. “What?” I ask.

“Need a ride?”

“No,” I say blindly reaching into the passenger side of the car, looking for my cell, and coming up empty handed. Thinking hard I remember leaving it on my bed.

Double. Fucking. Shit.

~~

“That girl didn’t care that you are giving me a ride home?” I ask him as I place my hands over the heater in his car.

His large hands reach over to turn the heat up and he chuckles. “That girl’s name is Wendy and no, she doesn’t care.”

We finish the rest of the drive in silence and when he pulls in front of my apartment I ask, “Is she your girlfriend?” I can’t *help* but ask. I guess because I am looking for more fuel for him to tell him to stay away from me.

Pausing for a moment to think he leans over, brushing his finger over my resting hands on top of my lap. My instinct is to pull away but I can't. I can't do a lot of things while he is around.

He pulls into my parking lot in front of my apartment. "Would it matter?"

I shake my head and finally pull my hand away. "No. It wouldn't. Thanks for the ride."

I slam the door as I step out, keys in hand ready to go inside and call Braden when I hear Ryder's door slam shut. I throw my head back, glancing up to the clouds in the sky.

"Get back in your car, Ryder," I request keeping my eyes trained above me.

"Just tell me where you went?" His voice sounds defeated.

It's a broad question but I know what he is asking. He wants to know where I ran off to.

My shoulders slump as I turn towards him. "It's not your business."

His head shakes from side to side. "I drove you home so I should at least get one of my million questions for you answered, and when you left you were my business."

I blow out a foggy breath, giving in. "CHS."

His face morphs into excitement and then drops. Stepping towards me he seems as though he wants to pull me into his arms but then thinks better of it. "Is that why you left? To go to the art school? We could have made things work, Hadley.

You didn't have to leave me."

"You got one question, Ryder. I answered. We're done," I say pointing my gloved finger towards him. I carefully walk on the iced over sidewalk to my stairway and hear him mutter "for now" before his car door slams.

After taking off all of my wet clothes and throwing them on my kitchen floor until I could take them to the communal dryer, I hear the ring of my cell phone from the bed. I run to pick up seeing Janie's name pop up on the screen.

"Janie!" I answer excitedly. She works with Braden and runs the annual Christmas party.

"Hadley! I need your help! I have no time to plan the holiday party this year. Do you think we could hire your company to do it?"

After a few more minutes on the phone and a quick text to Noe about the new event, I dial up Braden to tell him all the good news from today. I also let him know I need a jump for my car and even if he doesn't plan to attend the party I will be.

Chapter 8

Ryder

It's seven a.m. on Monday morning and I'm sitting in my car, head against the headrest staring at the stairs leading up to Hadley's apartment. I can see the ice that has formed on each step overnight. I can see a light glowing from what I assume is her living room but I don't see her car in the parking lot. I'm guessing she never went back out to get it.

I'm not a stalker. I didn't know she lived in the complex that I've driven passed every morning before work and every afternoon on my way home. I had the means at the station to find out where she lived but never used them. For four months, I have unknowingly gone past her apartment twice a day and now that I know I couldn't help but stop, especially since I see that her car isn't in here.

Checking to make sure she doesn't still need help would be the gentlemanly thing to do. What's holding me back is the possibility of her boyfriend being there too. I don't want to knock on the door only to have him answer. I'd hate for a fight to start that I would have to finish.

As I sit and debate whether or not to grow some balls and head up the icy steps I think about what she said just fourteen hours earlier.

She ran off to Chicago High School of Arts and didn't tell me. We had talked about it extensively the summer before our senior year on how we would make it work. We had it all figured out. We could talk every night, and I would drive down to see her every weekend. I know she was hesitant to switch schools at the end of her high school career but we both knew she really wanted to go, and I was doing all I could to support her and push her to go. She ended up not getting accepted or at least that is what she told me. She must have lied and for her just to drop everything and leave for Chicago without a word guts me. I was always her biggest supporter. Maybe she just wanted a clean break and to not have to worry about our relationship while she went and lived her dream. I could understand that. Then I think about the job she has now and shake my head.

The past four months have seemed like an eternity. It felt longer than the seven years that I hadn't seen Hadley. I tried hard to keep myself from going to her work, to avoid texting her. Asking Jace to find out from Noelle how she was doing was out of the question since he lost her to that other guy. So, I kept to myself, remodeled the house a bit, went to the gym more, and hung out with Wendy. Then all of the sudden she slams into me, literally, and I couldn't help but gravitate towards her. Ditch everyone I was with and take her home, even though I probably could have helped her get the car started. I know I could have but I wanted alone time with her.

At some point I must have gotten out of my car and made my way up the stairs because before I realize what I am doing my hand raises and gives three loud knocks on the door. I wait a minute before deciding this was a really bad idea.

I should just go to the gym.

I turn around, grabbing the railing, and her door swings open.

"Braden, why the hell..." she starts but her words cut off when I turn and she finds it's not him.

It's me.

She pushes the door halfway closed so that only part of her body is hanging out. Her beautiful toned leg shows through the bottom of her way to fucking short pink cotton shorts. Her arm is raised, holding the edge of the wood tightly.

Her eyes meet mine as I'm still grasping the railing. "What are you doing here?"

I look away from her and down the stairs towards the parking lot looking for the answer. Then I remember. "I didn't see your car. I wanted to make sure it had been taken care of."

When I turn back her head is down, looking at her bare feet. Her toes, painted a bright red, dig into the threshold. "It's not. I...ah..." she stutters through. "I couldn't get a hold of Braden."

We just stand there for a minute. Her looking down and me looking at her.

"I can take you..." I start to say at the same time she asks, "Do you want to come in?"

I nod and she opens the door the rest of the way, letting go so I can enter. When I walk in I'm surprised to see how small it is but it's one hundred percent Hadley. Above her kitchen table is a beautiful painting of a waterfall that is so lifelike it looks to be a photograph but I know her work.

"I painted that," she confirms, her soft voice coming from behind me.

I glance back taking a closer look at her. Her hair wild from sleep and her nipples taut from the cold outside breeze I brought in and pushing at the fabric of her sheer tank top.

"Do you always sleep like that?" I ask extending a finger towards every man's damn fantasy.

Screw lingerie. Hadley looks edible in exactly what she has on.

Her face scrunches, the lines between her eyebrows forming as she brings her hands to her hips. "Did you need something?"

I chuckle, which makes her even angrier. I love an angry Hadley. "Did you?" I ask turning the question on her.

A growl comes from between her lips. "Ryder."

I take a step closer. "I love the way my name falls from your lips."

Her eyes drift to the side. I follow them finding a wall clock. "What can I do for you at seven in the morning?" she asks seemingly annoyed but her rapid breathing gives her away.

Walking over to her couch I sit down, sliding my ankle over my opposite knee. "The question is 'what can I do for *you* at seven in the morning?' I saw your car wasn't here and I can only assume since you cannot get a hold of your so-called boyfriend that you might need some help getting your car started or a ride to work." I drag my finger across my mouth, watching as her eyes take in the action. "Do you need a jump...or a ride, Hadley?"

She doesn't move. She just stares taking in the double meaning of my words. Boyfriend or not, I don't know if I could turn her down if she asked to ride me right now. It would be so easy if she just straddled me, and I could push aside the flimsy material she calls pajamas and slip right in. I could grab her face and claim her mouth, her chest, her stomach, her thighs.

"RYDER!" she screams, and I jump right out of my daydream.

I adjust myself where I sit hoping she doesn't kick me out for the raging hard on I just caused myself. "Yes?"

"Did you hear a damn word I said?" She shakes her head walking over to the window and looks out. The light from outside shines through her shorts and I can see the curve of her ass. "I think I just need a new battery. I talked to my cousin and he thinks that is the problem but he can't get over here until this afternoon. I was just going to call out of work but since you're here you can help me." She doesn't turn my way as she continues, "I have a new contract and I want to get started so I kinda need to go in."

I lean forward, covering my mouth with my hands, trying to hide the smile that I can't prevent. When I get myself controlled I ask, "What about your boyfriend?"

She finally turns, shooting daggers with her

eyes. “What about him?”

“Won’t he get pissed if some other guy is jumping you?”

I know how that sounds. I said it that way on purpose.

Her eyes roll into the back of her head, and her hips sway on their way to what I assume is her bedroom. Her voice is muffled but I can hear her loud and clear. “You’re not jumping me, Ryder. You’re giving me a ride to the parts store and helping me put in a new battery. After that you can go jump some other girl for all I care.”

Ouch.

The ride to the auto parts store is short and quiet. When she emerged from her room, she had on tight jeans and a flowing white shirt that covered up her amazing ass. When she put on her black boots my dick went into overdrive. Nothing is sexier than boots that come up to a woman’s knee...and they zipper. A vision of unzipping them with my teeth came to mind, and I had to shake my head several times to get my mind out of the gutter. It didn’t work.

So, now she’s riding passenger, again, and I am surprised at how comfortable this feels. We used to drive around for hours in my car. My hand would navigate its way to her thigh and sometimes I would raise it higher and higher up her shorts until her delicate fingers stopped me. I was always pushing it with her but respectful. Always respectful.

We get a new battery, drive the few miles to

where her car is located and switch the old with the new. After a few minutes, it starts right up, and we let it warm up while she waits in my car.

"I owe you," she says quietly and when I look over her green eyes look vulnerable. She seems torn. About what, I don't know.

"Okay, well, I'd like my fee paid now if you don't mind," I tell her pushing a strand of her hair behind her ear.

Her eyes close and I see her instantly relax. Her chest rises and falls before asking, "What's the fee?"

When I don't answer right away her lashes flutter open and she peers over at me. "Ryder?"

"Hadley?"

"Ryder?" She chuckles, hitting me in the chest.

"I want another question answered. I help you, you answer a question."

Without hesitation, she turns me down. "No."

I reach over, hitting the button to lock all the doors. Her eyes go wide as she pulls on her handle. It doesn't budge.

"Open the door, Ryder." Her tone comes out as a warning.

I shake my head. "You have two options, Hadley. Answer one simple little question and I'll unlock your door, or climb over me and use mine." I pat my thighs for emphasis.

I wink at her as disbelief plays over her features and she crosses her arms over her chest. Part of me wants her to answer my question. The other part would love for her to climb up over my lap.

"What do you want to know?"

I turn in my seat, letting my knee lean up against the console. "What happened with your boyfriend that I'm here helping you out and not him?"

For a moment I think she might not answer. Maybe she will make my fucking week and climb over me.

"I don't really know." She sighs. "Last night I asked him to go sledding and he said no. Then I brought up his work Christmas party and he practically jumped down my throat about it and left. I haven't heard from him since."

She sounds sad. I feel bad for her. It sounds like this Braden douche isn't good enough for her.

"What does he do? Where does he work?" I ask as I hit unlock on the door.

She makes a tsking noise with her tongue and pulls her handle. This time she is successful in opening it. "Only one question per save, Ryder."

~~

By the time I get to work we have call after call and I have barely any time to catch my breath. After all the training with James a few months ago, he was moved for promotion purposes. As much as I wanted to get along with him we just could never see eye to eye. I got a new partner, Nate, but I see James all the time and right now he is listening to Nate give me shit at the end of our shift on why I'm so fucking happy today.

"You've been walking around here lately like your dog died and today you come in here like you got the greatest fucking pussy last night," Nate says shoving his shoulder into me.

James is leaning against a locker staring at our interaction. His stance is menacing.

"Fuck off," I tell him. Nosy asshole.

"For real though," he continues. "You gettin' some good shit now?"

Nate knows that Wendy and I are just friends but tend to scratch our itches when we need to. We're just having fun, but I know the reason for my mood change.

"Nah. Something better," I answer back, desperate to tell him like I'm some teenage chick. "That girl I went to high school with. I saw her last night when our group was up at the hill to sled. She came barreling down and ran right into me. Well," I continue. "Her car wouldn't start and she didn't have a cell to reach that asshole boyfriend of hers so I drove her home. When I passed by this morning I stopped to make sure she had a car and he still hadn't called, so I gave her a ride to her car. I don't know, man. Even though she was standoffish I feel like maybe I might be able to get somewhere with her. That guy seems like he is going to make it easy on me." I laugh, feeling bad for that poor bastard.

Okay, I don't feel bad at all.

James' phone rings and he excuses himself. Nate continues to pump me for more info on Hadley.

"This chick has got you strung up this badly, even years later? Even after she dumped your ass without even dumping your ass?"

I don't expect Nate to understand. He has a wife and a son but they always seem to be the last of his priorities. When I was with Hadley I always put her first. For a brief moment, I allow myself to think about where we could be right now if she would have given me the chance to be there for her. To show her my support of her dream.

Kids? I don't know

Married? Maybe.

Engaged at the least.

Working where we are? Me? Yes. Her? Hell no. I would make sure that the job she had would be one that she loves.

Maybe she does love event planning but I doubt I would see the love and lust in her eyes that I saw when she painted a picture. I think about that waterfall picture in her house and imagine her smiling with each stroke of the brush as she painted it.

Nate throws questions like rapid fire at me, and I answer them as much as I can always respecting Hadley with each answer. I never really talked to anyone besides AJ about her, and it feels almost therapeutic to get someone else's opinion. Just like James did months ago, Nate tells me that if there isn't a ring on her finger, then there is still a chance.

I'm never one to mess with someone's girlfriend, and I still have no idea why she left in high school without telling me. Now that I think about it, maybe that should have been my question earlier in the car. I could have found out her true reasons for ditching me. Even if the information that she and her boyfriend may be on the fritz can be used to help me out I would still like to know why I couldn't even get so much as an email when she left.

"I need a drink," I state clutching my bag into my hand.

A huge smile comes across Nate's face. "Hooligan's?"

We get our shit together and decide to catch happy hour with a few of the other officers who do traffic. They all exchange stories of conquests during their days in college and I just sit back and think about how I am going to "save" Hadley again so she has no choice but to give in and tell me why they hell she left me.

Chapter 9

Hadley

I walk into the office and stop mid-stride when I hear a weird noise. A table scrapes the floor. A chair shifts.

"Yea, Sunshine. Just like that." A rough male voice groans out.

Oh my God. I can't believe Noe and Trent are at it again!

I slam my bag down on my desk hoping they hear it and stop their almost daily game of hide Trent's dick somewhere inside Noelle.

They don't.

Ever since those two crazy kids got together they never separate. They literally don't separate. I wouldn't be surprised if Noelle got knocked up soon with how many times I've caught them having sex or how many times she has told me they have. I'm happy for them though. Trent just lost the mother of his son to cancer two months ago and even though they weren't together he had a rough time with all of it. He's always had a thing for Noe but I think it took a hard push from Alex, his ex, during her final months to get him to really realize what's important. Alex wanted to leave knowing that Jason, Trent's and her son, had a great mother figure around. Noe loves Jason like her own.

I pick up the phone and check our voicemails not daring to make any return calls until Noelle and Trent have finished their rendezvous in the conference room. I've made that mistake once and will never do it again. Luckily no one else is coming in today and we have no appointments in the office.

Twenty minutes later, I hear the door open and the fornicators come down the hallway finding me.

"Oh shit!" Noelle yells, jumping back like I scared her.

Trent kisses her on the cheek and gives me a big cheesy smile. "What's up, Hadley?" he asks just before making it to the door. He looks disheveled and sexy. His Decker Construction polo shirt squeezes the muscles all that manual labor gave him.

I continue typing away at an email. "Obviously you were."

A boisterous laugh leaves his lips, and I look up finding a proud look on his face.

"Well," Noelle says walking towards him, running her fingers over his biceps. "I took care of that for you didn't I, Trent?"

He grabs her face with one hand and pulls her in for a long kiss. "That you did, Sunshine. That you did."

After he steps out Noe walks down the hallway,

probably to sanitize the table in the conference room. When she returns, I inform her about the Christmas party for Braden's work and how since he pitched a fit about even going last night that he won't be happy about us planning it.

"Why is he being such a douche?" she asks sipping away at her fresh cup of coffee.

I slump into the back of my chair. "I don't know. He's wanted to go every year! Plus, my car broke down last night and I couldn't get a hold of him. Ryder had to take me to replace the battery this morning."

"*Ryder* had to take you?" Her voice raises an octave and I almost have to cover my ears.

"It's not a big deal." I wave a hand at her knowing full well she will. "Don't make it a big deal, Noelle." One girl's night I had too much to drink and told her all the sordid details. How I was infatuated with him in high school. How he went full force after me once the summer before our senior year started and how he ripped my heart out there underneath the bleachers of the football stadium. Not to mention how just weeks after I left he was nailing down any girl he could hammer. I found out after I confided in Emie.

"I have to call him." I think to myself, glancing down onto the black and white tile floor of my aunt's guest bathroom as I chip away the polish on my fingernails.

I take a deep breath and dial the ten numbers to talk to Ryder for the first time in three weeks. Just as I'm about to hit the send button I see Emie's name pop up onto the screen.

"Hey, Em," I answer sounding as torn down as I feel. I've never felt so alone in my life as I do right now. Sure, I've made some friends at the arts school and I talk to Emie on a daily basis but right now, well, I know things are about to change in a major way.

"I miss your face, Hadley. Come back to school," she replies making me smile for the first time since this morning. When I don't respond she asks, "What are you doing?"

I look at what sits beside me where I sit on the floor and my stomach drops, again. "I was about to call Ryder."

"Ugh." She groans. "Why would you want to do that? If he isn't even asking about you why should you care?"

After I left I broke down and told her everything, and she has been keeping me in the loop of all things Ryder, even if I don't want to hear them. Most of them I don't want to hear.

"He still hasn't even asked about me?" I ask dejectedly into the phone.

I can hear her blow out a breath into the receiver. "Nope. Not once, and he knows we're best friends. But he's too busy with half the cheerleading squad to bother seeking me out to find you. I wouldn't hold your breath, Hads. Do NOT call him."

My head falls into my hands as tears threaten to spill. "He's onto cheerleaders now?"

I hear tapping in the background, most likely on her computer. "Well, he's really into Bridgette Tate lately." She giggles to herself before she twists the knife in my chest more. "Mentally and physically if you know what I mean?"

I can see it even through the phone. The wink Emie gives when she turns something innocent into something sexual. But her words strike me like lightning. Bridgette Tate. I hate that girl and now here I sit, my future literally in my hands, and he probably has Bridgette in his. I'm mad. Pissed. At Ryder. At Bridgette. At Emie for acting like what she's saying isn't crushing me.

"I have to go." I lift my finger up to hit end waiting for her to say bye.

"You're not going to call him, are you?" she asks frantically acting as though she didn't just rip my heart out all over again.

"No but I'll talk to you later, Em. Love you." I hit end and lay down letting the cold tile soothe my heated body.

He's out there screwing around while I'm here dealing the consequences of our supposed "love."

I pick up the long white plastic test that lies next to me, gaping at it. The plus sign staring me dead in the face.

Pregnant.

"Someone looks deep in thought," Noe comments, interrupting my miserable trek down memory lane, while she reads the messages I left on her desk.

Getting myself together I look over and smile at her.

"Kinda," I start. "I have to go meet Janie this

afternoon to talk to her about what she wants to do this year for the annual Christmas party. I have so many great ideas. Do you want to come with me?"

A chuckle escapes from her belly. "I'm good. I just came with Trent but you go ahead. Let me know how it goes."

I shake my head at her. "I should be shocked by the things that come out of your mouth."

Her shoulders rise in a shrug. "Usually come goes in my mouth." She winks and goes back to her messages.

I try calling Braden three more times before I head over there, hoping he has listened to his messages. I'd hate to blindside him just showing up to his work.

~~

My car gave me no issues when I started it up and now I'm sitting in front of Braden's job, trying again to call him and looking at his car wondering how this is all going to play out. I still don't understand what went wrong. Why he doesn't want to go. Why he walked out of the house and hasn't returned my phone calls. Why it seems like we're back on our downward slope. Why I'm nervous to walk in those doors knowing that he is in there. Somewhere.

I step out and just as I slam the door shut my phone rings in my hand. Looking down I see Braden's name and reluctantly pick up. "Hello," I answer making sure to sound as annoyed as I feel.

"Hadley!" He practically yells causing me to pull the phone away from my ears. "Where the hell are you?"

Taken aback I stop midway through the parking lot. “Excuse me? I don’t hear from you for twenty-four hours and that’s how you greet me?”

I can hear him hiss and know that he is seriously mad. “Where. Are. You?”

My feet finally start moving again, and I open the door to the building. “I’m walking into your building. I’m meeting Janie in five minutes. I saw your car in the lot but...”

I’m pulled into one of the unoccupied offices halfway through my sentence. I don’t have to look to know who it is. “What the HELL, Braden?” I ask using force to pull out of his grasp.

He looks over my shoulder towards the door and puts his phone into his pocket. “Shh.”

“Don’t shush me!” I push off him trying to distance myself but his grip is strong. “Braden, can you please release me?”

Voices fill the hallways, and I turn around to see who it is but in an instant his lips are on mine. Pushing, pulling, prying but I don’t relent. I’m pissed that he would ignore me for a day and then try to kiss me without so much as an apology.

“Get off me!” I yell between tongue thrashings. He pulls back, his chest bobbing up and down with heavy breaths. “What the hell has gotten into you?” I ask.

His eyes stray towards the door again as more voices fill the hallway before returning to mine. The hair on the back of my neck stands up with suspicion.

“Did you get your car fixed?” he asks in an ominous tone.

Throwing my hands in the air I adjust the strap on my bag. “Yes, no thanks to you!”

He doesn’t flinch. “Did your cousin help you?”

Hesitating, I search my brain for some way to tell him about Ryder without him flying off the handle and making our tense situation even worse. I don’t feel like I did anything wrong yesterday before he left...but after, well I can’t help but feel like I shouldn’t have let Ryder into my apartment.

But he left me no choice.

He asks again, growing impatient, stressing every word. “Did your cousin help you?”

“Yea, he did.” I lie not caring about the consequences if Braden should ever find out though I make a mental note to call my cousin Chris later and fill him in.

Braden’s eyes search the ceiling for something but when he doesn’t find it he looks back to me. “Let’s go home.” He reaches for me but I step back.

“What part of ‘I’m meeting Janie’ didn’t you understand? I’m planning your party and whether or not you go, I am.”

I turn around, walking out of the door and towards Janie’s office.

Before I get there Braden turns me around and pulls my face within inches of his. “I love you, Hadley,” he tells me, his voice laced with desperation.

I search his eyes and it feels like hours before I respond. “I love you too,” I tell him.

I swallow hard as the words leave my lips. For the first time in a long time I feel like we might be falling apart without a chance of being put back together. I don't know what changed from Saturday until today but something has shifted and our world is off its axis. I think he is hiding something and I know for a fact I am. Even if Ryder and my interactions so far have been innocent, a lie is a lie.

Chapter 10

Hadley

It's been a rough week. Between my run in with Ryder on both Sunday and Monday, and barely seeing Braden for the past five days my strength is deteriorating and fast. After my meeting with Janic, I tried to call him and see what his plans were for the week so we could talk with yet again no answer. I've heard more from Ryder texting me than Braden and it's starting to wear on me.

A million thoughts run through my head as to why Braden would be acting this way and all I can come up with is that he is cheating on me. Either that or he wants to break up. What other explanations can there be? He has successfully avoided me, and as I sit here tapping my fingernails on my desk, I wonder what the hell I'm going to do.

"Ugh," Noelle groans. "Can you please stop doing that with your nails? It's driving me crazy!"

I turn one hundred eighty degrees in my chair to face her. "I can't. This thing with Braden is making me sick to my stomach, Noe," I tell her as nausea settles over me. "I don't know what's going on with him!"

Sure, things between us are far from perfect but I'll be devastated if he is running around with someone else. I think the blow of a break up would hurt much less than finding out he is cheating.

"Ask," she states simply.

Like it could be that easy.

My head falls back into the chair and I look up at the ceiling wondering if it is truly in fact that easy. I've done everything but ask him what the hell his problem is. I've called him, texted him, invited him over for dinner...anything I could think of and he just isn't taking the bait. I don't know what else to do...except maybe to back him up into a corner with no place for him to go and fucking ask.

Turning my chair back around, I grab my phone and shoot off a text to him before I chicken out.

Me: We need to talk. Meet me tonight or I'll assume we're over. I can't live like how I have the past week.

Our relationship seems like a roller coaster. One minute we're up and the next we're plummeting down to the ground only to be saved yet again by the incline. Right now it seems like we are falling with no steep hill in sight...and Ryder coming back into the picture is not making it easy on me.

My emotions are running wild trying to figure out how I can hate what Ryder did to me. Hate that he wasn't there when I desperately needed him the most but feel my body come alive whenever he is around me or how my heart flutters when I get a text from him. All I can do is attribute it to him being my first love, and you never forget your first, but maybe that is just a lie I tell myself so I can feel better about hating to love him.

All week he's been checking up on me, on the car, asking to go out for coffee or just to talk. As much as I want to I just can't. I need to figure things out with Braden and sort through the feelings of letting Ryder back in my life–if that is something I choose to do.

When Ryder isn't around it's easy for me to think clearly. Just to let it all sink in that he hurt me, scarred me but anytime he is near all that goes out the window and I can't think straight. I let him in my apartment. I let him help me. I let him back in just a little and now he's pushing for more knowing very well that I'm taken. Not that our relationship is stable at this point, but Ryder doesn't know I haven't spoken to Braden in a week.

My text pings and I quickly pick it up.

Braden: Just tell me when and where.

~~

I feel nervous as I get ready for my meeting with Braden. It seems weird to call it a meeting since he is my boyfriend. I throw some liner on to make my eyes look smoky and a tint of pink gloss over my lips. I leave my hair down the way Braden likes it. The red highlights have been dyed back to match the rest of my hair color so that I stop looking "like a teenager" as he so delicately tells me.

I pull the towel off of me and slip into a pair of skinny jeans and a purple sweater adding the small diamond stud earrings he gifted me last Christmas. It makes me think of the upcoming holiday. A week ago I thought maybe it would be when he would propose. Now, I'm just wondering if we will even be together.

My cell pings with a text and I throw some deodorant on and a spritz of body spray before picking it up.

Ryder: Drinks tonight?

He's relentless. It's two innocent words but they hit me right in my core. How sad is it that I would rather go get drinks with Ryder than deal with the possibility of ending my relationship with Braden. At this point I'm torn between wanting that and wanting to fight for what we've worked hard on the past two and a half years. I have to do the right thing. I respond to him for the first time since Sunday.

Me: Sorry. I have plans.

Ryder: She answers, finally!

Me: Haha. I've been busy.

Ryder: Not even one drink. Just one. I'll buy.

Me: I can't. Meeting Braden.

That should deter him. When I don't get an immediate response I put my socks on and head to the door, slipping my boots, coat and gloves on. Once my door is locked, I run through the crisp December air to my car, turning it on and blasting the heat, waiting for it to warm up. Curious, I glance back to my phone and find another text.

Ryder: I'd be much more fun ;)

I smile down at the phone but don't let it

distract me from tonight's mission to find out what is going on with Braden and me, even if going out with Ryder does seem like more fun.

~~

The bar is almost completely empty with the exception of a few patrons. I sit down in a quiet corner booth at promptly six o'clock and order rum and Coke from the waitress noting how completely bored she looks. I used to be a server. I know how much it sucks to work on a Friday night and have it be completely dead. My parents didn't have much money so I worked my way through college based on the tips of other poor college students. I barely made enough and I am still working through my student loan debt. The job at Events Unlimited saved me from not only being up to my ears in bills but also kept me from the lifestyle of a starving artist. I started off as a receptionist there but have slowly been trained to take on some events. The Christmas party being my first official one I plan from minute one.

I had tried to sell the paintings I made but no one is interested in them unless it's from a famous artist. Sure, I could go work at a school as an art teacher but unfortunately those classes seem to be the first to go during budget cuts. Even though I would love to spend my days painting in overalls outside on a beach somewhere I still like my job at EU and have fun letting out my creative side when I have free time–which isn't much.

Halfway through my drink I look at my cell finding it's already twenty after six. Swiping the screen to the side, I dial Braden's number, immediately getting his voicemail. I wait another minute in case he is trying to call me and when my phone doesn't ring I try him again.

Voicemail.

A sinking feeling takes over in my chest when I think that he might not show up. This could be the end of us. If he doesn't get here soon I know it's over. Even if we have tough times it always sucks when something you worked so hard at is over.

Without asking the waitress takes my drink off the table and returns with a new one. I must look like I need it. I make a mental note to tip her well.

An hour later, after five calls to voicemail, ten texts remain unanswered and three more rum and Cokes, I'm sad, angry, happy and downright confused. I could be worried that something happened but right now all I can think about is how much Braden doesn't care about this relationship.

Crossing my arms on top of the table, I lay my head down wondering who I should call to come pick me up. I'm in no shape to drive. When I finally decide that I should just call Emie the sound of heavy footsteps getting closer to my table fills my ears.

"Oh, now you decide to show up?" I say, my voice muffled into my sleeve.

I hear a chuckle and then a voice that most definitely does not belong to Braden. "I would have decided sooner if I knew you were waiting for me. In my defense, I did ask you to join me tonight."

I pop my head up and take note of the dizzy feeling I have from my five drinks. "What do you want?"

"Nothing, Hadley. I saw you over here and I wanted to say hi. Can't I just say hi?"

Through the haze of my tipsiness I take in his stance. It's strong, powerful and towering over me. His hair is messy in all the right places, and a huge smirk showcases the small dimples he has. His Adam's apple bobs as he swallows and his chest takes in slow shallow breaths. The leather jacket he is wearing is unzipped and I get a hint of the dark blue shirt he has on. A black belt wraps around his waist and between my thighs clench when just a quick flash of what is underneath the jeans that belt holds up enter my thoughts. I'm sure his body is much more toned now than back then, but then I remember how many others have seen what's underneath those clothes since.

"Okay, you've said hi. Now you can go." I wave my hand around dismissing him. I don't need this right now. I'm mad at Braden and I'm not thinking straight.

"Who were you waiting for?" he asks, his brows quirking up.

I roll my eyes and breathe out a sad sigh. "Braden. I told you that earlier. So, you should go," I tell him just as the server walks by. "A shot of tequila please?"

"Make it two," Ryder requests. "My tab."

He takes it upon himself to sit where I was so sure Braden would be sitting while we mended our reoccurring broken relationship. Braden should be here. Braden should've been there all week. He should have been the one helping with my car.

Taking a deep breath I try to be nice to the man who has done nothing but be nice to me despite my bitchiness. "Thank you for the other day, Ryder. For driving me to get the new battery."

"Of course. What are friends for?" He winks before taking a pull from his beer.

Our shots are placed down in front of us and I don't grab it immediately, unsure if getting drunk with Ryder just a foot away from me is a good idea, not that I'm not halfway there.

Ryder pushes one shot my way and pulls one towards him. "Where is he? Braden. If he hasn't decided to show up yet?"

The question irritates me only because I don't have an answer. "Where's your girlfriend Wendy?"

We sit in silence for a few minutes, neither one of us drinking the tequila. Neither one of us giving into the others questions.

His hand falls down on the table startling me. "How about this. I'll ask you a question, and you answer it. Simple. If you don't want to answer then you have to take the shot."

I snort. "How does this benefit me?"

"Well, I do the same. You ask. I answer or I take a shot–and I hate tequila so I'm pretty much up for just giving you the truth. I'm sure, just like myself, you have some questions."

Eyeing him skeptically, I ponder over it for a minute. "Okay. I get to ask my question first."

"Fair enough. Go ahead." He nods his head pushing me to ask anything.

Shifting my body to get more comfortable, I bring my legs up onto the bench, pulling my knees to my chest. "Is Wendy your girlfriend?"

"No." His answer comes quickly and certain.

“So, what is she to you?” I continue.

His hand comes up, his long finger waving side to side. “Ah, ah. It’s my turn. Where is Braden?”

“I don’t know. He was supposed to meet me here over an hour ago.” I don’t rest before I ask my next question. “What is Wendy to you?”

“Just a friend.”

“She didn’t seem like just a friend,” I state taking a sip from my mixed drink.

“She knows where I stand. Why are you still sitting here if he ditched you?”

“Just contemplating. Trying to figure out if he is cheating on me,” I answer honestly. “He’s been avoiding me all week. I got roped into planning his work party and ever since then he acts like he doesn’t want me around his job. I think he has a secret side fuck there.”

I lift my eyes to him.

The features of his face grow sad. “You were never a side fuck, Hadley.”

“But I was a secret,” I counter.

He shakes his head. “Hadley...”

“Where does Wendy think you stand?” I continue not wanting to talk about the past. Not yet.

“Right next to you if you would ditch the fucker who doesn’t know what a treasure he has.” He admonishes, his dark blue eyes piercing me with his stare.

“Ryder...”

Interrupting my though he asks, “Why didn’t you call me to tell me you were leaving?”

I reach in front of me, picking up the small glass and pouring the amber liquid down my throat. I don’t flinch when the taste of it burns its way down to my stomach.

“You’re not going to answer that?” he asks unbelieving.

“No. How many girls have you slept with since me?”

He grabs the glass in front of him and pours it into his mouth, slamming it down when he finishes. Turning to the passing server he grabs her forearm. “Four more shots please.”

Chapter 11

Ryder

I sit staring across the table taking in how beautiful Hadley looks, even sad. She's dressed in a pair of blue jeans, Ugg style boots, and a long purple sweater. Her dark hair flows over her shoulders down to her perky breasts. When my eyes meet her lips, she is biting the bottom one and it causes my dick to come alive. Her mouth curves into a smile and when our eyes meet I can see she knows what she is doing.

Hadley biting her lip is my weakness.

"Stop it, Had," I warn her just as the server brings us our four shots.

Her head tilts to the side, sizing me up. "Stop what, Ryder?" she asks innocently.

I lean in towards her, almost all the way across the table, lowering my voice so only she can hear me. "Biting your lip, Spark. You know what it does to me."

"Oh, I know but you can't touch me. I'm

Braden's."

I glance around the bar noting the lack of customers before turning back to her. "He's not here."

"I noticed. Thanks."

Anger raises inside me as I see how defeated she looks that he isn't here. What a piece of shit. If she was mine I would never stand her up.

Earlier, when I walked into Hooligan's searching for Nate, my text went off. I pulled it out of my back pocket, sliding the screen over to see a message from him that his son got sick and he wouldn't be able to meet me.

Glancing at the bar, I had found a vacant spot at the end and took a seat. After I ordered a beer, I pulled my phone out once again to see if AJ was available. Before hitting send on the text something caught my eye from the corner booth.

Hadley.

The bartender dropped the beer in front of me and I handed him my card. "How long has she been here?" I asked him pointing towards her.

He looked at his watch and then at her. "About an hour and a half or so."

So now, here we sit in silence, neither one of us drinking the tequila. Neither one of us giving into the others previous questions.

"So, you're seriously not going to tell me how many girls you've been with? Or do you not remember." She laughs.

"I know how many, Hadley." My eyes go wide. That's a messed up thing to say. "I'll tell you my number if you tell me yours."

She goes to pick up the shot glass before thinking better of it and sits up straighter. "Two."

"Two what?" I ask confused because a beautiful girl like that has to have had more than two suitors, even if it does make me all kinds of jealous.

She huffs. "Guys, Ryder. I've had sex with only two guys." Her eyes roll and she takes the shot of tequila anyways.

"So, Braden and me?" I ask though it's a dumb question. I know I'm one of them and she's been with him for a while so he has to be the other. "No one in college?"

"Ah, ah, ah." She mocks. "Your turn to answer. How many Blake? How many girls has the sexy Ryder Blake slept with?"

A smirk as wide as the Grand Canyon spreads across my face. "You think I'm sexy?"

Her face flushes when she realizes what she said but the liquor doesn't keep her embarrassed for too long. "Of course you're sexy," she says waving her glass around. "You have the body of a Greek God and did half of the girls in our graduating class in high school."

"What are you talking about, Hadley? I slept with two girls in high school." I don't tell her about my college years wasted between the legs of many co-eds. In high school, it was just her and Bridgette Tate. Though many tried, her best friend Emie included. I was too devastated by her disappearance to want anyone else.

My entire senior year of high school was spent playing football and going straight home. There were only very few occasions that I went out. I even sat out the school dances because I had envisioned Hadley on my arm as we entered them.

She hasn't spoken a word but just looks at me, furious. "I don't know where you got your information," I tell her.

Abruptly she stands from the booth, catching herself before she stumbles back. "Emie. My best friend. She told me all about how just a week after I left you had the cheerleading squad all lined up. Don't give me your bullshit, Ryder."

As my body tenses up I have to calm myself down before I say anything stupid. I take a deep breath. "Emie?" I ask to be sure. "Emie told you this?"

She nods crossing her hands over her stomach. "Yes."

"Sit down, Had," I tell her, readying myself to give her the news that her best friend is a bitch. "We need to talk."

Stepping away from the table, she uncrosses her arms and starts to walk away. "No. I have to go to the bathroom."

I watch her all the way to the bathroom making sure she makes it there okay.

I can't believe Emie told her I was sleeping around. That girl probably had more notches on her bedpost by the end of senior year than all the girls in our class put together...but never me. Not that she didn't try numerous times. Just three days after Hadley left, Emie was waiting by my locker asking me to take her to the homecoming dance. I thought, at the time, that she didn't know about Hadley and me but after what I just heard, I think she was bullshitting both of us.

I had asked Emie where Hadley was, begged her to get info out of her parents but she claimed she had no idea and they wouldn't tell her.

"Okay." Hadley plops carelessly back into her side of the booth. "The total number. I wanna hear it."

I peek down at the three remaining shot glasses then back up at her. Despite the crap she is going through with that piece of shit boyfriend of hers she is smiling. Probably from all the alcohol she has in her. "Twenty-two," I state, deciding to drop the bullshit Emie pulled on us so long ago, for the moment.

Her face drops and she looks away, seemingly disappointed. "Next question for me."

I bow my head ready to ask a question I don't want to know the answer to but take the plunge anyways. "Do you love him?"

She takes another shot of tequila but still answers. "I thought I did, but is love supposed to be this hard?" she asks before her attention is directed to the door where a few others have come in. She looks down at her phone and frowns. I want to reach over and kiss her sadness away.

"Well," I start to tell her. "I've only ever been in love once so from my experience no–but it does make you vulnerable enough to have your heart ripped open."

A snort escapes her. "I know how that feels, Ryder. You don't have to tell me how that feels."

"So, if Braden ripped your heart open then why

are you with him."

"No, not Braden. You." Her words cut me to my core. "You ripped my heart out."

My stomach twists in knots. I did everything but hurt her. Yes, we kept it a secret but I never did anything besides love her and make sure she knew that I did. Hadley was my world and when she left it felt like I was stranded in the middle of the ocean with no paddle in my one man boat.

"Well, you ripped mine out too," I tell her before taking another shot. I know she is open, answering questions, but she can't just put all the blame of what happened on me. I didn't leave her without any idea of where I went. She left me and she left me broken. "But unlike you I haven't been able to have a normal working relationship since."

Her eyes lift to mine throwing daggers at me with each second that passes by. Throwing her hands up her voice gets loud enough to draw attention. "Normal? Is this normal to you? My 'normal' relationship is hanging on by a thread right now. And you..." she points at me, "ever since you came back it's like that thread is rapidly unraveling!"

I quickly jump out of my side of the booth and slide into her side. Her eyes grow wide and she cowers into the back of it. Every inch I move in she pushes away until her back hits the wall and her knee comes up to block me. That one sentence, that one beautiful sentence has given me what I didn't even know I needed to hear.

Leaning in as close as I can get without tasting those beautiful lips of her I whisper, "Maybe that should tell you something, Had. I make no apologies for unraveling you and now that I know I'm helping dwindle the flimsy string that is holding the joke you call a relationship together," I breathe in closer. "I plan on watching it fall to the floor and then I'll secure you with nice, strong rope. Tie us up so tight you can't move...not that you would want to."

Her body shakes but not from being scared. It's quivering. I'm making her quiver, and her labored breaths are causing a stir behind the zipper of my jeans. If she wasn't taken I would claim her mouth once again.

She doesn't say a word but just stares between my lips and my eyes, her tongue coming out to wet her mouth. She wants me to kiss her.

Fuck it.

I lean in, pushing her erected knee into her chest. Her breath hitches as I bring my hand up to her cheek, caressing it softly, her head falling hesitantly into my palm. Bringing my lips closer she rewets hers, and I take that as my cue to grab the other side of her face and pull her towards me. Our lips just millimeters from one another, our eyes locked on each other.

I pull on a tendril of hair. "I miss the red. It suited you."

"Ryder," she whispers, the alcohol from her breath intoxicating me.

"Hadley," I breathe back into her.

Her eyes blink back a tear and it breaks my heart. "I loved you."

Taking another move getting so close I can feel her lips graze mine as I say, "I loved you more."

"There's something I need to..." she starts but a notification from her phone makes us jump as though we were doing something wrong. The look on her face tells me that she thinks we were.

Picking up her phone, she glides her fingers over it.

Sliding back over to my side of the booth I mutter "saved by the bell" under my breath before taking my original spot across from her.

She shoots back a text to whoever interrupted our moment and looks up. Her delicate fingers holding the phone like a lifeline as she just stares at me. After what feels like an eternity she speaks, "I have to go."

"Wait," I command reaching across the table just as she pulls her hands away. "You were going to tell me something."

Her stare is deep, unmoving, like she is fighting on whether or not to finish her thought.

"I can't. I want to go," she says, her green eyes contradicting her words.

"Let me call you a cab. It's my duty to make sure you get home safe." I stand up with her. "We can share. Your house is on the way to mine."

Pulling her jacket over her shoulders she motions toward the door. "Braden is here to pick me up."

My heart stops for a brief moment. I plaster a fake smile on my face. "Think he can give me a ride too?" I joke.

She snickers while she fastens the buttons her coat. "That would be something."

"Well," I say fingering the last shot on the table. "Sudden death?"

Her gaze falls to the door and then back to me. "What does that mean?" Her hands find her hips.

"One more question."

She points to the glass I've now picked up. "There is only one left, Ryder."

I love when she says my name.

"I know," I say stepping towards her. She doesn't back away. "I ask a question. You don't answer you take the shot. If you do then I'll take it."

A slow smirk presents itself. "Okay, shoot."

With my free hand, I lift her chin up so that I can look deep into her eyes and find the truth. "If not for that asshole outside waiting for you...would you have let me kiss you tonight?"

I need to know. I need to see how serious she is about this man. Is their relationship so broken that she would have risked it for a kiss with me? But the Hadley I know, that I remember was faithful and trusting to a man she loved.

She blindly grabs the shot from my hand and tips her head back to take it before turning away, her eyes never leaving mine.

I fall back into the booth, my head down, swimming in a sea of tequila and unanswered questions. More than I had before I walked in her tonight.

"Ryder." Her beautiful voice calls me from a few feet away. I look up and she is smiling. A true genuine smile. One I haven't seen on her since I found her again. "Yes. I would've let you."

My heart starts to beat faster. I want to jump up and grab her and slam my lips to hers but before I can even think straight she is out the door.

Chapter 12

Hadley

The door of the bar slams shut as I approach Braden's car. When I don't immediately open the passenger side door he rolls the window down.

"Get in the car, Hadley." He growls. I stand there, unmoving.

After another command to get in I place both hands down lowering myself so that I can see into the car.

He looks over, the green of his eyes have grown dark with dread. I can see he is upset. "Please," he asks. "Get in the car. I'll take you home and we can talk."

I sigh before relenting and getting into the car. "Nice of you to show up, Braden," I comment once my seat belt is secure.

I watch through alcohol infused eyes as Braden's jaw clenches and unclenches. His knuckles are pure white from the tight grip on the steering wheel. It almost makes me giggle. He has the audacity to be pissed and has yet to even explain where he has been for the past–taking a glance at my watch–two hours?

A growling sigh comes from between his teeth. "What's funny, Hadley?"

Maybe I laughed out loud. I don't give a shit. He has no right to be mad at me. I've done nothing but reach out to him all week!

"This relationship!" I yell letting him know how truly angry I am come through. "This relationship is such a fucking joke, Braden, that it makes me laugh."

I'm not even sure it makes sense to him, but to me, right now, it does.

"Obviously." He snorts, flicking the turn signal on. "Obviously you think it's a joke, Hadley."

I roll my eyes in disbelief.

Is he kidding?

"Me? Are you serious?" I screech pulling the door handle as, minutes later, he parks in the parking lot of my complex. I look over at him, my eyes forming into slits. "I'm not the one that checked out this week. I'm not the one cheating!"

After slamming the door I grab onto the hood of his car when I slightly slip on a small patch of ice, I push off and stomp my way up the stairs. Just as I push they keys in to open the door Braden's hand wraps around my wrist.

"Let me go!" I yell ripping my hand away from him and pushing my way into my apartment.

He's quick to stop the door before I slam it in his face, striding in like he pays the rent here.

I point my finger into his chest. "Get out!"

He body stands firm but his eyes scream vulnerability. "I'm not cheating on you, Hadley. What the hell?"

Ignoring that lie I walk into the kitchen making myself a glass of water. When it quenches the parchness of my throat, I throw my purse and jacket off towards the table.

Braden hasn't moved an inch, and when I look at him I see a different man. The difference a week makes. It's sad, and I feel not only hurt but disgusted.

"Where the hell were you then, Braden...and not just today? All fucking week! I told you this morning that you needed to meet with me to figure all this out and you didn't show up. Didn't call. Didn't text until you were in the damn parking lot two hours late. Dammit! I feel like we're just falling apart!"

He flinches. I'm not sure he has ever been the recipient of my anger. As he steps closer he uses careful movements like he is confronting an angry animal. His eyes find mine, and his teeth snatch up his bottom lip.

Immediately remembering Ryder and what me biting my lip does to him. Guilt instantly creeps in when I think of how close he was to kissing me. How I almost let him and how Braden, who was just outside in the parking lot, could have just as easily walked in and seen how close we were.

My knees start to go weak at the thought of hurting Braden even just a sliver of what I felt the night Ryder betrayed me so long ago. Even though

Braden has done nothing but hurt me this week he doesn't deserve to feel that pain like I did, even if he might be cheating on me. I don't know how I will be able to move on after another blow like that. I silently pray he isn't stepping out on me...and then I try to imagine how I would feel if I caught Braden in a bar, his lips just a fraction away from another woman's. It makes me sick.

I feel like a hypocrite saying it makes me sick to think of Braden doing what I almost did.

"I could never cheat on you, Hadley. I'm so deeply in love with you that I can't even imagine getting to know another girl." He reaches out for feelings of guilt. I can feel myself climbing back up the hill of the roller coaster that is our story.

He pulls me into him, his arms circling around my body, and my head falls into his chest. It feels warm and comforting. He smells like home and I just want to curl up with him and have him caress my back and tell me everything will be okay, but I have to get some answers.

My voice is muffled into his jacket. "What happened, Braden? Where were you this week?"

His chest rises and falls with a deep breath. "Right now, baby, I'm just dealing with some stuff and I'm trying to figure out how to deal with it the right way."

I pull away, looking up into his now distant eyes. "Talk to me, Braden. We're supposed to be a team. We should be able to tell each other anything."

Every muscle in his body tenses up as the shade of his irises turn darker. "We should, huh?"

he asks seemingly baiting me.

I take a hard swallow and try to see what he wants me to say. I just nod and he pulls away, disgusted.

"So if we can tell each other anything, tell me who Ryder is, Hadley?" he yells, his voice booming off of my patio door, shaking the glass. "Who is he to you?"

Time stops. The world comes to a halt and all I can do is just stare at Braden. Watch as the vein in his neck becomes prominent. Watch it flicker with each beat of his heart and watch as he steps closer to me, daring me to answer.

"How do you know about Ryder?" I ask trying to avoid the question I don't know how to answer, when I finally find my voice.

"How do I know abo…" He stops mid-sentence, shaking his head and pulling his hair through his fingers. "Are you sleeping with him?"

"No!" I deny instantly.

"Then why did you lie?" His voice grows more heated than before, if that's even possible.

I sway for a brief moment, the final shots of tequila reaching my system. I lean up against the couch to keep my balance. "What did I lie about?"

He picks up a pillow, throwing it across the room. "Your cousin didn't help you fix your car, Hadley. Ryder did! Now, do you want to tell me about him? No fucking lies."

Thoughts race through my mind. I didn't tell anyone about Ryder's help except for my cousin, who hates Braden with a passion, and Noelle.

Neither would say something to him. Then it hits me.

"You and your damn friends are such stalkers! Don't you have anything better to do at work? So, you ditch me on Sunday and have me followed?"

"Yea, Hadley," he says sarcastically. "Because that is the worst of the two issues here."

"Wait!" I stare him down wanting my own answers. "That all happened after you hightailed it out of here on Sunday and then refused to answer my calls, and why the hell didn't you say anything when I came to your work on Monday?"

More things come into focus as others become more confusing.

"I wanted you to tell me the truth!" he yells. "I wanted my girlfriend of two years to tell me some other man helped her. A man who I have never even heard of before!"

I stalk towards the kitchen to get more water. I suddenly feel like I need it. "Are you kidding me? He had to help me because you wouldn't answer your damn phone."

As water from the faucet fills up the glass Braden continues, "No one else could help you, Hadley? It had to be some guy you've never mentioned before?"

"He stopped by." I realized my slip up when the drink is halfway to my mouth, but he seems unaffected like he already knew he'd been here.

"What happened Sunday that you couldn't bother to answer my calls in the first place?" I say before he can dive deeper into that last admission. "Is it the party? The fact that I'm planning it or the fact that I'd like to go and you seem dead set on not going?"

"We're not going." He slams his hand down on the counter, shaking my spice rack "You're not going."

"I don't have a choice!" I yell throwing my hand up. "I'm the event planner! Don't you want to go?"

"I do want to go," he confesses, his face turning a dark shade of red, before walking back into the living room and sitting on the couch. His hands go straight to cover his cheeks as his elbows rest on his knees. He looks ten years older right now, stressed beyond his years.

"So what's the problem then, Braden?" I ask not being able to hide the annoyance in my voice. It's not working.

He jumps up, pointing a finger in my direction. "I don't want YOU to go!"

My jaw drops to the floor.

And there it is.

"Me?" I point a finger into my chest. "You don't want me to go? Are you going to take the woman you're cheating on me with? Is it Janie? Huh? Who is it, Braden? Who would you rather take than your own girlfriend?"

"You've lost your mind, Hadley!" His voice rising to a level I've never heard before. "I'm not cheating!"

The volume of his voice causes me to jump.

"We're not going," he continues. "You're not going. I'm not cheating and I won't tell you again.

End of discussion." His voice is low, like he is trying to fight a losing battle, which he most certainly is.

I walk to the door and open it, letting a cold breeze filter through the apartment. "Leave."

He strides to the door, slamming it back shut. "No! I want to know about Ryder. Now."

I bring my chest to his, looking up to show him how pissed off I am. "Tell me where you were tonight then."

His eyes drift down to my lips and I think he may kiss me, until they meet mine again and I see hurt. Anguish.

I swallow the lump down in my throat. I suddenly feel bad but we both want answers and neither of us wants to give in. However, if there is any chance of making things right I have to talk to him. If his avoidance of me this week was because of my lie about Ryder, and if I have any chance of fixing this, I need to be honest.

"My ex from high school," I say starting up the conversation we need to have. He needs to know what happened.

We make our way to the couch to sit down and I tell my story first. How Ryder and I met and kept it a secret. How I got hurt in the process and left without telling him. I tell him that Ryder's and my parents hated each other and how Ryder, a few months ago, showed back up in town. He says nothing, but just listens to what I have to say, taking in each and every word. When he hears about the sledding incident and how it all happened with my car his body tenses and stays that way until I finish. I don't dare tell him about seeing him tonight. When I'm done he just looks at me, expectantly, like he wants more.

"Is that it?" he asks.

I deflect his question by asking his whereabouts this week. He breathes out a sigh but his only response is, "I was trying to figure out what to say to you. I was thinking. I needed some space."

I shift on the couch, pushing myself back into it and away from him. "Don't you think that you should have clued me in on that, Braden? We were fine Sunday until the mention of the party."

"I don't want to go," is all he says essentially starting round three of this fight.

"No," I counter, shaking my head. "You said you don't want me to go."

"That too." He shrugs before continuing in a more heated tone. "You were pushing to go. I don't think it's a good idea. Then I turn my phone off to get some space and find out the next day some guy, who you have never mentioned to me before, is giving you rides and fixing your car. How can you expect me not to take a break from you, Hadley?"

Anger rises in me. I'm pissed. He disappears all week without as much as a phone call. "If you would have picked up when I called I could have told you about him. Then this week from hell could have been avoided!"

"Would you though, Hadley? Would you have told me about him? You didn't tell me you saw him in the bar a few months ago?" His voice grows colder. "This guy fucks you up for years and you allow him back in your life, not to mention hide him from me, your boyfriend who NEVER hurts you?"

I lower my gaze to my fingers. “Until now,” I whisper.

“Excuse me?”

“Until now you’ve never hurt me.” I look up stronger than a moment ago. “This week was nothing but me getting hurt.”

The cushions move as he stands up. “I’m not doing this anymore tonight, Hadley. You’re not the only one who was mind fucked this week.”

He slips on the jacket he took off and walks to the door.

I pull my knees to my chest. “You’re getting what you want, Braden.”

His hand halts on the doorknob before turning towards me. “What’s that?” he asks cocking his head to the side, confused.

I look up, finding the face of a man who I don’t recognize anymore. This is not the Braden I met over two years ago. Not the Braden who has been riding this up and down coaster with me the past few months. This is a man I don’t like. Someone I don’t know. “Your break. I’m giving you your break.”

“What the fuck ever, Hadley. Fine.” He throws the door open and slams it shut with his exit.

Tears flow freely down my face, my body racking with sobs.

I cry for the next hour going over every minute of the day and realize I still don’t have any answers. Then a thought runs through my mind.

I never told him it was a bar I saw Ryder a few months ago.

Chapter 13

Hadley

It's Saturday night and I need a girl's night. Not a "let's go out to a bar and let random assholes hit on you kind of night" but a "get in your pajamas and drink wine with friends" kind of night.

So after shooting off texts three hours ago, Noelle and Erin are here and Emie is on her way. Wine bottles line the kitchen counters and we're about four bottles in.

"Noelle!" Erin yells. "I do not want to hear about my brother's penis. Like ever!"

I laugh as I watch the back and forth banter between the two of them.

"Well," Noelle says raising her glass. "You said let's make a toast and I couldn't help but praise the fucking beautiful cock that lies between your brother's legs. I'm sorry." She shrugs. "I'm thankful every damn day he lays it in me."

"Don't you mean on you?" I ask trying to keep my laugh at bay.

"No." She shakes her head looking at me like I'm stupid. "Why would I want it on me? I'd rather it be in me."

My laugh gets out of control and Erin goes to get more wine. Noelle eyes me. "What are you laughing about Chuckles? Doesn't Braden have a nice dick?"

I almost spit my drink out.

Noelle can talk for hours on how amazing Trent is in bed. Erin will let a few things out here and there about Walker but as far as I'm concerned there is nothing spectacular about my sex life. Now that Braden and I are on a break there won't be in the near future either. I'm normally not the type of girl to talk about my sex life but the five glasses of wine I've had apparently unfilter me.

"Yea, it was okay." I raise a shoulder as I circle a finger around the rim of my glass.

Erin walks back into the room. "Was?" she asks as she sits down next to me, most likely thankful that the subject is off of her brother. "As in not anymore?"

Taking a deep breath and then letting it back out I look over at the falling snow outside my patio door. "Yes, was. We're on a break."

Noelle starts clapping her hands like a damn seal. "Finally!"

"Noe!" Erin chastises. "Can't you see that Hadley is hurting?"

"She's not hurting," she argues. "She's fucking free!"

I know that Noelle never liked Braden. She

said there was something about him that she just couldn't put into words which is saying a lot because Noelle is never short on them. But her saying I'm free strikes a chord. Am I really free?

No. I haven't been for a long time. My feeling of freedom was lost a long time ago. When I left Ryder and high school to go to CHS and I put myself into my art. No longer was I the carefree Hadley that jumped off piers into Lake Michigan or who wanted to skydive and bungee jump. I lost all that the day Ryder, the one person who I felt really understood me, spewed his disgust towards me to his friend.

I lost my drive. I lost my will to be carefree. I lost myself somewhere and I desperately want to get it back.

A knock at the door pulls me from my thoughts and I jump up to answer it. Emie walks in waving two bottles of wine.

"From Napa," she states going to work on opening them in the kitchen.

She just returned from a weeklong trip with some sorority sisters in Napa Valley. I've barely spoken to her since she left. She has no idea what I went through the past seven days. Even though she is my best friend, she sometimes makes it uncomfortable to talk to her about Braden.

Noelle greedily holds her glass up as Emie fills it. "What did I miss?" Emie asks looking over at us.

"Oh, not much." Noelle eyes me after getting her fill. "Just Hadley and Braden broke up and now she can go ride Ryder."

Both Noelle and Erin laugh but Emie just

stares at me looking for confirmation.

I nod. "The break thing is true but not the riding Ryder thing." I wave my heavy hand around feeling the effects of the alcohol.

"Well, good," Emie says. "I wouldn't think that is such a great idea."

"Are you kidding?" Erin chimes in. "Why wouldn't it be? From what I saw he is sexy and from what I heard Braden did to her this week she needs to find a new man. I don't know if he is cheating on her but I can tell you from experience it's best to just move on."

"What happened this week?" Emie asks taking a seat across from me and putting her feet up on the coffee table much to Noelle's dismay.

"Braden ignored her all week. Apparently he somehow found out that Hadley was seeing Ryder and checked out on her," Noelle tells her.

Emie's eyes go wide. "You were seeing Ryder? Hadley?" she says with disapproval.

The wine falls smoothly down my throat. "I wasn't seeing him. He helped me out with my car when Braden wasn't answering my calls. Somehow Braden found out and ignored me all week." I shake my head. "We were supposed to meet last night but he didn't show up until two hours later and we got into a fight. It would have been worse if he knew I had been taking shots with Ryder at the bar while I was waiting for his ass."

My hand slaps over my mouth. I hadn't told Noe or Erin that. I wasn't planning on it. I just keep sticking my foot in my mouth.

"The plot thickens," Erin comments then

laughs.

“What kind of shots?” Noelle asks. “Like protein shots.”

Emie spits out her wine across the floor. Noelle jumps up, runs to the kitchen and grabs a rag and some carpet cleaner. This causes Emie, Erin and me to erupt in a fit of laughter. It’s not even her house and she is freaking out over the wine on the floor.

“Noelle,” I laugh her name out. “Don’t worry about the carpet.”

She looks up from her spot on the floor. “Don’t worry about the carpet?” she asks astonished. “Oh, honey, I keep all my carpets clean. All of them.” She winks. “Don’t you know a man loves a clean carpet?”

“Noelle stop!” Erin groans.

I laugh again, letting the wine talk for me. “He doesn’t have to worry about a clean carpet, just about buffing my hardwood floor.”

I’m even shocked by my admittance of having it all bare down there. All of them start whooping and hollering and I reach over to grab my phone to order us all Chinese, while Noe finishes up her cleaning. However, I am distracted by a text I missed. I can feel myself blush when I find it’s from Ryder.

Ryder: What are you up to?

I smile and while the girls continue to giggle and chat, I respond.

Me: Hanging out with some friends.

Ryder: I’m a friend. Can I come hang out?

Another smile presents itself on my face, and I put the phone down before my tipsy side tells them to leave and tell Ryder to come over. I don't know what a break with Braden means but I do know that it shouldn't involve me asking Ryder to come over. Even though he isn't here just the thought of our almost kiss makes me want to finish what we started.

I excuse myself to the bathroom. When I'm done I grab my credit card from my purse so I can pay for our food and walk back into the living room catching Noelle throwing my phone back onto the couch where I had it.

"What did you do?" I ask her but look over at Emie who is more interested in her own phone than the two bitches messing with mine. She has barely said a word since she got here which is not like her.

I wonder what that is about. It seems like anytime Ryder's name comes up she goes all mute on me.

"Nothing that you shouldn't have done," Erin says crossing her leg over the other.

I pick it up finding my texts with Ryder still open but it has significantly more than when I left.

"You texted him back?" I screech at the two of them looking at the messages that occurred while I was in the bathroom.

Me: You can come anytime.

Ryder: Really?

Me: As long as it's with me.

Ryder: Which one of Hadley's friends is this?

Me: The kind that wants her to get laid.

I'm horrified as the texts seem to be getting worse.

Me: She told me she wants to do some protein shots with you.

Ryder: Haha. I'm sure she did.

Me: She did. She said now that Braden is out of the picture she would love to wrap her mouth around your dick. Protein does a body good.

Ryder: Braden's out of the picture???

And that's where I must have caught them with my phone. I stare down at it wondering what the hell I say to him now. I opt for ignoring his question.

Me: I'm sorry about that. I should never leave my phone unattended around them.

Ryder: It's ok. They proved informative. Is it true?

He won't relent, and I'm not sure how to respond so I don't. The rest of the night seems off. I'm pissed that Noelle sent out those texts and told Ryder something I didn't really want him to know and Emie has been extremely quiet. She gives one word answers and anytime the other two joke about Ryder she doesn't even comment at all. When the wine is gone, the food is eaten, and the cabs arrived and picked them up, I slump down into the couch and grab my phone again seeing a text from an hour earlier.

Ryder: Just a yes or no, Hadley? Did you two break up?

I know he won't stop asking until he gets his answer. I always remember Ryder as a push and shove kind of guy. Never stopping until he succeeds at what it is he wants to succeed at.

Me: No, no break up. Just a break.

When he doesn't respond I decide to jump in the shower. The hot temperature, combined with the copious amounts of fermented grapes, cleanses the stress of the past two days. I stay in there for a while not wanting to step out into the emptiness of my apartment. When the water runs cold, I get out and put on a pair of yoga pants and tank top. I pull back the sheets and stop before climbing in when I hear a knock at the door. A glance at the clock tells me it's past midnight.

I reach for the bat next to my bed and walk quietly towards the door. Looking through the peephole my stomach flutters with excitement over seeing Ryder's face. I shouldn't be this thrilled to see a man that I love to hate and hate to love.

I swing the door open, bat still in hand, and watch as he takes me in. His eyes leave a blazing trail from my bare feet to my hardened nipples and then land on my own dilated pupils.

"Do you think an intruder would knock on the door, Hadley?" he asks looking at the bat in my hand.

I turn around and drop the bat onto my sofa. "Just be glad I didn't grab my gun."

He chuckles as he walks into the apartment and closes the door. I don't know why I'm letting him in but I can't stop myself.

"You know how to shoot?" he asks surprised.

I have to cross my arms over my braless chest before I turn around. “Braden taught me.”

He nods in understanding before taking a step further in and looking at the painting in my dining room. If only he knew that the color of the water reminded me of his eyes.

After what feels like an eternity I finally ask, “What are you doing here?”

A dark look crosses his features as he stops closer to me. His proximity causes me to drop my hands. “I still remember, Hadley.”

I watch as his fingers hover above my arms raising them as though he is trailing his touch up over my skin. They leave goose bumps in their wake and create a pool of desire. I try to clear my throat but my question still comes out hoarse. “What do you remember, Ryder?”

The atmosphere in the room shifts. It turns from tense to thick with lust. His muscles tighten in his forearms, his lips get closer to mine. My eyes involuntarily close.

When he answers I can feel the heat of his breath on my neck. “How your lips feel on mine and how your skin feels under my touch. I want to kiss you. Finish what we started yesterday.” My body tingles with how close he is to me. I want to push him away but pull him into me all at the same time.

“You can’t,” I say fighting the urge to let him ravish me.

I open my eyes, finding his looking down at my heaving chest. “Are you still his?” he asks.

“No,” I whisper.

"Then let me claim what is rightfully mine, Hadley."

"I'm not yours."

"You're not his anymore either. You're fair game."

I push off of him, upset by his choice of words. "It's not a game, Ryder! This is my life."

Angry and sexually frustrated I stomp over to my patio looking outside. It faces into the parking lot and even though the snow has cleared there are piles of it on every corner.

The taller ones remind me that just a week ago I was trying to be free and feel like the old me as I slid down that hill.

"I just want my life back," I say to myself but he hears me. I know he does.

I listen as he approaches and turn around so that I can make sure he keeps his distance. My mind goes to mush when he catches me off guard.

"Tell me," he urges. "What about it do you want back?"

I shake my head side to side as I look down. "Freedom. The freedom to be me. To take risks, take chances. Live life."

I feel like a broken record but I don't know what to do about it.

He points towards my room. "Go get dressed," he commands.

I look up at him curiously. "What? Why?"

"I want to take you somewhere."

Chapter 14

Ryder

I can't believe I'm about to do this, and I can't believe Hadley is trusting me enough to take her somewhere she doesn't know.

She got dressed and slipped on her coat without another word but the bouncing of her leg next to me in the car tells me she is nervous but curious.

My heart broke for her hearing that she has lost herself over the past half of a decade. I can understand that. Sometimes I feel like I can't be the guy I used to be when I was with her. She was the one who taught me not to care what the hell other people thought. The one that made me want to do adventurous things like mountain climb and parasail. For her to say that she misses taking risks, well, it makes me sad for her.

Just in the small amount of time I've spent with her I feel like she is just the shell of her old self and even though where I am taking her won't fix that I just hope she can come out little by little.

I pull into the parking spot of a nearby hotel and when I look over, Hadley's eyes are wide and angry. "If you wanted to fuck me, Ryder, you could have told me at my apartment so you wouldn't have wasted time or money bringing me here so I could say no."

I laugh. "Fuck you?" I shake my head. "Oh no, Spark. The first time I get myself between those sexy ass legs of yours again I won't be fucking you. I'll be worshipping you."

Her cheeks flush red, and her thighs push together I'm sure to ease whatever tension I just created down below.

Looking towards the building, her eyes scan the outside. "So, what are we doing here then?"

I put the car in park and turn it off. "You'll see," I give her a vague answer.

My words in the car about worshipping her must have been effective because she won't look at me and she sure as shit won't get closer than five feet away. Now that I think about it, my plan to get closer might not work out so well.

As we enter the quiet lobby we bypass the desk and head straight for the back of the hotel, the clerk never stopping us. The hallway is long and quiet, seeing as it's now one in the morning, except for the paddling of our soft footsteps. When we reach our destination Hadley looks between me and the glass windows confused.

"So, what now?" she asks looking back at me.

I motion behind her to the large room with a pool and hot tub. "We're going in."

Her laugh fills the hallway. "No we're not. We

aren't staying here and we don't have swim suits."

I push the propped open door and extend my arm inviting her in. The smell of chlorine greets us. "We don't need them." I wink at her. "Live a little."

When she makes no attempt to move and refuses to enter I pick her up and throw her over my shoulder. She goes to scream but I stop her. "Don't," I warn, slapping her on her ass. "You don't want to get caught do you?"

She quiets down but continues to struggle as I carry her over to a corner where we can't be seen. My friend owns the hotel so even if they caught us it's not like we couldn't get out of it. That and the fact that I'm a police officer would help if we did in fact get arrested.

Setting her down next to one of the long white chairs she gives me a deadly look, the shade of her eyes turning evergreen. "I'm not doing this, Ryder. You are not seeing me naked."

I throw my head back and let out a loud laugh. "Are you kidding? I can close my eyes and see you naked, Hadley. You might be more toned up now but there is no way I could forget how beautiful your body is."

She flushes again and subtly bites her lip.

"Plus, you can't tell me," I walk over turning the hot tub on, "this doesn't excite you. Didn't you say you wanted to feel free? Take a chance?"

She contemplates for a moment before zipping her jacket down and letting it fall onto the chair. "Turn around," she says, looking past me, most likely making sure no one can see us.

I do as she says and look out towards the pool

and start stripping myself hoping to God that I don't get too hard. "I hope you're getting undressed because if you aren't I'm going to do it for you," I threaten.

I hear her slip into the hot tub before she responds. "You can turn around now."

I have no shame doing as she asks while taking my boxers down over my ass. I find her in the hot tub staring directly into my eyes not wanting to look down. Spotting her clothes on the chair and knowing she is ten feet from me, naked under the water, has me trying to keep my dick at bay.

I slowly slip in to the warm water across from her watching as her toe peeks up through the water and steam. The bottom of her foot is smooth and I have to keep myself from reaching out and bringing it towards me. The water trickles down to her knee before she lowers her leg back underneath the surface.

A sound comes from just outside the pool area and her eyes shift towards the exit.

"What does a break entail, Hadley?" I ask distracting her. "Can you see other people?"

She stifles a laugh and brings her attention back to me. "I don't know. I've never been on a break before but since Braden and I were together for over two years I think anyone at this time would just be a rebound."

Hadley stares at me, waiting for a response but I take a moment to think about it. "A rebound, huh? Well, isn't a rebound defined as someone you use to bury the pain of a bad break up?"

She tilts her head to the side wondering what

I'm getting at while bringing water up and over her neck and chest. I swallow hard trying not to be distracted. "Yea," she says slowly, question in her tone.

"Well, I don't think," I tell her scooting myself around the tub until I'm as close as I can get without her moving. "That you would be burying any sort of pain. I think you would just be picking up where you left off. Where you should have stayed."

My hand comes out of the water, pushing her hair back behind her ears as I slide my fingertips down her neck. Her eyes flutter shut with the touch of them gliding over her collarbone. I watch as her lips part and her teeth snag her bottom lip. Her chest rises but never falls as she holds her breath. Reaching my hand up and around the back of her neck I pull her to me and gently hover my lips over hers.

"Ryder," she whispers but I don't respond. I just hold my lips so close that I feel her breath seep into my body. I watch as her eyes open, a tear pricking at the edge, threatening to fall over, and I lean a few inches back.

"Had, what's wrong?" My brow creases in confusion. Is she upset about her break up? Is she scared to be with me?

I drop my hands at the same time she drops her gaze down to the bubbling water.

"I just...I can't..." She stumbles through her words before looking up at me and I see the tear fall slowly down her cheek. "We need to be friends."

My breath catches as a gust of air exits my

lungs. I didn't expect five words to crush me like that. After yesterday's confession of hers that she would have let me kiss her and finding out today she is available I think maybe I got my hopes up too quickly.

"Okay." I shake my head reluctantly giving her more space. "I can do that."

"Really?" she asks with the sound of hope in her voice.

"Yes. I'd rather be your friend than for you to tell me to stay away. I just don't know that I could do that right now."

Her smile lights up the space and I can't help but smile too.

"So, as your friend," I reiterate the last word. "I think you should tell me what happened."

Her fingers wrap around her long hair, pulling it up on top of her head and holding it there. The action almost gives me a peek at her breasts. Her elbow comes to rest on the side of the hot tub so that she is leaning over and just looks at me for a moment.

"He knew about you," is all she says. I stare at her waiting for more but it never comes.

"So you told him we dated?" I ask.

She processes the question briefly. "No." She furrows her brow. "He didn't know that until yesterday. He did however know you gave me a ride to fix my car and that I lied to him about it. I told him my cousin helped but somehow he found out you did and decided to ignore me all week because of it. I don't blame him really. I'd be pissed if he lied to me."

A lot of things run through my head. One being that I'm sure he has lied to her before. What kind of man ignores his long term girlfriend of two years without confronting her with what he knew? The second thought I have to ask. "What else, Hadley? It just seems like something else had to have gone on between the two of you for it to escalate to a break up."

"A break," she clarifies. "And I don't know. I think he is embarrassed of me. Or cheating. Remember I told you he jumped down my throat about his Christmas party? Well we got into an argument over that again."

I'm happy she is finally opening up to me more without the help of alcohol but I hate that he is treating her this way.

The steam rises between us, and my body is starting to heat up. I know soon we will have to get out of the water, and I'm going to have to take a look at her naked body. I won't complain though. "You don't want to go?"

"Oh, I do, and he is more than willing to go. He just doesn't want me to." She shakes her head like she can't believe something. "He doesn't have a choice now. I have to go. I'm coordinating the event."

She looks sad. Defeated.

"Spark," I call her by her nickname that I gave to her all those years ago. The one that reminded her not only of how we started off as a little flame and blew up into a full blown fire but how she used to be a pistol. Someone that was a light everywhere she went. As she looks up at me I tell her, "If you were mine, I would be honored to have you on my arm whether at a Christmas party or a lunch at Burger King. It wouldn't matter. Any man should feel lucky to have you by his side."

An unladylike snort emits from her mouth. "Yea, just like in high school, huh?" Her voice grows cold. "I seem to remember hiding our relationship from everyone."

Her sudden irritation causes her to stand up without warning, showcasing her amazing body and my argument falls dead on my tongue. I think any fight with a man can be won just by taking off your clothes. He will forget his point, except for the one growing between his legs, and you win. Her bare pussy takes me by surprise and is scrambling the thoughts in my mind. Her soft breasts make me lose all sense of motor function.

Holy shit she is even sexier than I remember.

"Yea," she chastises walking to her clothes. "See, you have nothing to say."

"Wait a second," I yell as she starts to put her panties on. They are pink and lacy and all things feminine. They cover up very little of her lower half before she slips on her matching bra. Her eyes never leave mine as they wait for what I was going to say. "I didn't want to hide anymore, Hadley. I was coming to you. I was going to tell everyone all about us and you just fucking left."

I stand, careful not to slip, and pull myself out of the hot tub. This time Hadley doesn't even try to keep herself from looking at my dick. I'd call her out on it but I'm too invested in getting this straight.

"Just tell me why, Hadley? One sentence to let

me know why you left that day. The day I was going to ask you to homecoming. The day I was going to tell our parents to go fuck themselves. The day I was going to tell you that I planned to marry you and how in the future I wanted you to have my children."

Her face grows somber and she looks away, her body beginning to shake with sobs. I scramble to put on my boxers, walking over to her and pull her half-naked body into mine. "Tell me why you're crying. I just don't understand. What can I do to make it better?"

Her arms drape around my wet torso, her hair sticking to our bodies, as she continues to weep. When she begins to shiver, I look around for a towel spotting one on the far end of the wall. I manage to hold onto her and navigate to the other side of the pool and grab for one. She allows me to pull her off of me so I can wrap it around her before she sits on a nearby chair and I follow, wrapping the white linen around my waist. Her head falls into my lap, and we just sit there as her cries grow silent.

"I wanted that too, Ryder," she finally speaks. "I wanted all of that. I wanted to hear you say you loved me so much you wanted to marry me. I wanted to tell them all to mind their own damn business. I wanted you there for me when I needed you the most."

I rub her back as she tells me the words I longed to hear years ago. "Why didn't you stay long enough to let me tell you them? Why didn't you let me prove to you that our relationship could survive anything?"

She looks up from my lap, her eyes red with hurt. "I wanted to."

Her face splotchy from crying is tearing my insides apart. "I would have given you everything. Anything you wanted," I tell her, gliding my palms over her shoulders.

When her breathing calms and her tears stop she sits up. "I'd like to go home."

I nod my head and stand up following her over to her clothes. She picks them up and drops her towel but the swinging open of the door surprises us. We quickly move into the corner and I cover her. I can feel her heartbeat beating erratically out of her chest but can sense she loves the rush. Always has. I smile knowing I just might have given her exactly what she needed tonight.

After a minute of holding our breath, the door opens again and whoever it was leaves. I look down, just now noticing our bare skin touching. Her covered breasts are pushed up and her skin is prickled with goose bumps.

"Being friends is going to test all my self-control."

Chapter 15

Hadley

"Do you have everything you need?" Noelle asks through the other end of the phone as I'm walking into Chevy Chase Country Club for the final walk through. Tonight is Braden's work Christmas party and the guests are arriving soon.

It's been two weeks and I haven't heard from him, nor have I had an in person meeting with Janie. Despite him telling me he isn't cheating on me with her, or anyone else, I just prefer to be ignorant and use the break to clear my head. But all its done is messed with my mind more.

So many times I've wanted to call him. I just can't and so I poured myself into this event, booking more clients for Noe, working out and spending some time on myself.

"I think so," I answer, pushing the door open to the building where I'm met with the most amazing sight. "Wow!"

The venue is stunning. I ignore Noelle's continuous questions and hang up in complete awe of my surroundings. I know that I was the planner but seeing it all come to life almost brings a tear to my eye. I've helped on numerous occasions with different events but this my first solo one.

Entering the lobby, I find all the lights dimmed and snow globe candles illuminating every flat surface. Beautiful sparkling snowflakes hang from the ceiling and silver cloths adorn the end tables and coffee tables.

I slowly make my way to the room where the dinner and dancing will take place and am transformed into a winter wonderland. The walls are draped with white tapestries, spotlights of alternating gold and silver, shining on each one. The dance floor is towards the back of the room and the DJ seems to be finishing his set up. Each table is topped with the same silver tablecloth as the lobby tables and each are set up for ten people. The place settings consist of crystal and china. They have spared no expense and the commission off this event alone will pay my rent for six months.

Walking around I drag my hands along the chairs covered with soft fabric. The centerpieces are a larger version of the snow globe candles but are surrounded by stemless red and white roses. Each seat has a place card written by a calligrapher. Janie did the seating arrangement, so I have no idea where Braden is going to sit or if he is even attending. There will be over three hundred people here.

My phone vibrates in my hand alerting me to a text.

Ryder: I miss your voice.

I smile knowing that my friends don't text

things like that. He's been trying to get me to hang out with him again but I really need a clear mind and he truly clouds my judgment when he is around. He asked me to go out tonight but yet again I declined his invitation. So he has been sticking to sending messages like that every day. It's more than Braden has done.

When I'm finished going through the final checklist with the kitchen, I excuse myself to the bathroom before everyone starts to arrive. After washing my hands I take a look into the full length mirror making sure my eyeliner has not run and my lipstick is still intact. I turn to the side taking in the beautiful dress that I splurged on just for this event. It's a floor length off white gown. The top half is crystal beaded with a sweetheart neckline and spaghetti straps. It cinches on one side just at the waist and flows freely down with layers upon layer of chiffon. My favorite part is the slit that runs from the bottom of the dress on my left side all the way to my mid-thigh. It's formal and sexy and it makes me feel beautiful. My long brown hair is loosely pulled up on top of my head giving it a formal but casual look. I wear the diamond studded earrings that my grandmother gave to my mom. My thin silver bracelets clang as I smooth my hands down the dress before heading out into the party.

I walk out confident and ready to make sure the event runs smooth until I hear a voice that stops me dead in my tracks. "You look beautiful."

I whirl around to find Braden leaning up against the wall adjacent to the bathroom. His smirk plastered on his face as he takes in my dress and for some reason it makes my skin crawl. I can tell his thoughts are anything but pure and I can't even look at him that way right now especially since he is drunk.

I look down at my silver peep-toe shoes accepting the compliment. "Thank you."

When he doesn't respond I look up finding him walking towards me, his arms reaching out as if he wants to bring me into them. I step back not letting him anywhere near my personal space. "Don't," I warn. "Don't you dare touch me. Remember? You didn't even want me here."

The hurt in his eyes is evident but I don't care. He's here and he doesn't want me to be. I walk with purpose away from him and into the lobby filled with people dressed to the nines. Men in tuxedos and suits, and women in striking gowns. Husbands and wives using the excuse to get done up and go out. Others bringing dates they hope to impress.

"Hadley," a female voice calls out. I turn towards my right finding Janie nearing me. "Hadley, this is stunning. I'm in awe of it all. I'm so glad I hired you." She laughs. "If I planned it we would be at Lou Malnati's eating pizza in jeans and sweatshirts."

I smile at her compliments but have a hard time looking her in the face. She seems sincere, and I know she can tell something is up by the look that crosses her face. I instantly feel terrible. I have no proof Braden is cheating with her–or anyone for that matter.

"Thank you." I look around. "It was a combination of both our visions."

Bringing me in for a hug, she kisses my cheek.

"But it was you who made it come to life." She pulls back, her hands still on my upper arms, and smiles. "Walk around, enjoy. I put you and Braden at table eleven."

Great! I think when she finally walks away. He must not have told anyone and now I am torn on whether or not to sit with him so that he doesn't get embarrassed, not that he wanted me here anyways, or leave him to explain to the others why his date isn't at the table.

Fuck him.

He can sit alone.

The cocktail hour and dinner go off without a hitch, but I have this feeling that it's too perfect and something has to go wrong. I call Noelle and after five minutes of her telling me to simmer down I finally hung up when she says she needed to finish riding Trent. She always goes for shock value.

As the plates are cleared, the DJ changes from soft music to upbeat rhythms. A few attendees head to the dance floor, and I stand on the outskirts watching them be carefree. Their job is so intense that it's nice to see them relax. I haven't seen Braden since our run in outside the bathroom, and I am thankful that this will be over soon and I can go home, pop open a bottle of wine, and take a hot bath.

"Hadley!" Janie yells from the middle of the dance floor waving her hand frantically for me to join her.

I shake my head no but she runs over and grabs me by my elbow and pulls me out there. I hesitate for a second before deciding the hell with it and start moving my body to the sounds of Ariana Grande's "Break Free." Seems like a fitting song right now, and it feels amazing just to let loose and, as Ariana suggests, break free.

When the song changes to a sweet melody, I try to turn and get off the dance floor before it's flooded with couples. I freeze when firm hands grip my hips from behind. I roll my eyes at Braden's attempt to show nothing is wrong, but the look on Janie's face tells me something isn't right. She seems confused, and her eyes are wide as saucers.

I feel his breath on my neck before his words hit my ears. "I didn't know you could move like that, Spark. I'm trying not to get hard in front of all these people."

My heart flutters, his breath tickling my ears. My body immediately responding to his, molding into him. Our bodies sway to the soft beat but after a moment I remember where we are and scramble out of his arms, turning to face him.

"Ryder. What are you doing here?" I search him for answers but a scuffle behind me attracts his attention.

Confusion crosses his face as he looks across the dance floor. He braces himself, nudging me to the side and I get a better view of Braden coming full force at Ryder.

"BRADEN, NO!" I scream as his fist flies through the air towards Ryder. Ryder ducks down, missing the blow, and throws one of his own directly into Braden's gut. He hunches over in pain but still charges Ryder.

He hits his target, tackling Ryder to the ground, and all I can do is stare, my hands over my mouth. A few guys run up pulling Braden off of him and Ryder stands waving off the men who try to hold him back.

I'm in shock as I stare at Braden and then over to Ryder who is holding his bleeding lip but looking right at me. "Braden?" he asks confused.

I nod towards the man who filled my days for the past two years and feel tears falling down my face. The DJ stopped playing the music and the entire room is silent. Three hundred people all waiting to hear their interaction or to see whether they will go at it again.

Ryder points at Braden. "That's James. My old partner. That can't be Braden."

I follow his finger back to a seething Braden. If it weren't for his buddies he might still be trying to fight Ryder.

Braden speaks up, venom in his voice punctuating every single word. "Braden. James. Bolter. Hadley's boyfriend."

Everyone collectively gasps, including me, and a few things start to make sense. Braden has always gone by James at work, ever since he started there, so I understand how Ryder didn't make the connection. Ryder said Braden and he were partners. Braden is a police officer and that must mean Ryder is too. They both work for Buffalo Grove and in the same department.

It all makes sense now how Braden knew about Ryder and why he didn't want me here. Ryder must have been talking about me at work.

How did Ryder being a police officer never come up in any of our conversations?

Well, that's fucking great! Now I'll be the topic of everyone's gossip at the PD from now on.

I turn to the DJ motioning for him to put the music back on and storm my way towards the exit. Everyone is staring at me and I ignore the knee jerk reaction to flip them all the bird. I think I'm in shock because before I know it I'm back in the bathroom, door closed, head resting on the back of it. I hear when someone enters but I make no motion to move.

"Had." A soft voice calls out. Janie. "Hadley, come out and talk to me."

When I continue not to respond, I hear the door open back up as she leaves. I feel terrible. Here I thought Braden was cheating on me with her and all she has done is be nice to me. I've been a total bitch to her. I was short with her on the phone, ignored her suggestions of meeting in person.

After a few minutes, I feel it's safe to escape and find my phone. I can't leave because I set this party up but I can't stay either. Lowering my head, I walk through the tight spaces left by the hundreds of people here tonight, spotting my purse on a table. I reach out, pick it up, and finally raise my head. Across the table is Ryder. In the seat next to him is Wendy, the girl from the sledding hill, holding a pack of ice against his mouth. My insides coil up. My mind on overload.

He works with Braden.

He works with Braden.

Shit!

He works with Braden.

I stand there, unmoving, and watch Wendy pull the ice away from him and place a gentle kiss to the side of his mouth.

I swallow back the bile rising in my throat and give him a disapproving look. I didn't think it would hurt to see something like that, especially when I put him in the friend zone, and now that I know he works with Braden, there is no probability of us ever becoming more than that. I won't mess with their careers.

Rather than stand there looking like an ass, I pull my phone out of my purse and purposefully walk to the side of the stage to a quiet spot. Before I can hit send on Noelle's number someone snatches the phone out of my hand and whips me around.

When I get my bearings, I find Ryder's dark blue irises heating up with what, I don't know. Anger? Lust?

"Why do you keep running, Hadley?" he asks, his voice just high enough so I can hear it above the music.

"I figured you were busy with your girlfriend." I spit out causing him to smile.

"She's not my girlfriend, but your little boyfriend not only played me the past couple of months but took a swing at me." His tongue darts out and over his swollen lip.

"He's not my boyfriend," I breathe out, his nearness is undoing me. "And how'd he play you?"

Both hands wrap around each of my wrists and

he steps closer. My rapid breathing shows how affected I am by him and in this moment I could care less if we got caught like this. Even if it was by Braden. His mouth speaks into my hair. “I told him about you, Hadley. When I first transferred to BGPD back in August. He never mentioned you were his.” His leg moves between mine nestling itself between my thighs. The slit of my dress giving way and exposing one of them. “Hell, before he knew your name he even told me to go for you. Told me you weren’t engaged so you were fair game.”

“Go back to Wendy,” I say trying to distract him from making me come by just the brush of his leg. My resolve fading quickly.

Ryder’s head falls to my shoulder. “Are you jealous? My God, Hadley, tell me you’re fucking jealous.”

My body and my mouth betray my mind because I turn my head and whisper into his ear, “Yes.”

“She’s just a friend.” He growls.

I turn my head, exposing my neck. “So am I.”

He releases my left wrist and grabs the exposed skin of my leg pulling it up, his thumb brushing up the inside of my thigh. A tingling sensation follows the trail of his fingertip.

“Yes, but I don’t want to taste her. It’s not her skin I want on my tongue,” he says bringing his mouth to the edge of mine. I tilt my chin up bringing us to the same spot we left at the bar. The same spot at the hot tub. The point where all we would have to do is move a millimeter and our mouths would collide. I can’t take it anymore.

Despite saying I want to be friends, despite Ryder working with Braden–I want him.

The music stops and the DJ announces last call. Ryder slowly drops his hands and pulls back. Our eyes meet. “I’m coming over tonight,” he says, his tone implying it’s a threat. “I’d like to hang out with my *friend*.”

Chapter 16

Hadley

The event ends and since I was accosted next to the dance floor and left with soaking wet panties I'm rushing to get everything cleaned up. Noelle ignored my pleas to come help me and told me to put my big girl panties on. I finally found Janie, apologizing for the way I had acted the past couple of weeks. Thankfully, she understood. I don't see Braden again but his friend's wife told me after everything that went down he left, which I'm thankful for.

When I finally arrive home, I start a warm bath after putting my dress on the hanger and place a robe over my body. Walking into the kitchen, I pull a bottle of wine off of the wine rack and open it. When my glass is thoroughly poured I turn to go back to the bathroom when someone knocks softly on the door.

"One second!" I yell running to my room and slipping on a pair of shorts and a tank top over my head. After turning the water off in the bathroom I run over to the door and swing it open, a smile dancing over my lips. I wasn't sure he was actually going to come but I'm surprised at how excited I am that he did. My smile drops when I find not Ryder, but Braden standing in my doorway. Even drunker than before.

I try to slam it shut on him but he blocks it and trips as he crosses the threshold. "Hadley. Let's talk," he stammers.

"Ha!" I laugh, picking up my wine from the counter. "You've had three weeks to talk and now you want to. Get out."

"No," he says, leaning up against my table, most likely to keep himself from falling on his face.

"Yes. Or I'll call the cops." I threaten but even I laugh at that. He is the police and so is Ryder, who I now really hope doesn't show up anytime soon.

He slumps into the chair, his tie gone and the top three buttons unfastened. His eyes are glazed over and his blond hair sticks up everywhere like he has been running his hands through it. I walk over to the kitchen getting him a glass of water and handing it to him.

"I hope you didn't drive here, Braden," I tell him taking a seat in a chair across from him.

He takes careful sips as he watches me.

"So, you were Ryder's partner?" I ask and he nods. "When did you find out he knew me."

I can smell the alcohol from across the table as he speaks. "I found out the day you got the flowers from him."

Surprised, I grab my chest, cringing at the thought of Braden knowing for that long. I should have told him about the flowers but I had thrown them away after Ryder left. That was the day I came home to him making dinner and he claimed my body.

"He was a rookie and I was taking him under my wing. Fuck, I even told him to go for you." He lifts the glass up waving it around, spilling some on the table.

My fingers drum against the table. "Why didn't you say something to him? To me? I mean, you've been somewhat possessive our whole relationship and you didn't say a word."

"Sergeant," is all he says.

I stare confused. "What does that mean?"

His hand glides through his hair making it more of a mess. "I've been working towards Sergeant for a while now."

A sense of pride consumes me. I know he has been working hard to get promoted and I had no idea. "Why didn't you tell me?"

"I wanted to surprise you, Had." His head falls down, defeated. "I wanted to tell you after I got my chevrons and when I found out our new hire was your ex boyfriend from high school I almost lost it. I couldn't though. I needed to keep my head on straight to get promoted. So, I put in for a new partner and thought after that day you would never see him again. I guess I was wrong."

He stands up abruptly and walks to the bathroom. My phone buzzes from the counter. I check it, finding a text from Ryder.

Ryder: On my way.

My body tenses with panic. I can't have Ryder come over when Braden is here.

Me: Can you stop by tomorrow? Braden is here. He's in bad shape and needs to talk.

Ryder: No. I'm coming over.

Me: Please, I promise I'm fine.

Ryder: Call me when he leaves. I'll wait up.

As I wait for Braden to return I think about what he said. He was up for promotion and didn't tell me but if he would have told me he worked with Ryder, I could have made it easier on him. Even though I asked Ryder back then to leave me alone I would have never let him into my life this much the last month knowing that it could possibly hurt Braden's career if he flew off the handle with jealousy.

The chair scrapes across the floor with Braden's return. He looks better, like he splashed some water on his face and fixed the craziness of his hair.

"Feel better," I ask grabbing his glass and refilling it.

When I sit back down Braden takes my hand into his. I don't pull away but it feels foreign, like we've grown so far apart nothing feels the same.

"I got it," he says, squeezing my hands lightly. "I made Sergeant."

A proud smile takes up half of my face. "I'm so happy for you. When did you find out?"

He blows out a breath, letting go of my hand. "The Friday we were supposed to meet. That was why I was late." He looks up to the ceiling like he is searching for something that isn't there. "I got promoted and the boys kidnapped me and took my phone. I was late because they wanted to congratulate me. Then I pull up to find Ryder's car and your car in the parking lot. I walk in to find you two on the same side of the booth. God, Hadley my heart sank."

There are no words to describe how much I hurt for what this man saw. "Braden," I plead. "Nothing happened. I promise."

"I know, Hadley. I know because my text stopped you. I watched you two get closer and closer." He shakes his head side to side as if he is erasing the memory. "So I sent that text and you two jumped apart. After that I went outside and waited in the car."

"Braden." I reach out for his hand but he pulls it off the table and places it in his lap. "I'm sorry."

It's all I can say. Nothing I do can make any of this right and nothing he says can fix any of this at the moment.

Silence fills the air, and I'm unsure what to say or do. I apologized, but it doesn't feel like enough. Maybe I should call him a cab? I don't know.

"I saw you tonight and you looked so beautiful, baby." He reaches into his pocket and pulls out a box. "I just wanted to drop to one knee and give this to you."

A hitch in my breath causes me to literally choke up. He places the unopened box on the table just staring at it. Part of me wants to see what's inside, though I have an idea and the other part of me doesn't.

He twirls the box around. "I've had this for two months now but was just waiting for the perfect time. I was going to give it to you the same day I showed you my chevrons. Can you imagine how it felt to carry this around knowing the person I was going to ask to marry me was lying? Too bad all of the extra effort I put in the past few months wasn't worth it." He pushes back in his chair–picking up the box.

"I felt like we were falling apart." I try to reason.

He shakes his head as he looks at the floor. "I did too but I didn't want him to have you."

I straighten my shoulders. "So all that extra attention wasn't because you wanted me but because you didn't want him to have me?"

He doesn't answer my question but only lifts the box from his side. "You don't deserve this."

I watch, mouth agape, as he walks to the door. I'd stop him but his last words of me being undeserving simmer in my thoughts.

"Braden..."

His hand comes up to stop what I was going to say. "Don't."

I nod holding the door open for him. He places a kiss on my cheek and eyes me with disgust. "That's the last time I will ever touch your lying, dirty skin. I wasted time and effort getting you to comply. I hate that my time invested in you was for nothing."

With his last, harsh words he leaves.

Before I know it tears are streaming down my

face. I run to my bed and crawl under the comforter hoping to keep the world away. It's just too much to process.

Tonight put the final nail in the coffin on our relationship. How do you come back from this? Two people who hurt each other over the past couple of months.

All those things he did for me was in vain.

I throw a pillow over my head.

~~

An extremely loud banging awakens me. I try to pry my eyes open. They are sealed shut from all the crying I did last night. The noise gets louder and I jump up, throwing the covers off of me and stomp to the front door. Taking a glance through the peephole, I find a wide-eyed Ryder waving a Styrofoam coffee cup in front of him.

I pull the door open, immediately grabbing the cup out of his hand and walk to my couch. Placing it down onto my coffee table, I lay across the couch, covering my eyes with my arm. I can hear his laugh get closer, and my legs are lifted up and then back down onto Ryder's lap.

"What time is it?" I growl, but it turns more of a moan as his fingers go to work on my tired feet. Those heels did me in last night.

"Seven," he says, his first word since walking in, making it sound sexy.

I peek out from under my arms, stealing a glance at him as he eyes the length of my legs. His left hand continues the ministrations on my feet but the right draws circles on top of my skin. He catches me watching him and smiles.

He looks relaxed and refreshed. His eyes glow against the rising morning sun and his dark hair is perfectly managed. He's wearing a dark long sleeve shirt that must have been underneath the jacket he was wearing when I answered the door.

"You never texted me," he says, no worry to his tone.

I sit straight up but he doesn't allow me to move my feet. "I forgot. I'm so sorry."

His hands glide over the smooth skin of my legs. "It's fine. I made sure he left last night before I went home."

"You were here?" I ask as I pick up the coffee and lift it towards him. "Thanks for this by the way."

He smiles. "You're welcome and yes. I wanted to make sure that there was no trouble but I left after he did. I hope that was okay?"

His question catches me off guard. "Of course it's okay. After what happened last night I don't blame you for being worried."

"So," I start to ask. "A cop, huh?"

He shakes his head laughing. "Yea. I figured after giving them a run for their money I would pay for my sins by becoming one."

I nod. "I see."

"Plus," he wiggles his eyebrows, "I'm kinda into the handcuffs."

My mouth opens wide in shock but he pats my legs. "Get dressed. We've got to go."

The large sip of coffee I take burns my tongue.

"Where are we going?"

My feet are lifted as he stands and turns them to the side. "To be free." When I don't make a motion to move he says, "It's a surprise. Come on. Jeans and a t-shirt."

I quickly got dressed, excited to find out what he has planned.

After our first stop at a diner just off Dundee Road that I pass all the time but never go in Ryder starts heading down Milwaukee Avenue towards Rosemont. When he pulls into the parking lot I look at the tall building–confused.

"What's this?" I ask opening the door and stepping out of the car.

The temperature has taken a nose dive and I pull my jacket around me tighter.

He walks over to my side of the car, holding his elbow out for me to take "iFly," he says. "Indoor skydiving. I assume you have never been here."

I shake my head side to side and nerves take over my body. When I was younger I wanted to go skydiving and bungee jumping but as I grew older I got scared and realized those were very stupid risky things to do. But this–this is perfect.

We walk in just as they open and are immediately pulled into a room where they give us an overview of the signals and rules. Ryder sits next to me, his leg rubbing against mine, sending old feelings shooting through my body. It's distracting, and I'm afraid I'm going to screw up my flight because of my lack of attention.

His shoulder nudges mine. "Are you okay? You seem like something is wrong."

"Perfect," I tell him, nudging him back. "Just nervous."

He reaches down and grabs my hand into his, our fingers wrapping around one another. I'm not sure friends do this, but it's comforting and even though a lot of our skin isn't touching I can feel my body humming. "Nothing to be nervous about. I'll be right there."

When the class is over, the instructor takes us to another room for us to put our flight suit on. As I put the pink and purple material over my body my nerves start to go into overdrive. I sit on the bench and lower my head between my knees trying to calm myself down. When I feel I have myself in check I walk out and find Ryder in the same ugly suit as me but his is blue and green. He spins around slowly. "Like what you see?"

I laugh. "Very sexy," I tell him as I pull my hair back into a ponytail.

He takes my hand into his again and we are led into another room. Its ceiling reaches the height of the building and in the middle of the room is a large glass tube that is currently occupied by what appears to be a ten year old. She is flying, doing flips and spinning around as the air below her keeps her body floating. The tube is surrounded by onlookers and they all clap everytime she does a flip.

Seeing a kid do it doesn't ease my nerves. If anything, it makes it worse. I'm going to look like a fool out there.

Ryder squeezes my hand. "You'll be fine." He comforts me, seemingly reading my mind.

When it's our turn Ryder allows me to go first and watches as the instructor leads me inside the glass.

As soon as my body hits the air I go flying up. My body floats effortlessly. I close my eyes–nerves disintegrated–and imagine myself flying over the ground, seeing the curvature of the earth. When I was a teenager my reasons behind wanting to skydive wasn't for the risk. It was to see how small we all our in this big world. To see how each and every one of us make up such a large space. I can see that under my eyelids. When I open them, my eyes immediately lock onto Ryder's deep blue ones just outside the glass. His teeth shine bright underneath his wide smile.

He did this for me. He wanted me to feel free and right now I've never felt freer. I forget all the hurt, all the drama, and just smile knowing that he gets me like no one ever really has.

When my time is up, I excitedly run out to his awaiting arms and jump into them. He picks me up with ease and our lips collide without hesitation. My body tenses. It wasn't intentional but the spark that it ignited lit me on fire.

We pull apart, his blue irises meeting my green.

"I'm so sorry," I whisper.

He slides me down his body, dropping me to my feet and takes my cheeks into his hands. "I'm not."

Placing a light kiss on my nose, he releases me and walks over to the instructor for his turn.

I stand there dumbfounded not only by the

accidental kiss but also as I watch Ryder flip, turn and fly so high up in the glass that he disappears out of my line of sight. He's had to have done this before.

After a few minutes of showing off, he walks out pretending to run to me as I did to him earlier. I outstretch my hands, laughing, as he mockingly tries to get me to catch him. This time though he purposely kisses me chastely on the lips.

My heart, the butterflies in my stomach, and mind all tell me I'm a goner.

The smile on Hadley's face has made my week. Ever since she told me she feels like she lost herself I have made it my mission to figure out things that I could take her to do and show her that she can live life the way she wanted. The way she dreamed.

Last night was a game changer and a total mind fuck. I was shocked to see Hadley there dancing in the middle of the floor with Janie, our human resources girl. She looked amazing in that dress and that fucking slit up the side was my undoing. I watched her body sway and I wondered why the hell she was there. When a slow song came on I had to use the opportunity to snatch her up but I didn't expect what followed to happen. I shouldn't have been surprised that James was her boyfriend. The way he acted towards me after that first day I told him about Hadley should have been my first clue. When he had me change partners I was surprised. You just don't put the new guy with a rookie. Granted I have been an officer for a few years now but I wasn't experienced enough in the

Buffalo Grove department to take on a brand new guy. Now James, or Braden, or whatever the hell his name has just has been promoted to Sergeant. I'm not sure what that will mean for my happiness at the station but if winning Hadley back means I have to find another one then I'll look at the surrounding areas. I want this girl and I don't care what it takes to keep her.

Right now, though, taking it slow seems to be my best option, however, that little accidental kiss isn't helping.

"You looked like Charlie and his grandpa when you flew up to the ceiling." Hadley giggles from beside me in the car.

I laugh, confused. "What?"

"You know," she starts, shifting in her seat to turn her body towards me. "In Charlie and the Chocolate Factory when they drink that drink and it causes them to float to the ceiling."

I think about that scene in the movie and laugh again. "Oh, yea. That's funny." I reach over squeezing her thigh and wink. "Can I call you my Chocolate Factory?"

Her brow scrunches in confusion, a stray hair falling into her face before she blows it away. "Why?"

I face the road again, turning left at the light. "So I can own you."

She's quiet and when I am stopped at another red light I look over. "Did I say something wrong?"

"You can't own someone, Ryder."

"I think that's untrue." I reach out pulling her

chin so she is looking back at me. "You've owned me since our first kiss."

Her tongue darts out to wet her lips and she snatches her lip up between her teeth. I'm mesmerized by the action until someone honks their horn. She doesn't say another word until we reach her apartment.

She lets out a soft sigh looking up to her door. "Do you want to come in?"

"I can't. I promised my sister I would stop by."

"Okay," Hadley responds and I can hear the sadness in her voice. I don't know what it's about but I'm hoping it's because she doesn't want me to leave.

I tap her hand gently. "Unless you want to join me."

She smiles and I reverse out of the parking lot.

~~

We arrive at my sister's house thirty minutes later and as soon as I'm out of the car I'm greeted by two crazy girls. My nieces Macy and Marcy come barreling out of the house towards me. Their four year old bodies knock me down into the snow and they circle their arms around me as much as they can.

"Uncle Ryder!" They both scream simultaneously, blowing out my eardrums.

"M and M!" I yell back, playfully throwing them off of me into the yard. They take advantage and begin making snow angels.

Hadley walks up beside me after I get to my feet, smiling. "Twins?"

"Yup," I answer, leading her up the sidewalk to the front door. "Identical ones. Macy and Marcy."

"Cute," she comments as the girls mow us down to get into the house first.

Veering to the right, we enter the kitchen where Julia is making lunch. She looks up–her blue eyes tired from working late nights bartending–finding Hadley next to me. She wipes her hands on her apron.

"Hadley," she says extending her arms and bringing her in for a hug. "It's so nice to finally meet you. Ryder has told me so much about you."

Julia was a sophomore when Hadley and I dated. She never knew about our secret relationship until after our dad died. He passed away from a heart attack just after the guy who knocked Julia up left her to become a single mother of twins. After he died there were a lot of questions on why my relationship with my dad crumbled during senior year.

When Hadley left and her parents wouldn't cough up her whereabouts, I was heartbroken and distraught. I thought my dad could help find her. He was a lead investigator after all, but he yelled at me for even thinking about "that man's bastard child." I confronted him about leaking private information on Hadley's dad to keep him from promotions at his job at the bank. He never moved up past a teller because my dad successfully kept him there. I barely spoke to him when I came home from college. When he died, I regretted almost every word I had not said to him but never the words he did hear from me. I loved Hadley, hell I still do, and feel that she is worth all the trouble and harsh words.

I watch Hadley's face blush when all Julia can do is just stare at her.

"She isn't an exhibit at the art museum, Jules. Stop freaking her out." I laugh, pulling her in for a hug.

She playfully slaps my arm. "I know. I'm just excited to meet the famous Hadley." She walks back over to the stove. "I was getting tired of seeing that Wendy chick here."

The air in the room stiffens. I haven't hidden anything from Hadley when it comes to Wendy but she doesn't know that we've slept together a few times just to scratch the itch. We both have a mutual understanding that we are in love with other people but need a little release here and there. Wendy has only met Julia twice and those were both when she was dropping off the twins at my house to babysit. Besides the very minimal sex we've had, Wendy is like a best friend. Never once has she pushed for more, not that I would give it to her. I think Julia is trying to get me into some trouble. It's not going to work.

I glance at Hadley, who looks almost murderous. Maybe it will work.

I lean over and whisper in her ear, "You look fucking hot when you're jealous."

Her vicious eyes turn on me. "What do I care? We're just friends."

The girls come flying into the kitchen and tackle me again. This time I stay standing. I pick them up, one in each arm, and walk into the living room spinning them around in a circle until they scream for me to stop.

A dizzy Macy asks, "Are you babysitting us today?"

As a single mother Julia not only has the bartending job but also has a waitressing job during the lunch shift on weekends. This supplements the income she gets from assisting at the girls' preschool. When I can help out on the weekends and weeknights I do. I also send friends to see her at work who leave astronomical tips since she won't take money from me. Though she couldn't go to college, she does still owns her own home but money is always tight. I'm proud of her. Once she had the girls, she would never take a cent from my mother either, even though my mom has an abundance of it.

"Of course! What kind of uncle would I be if I didn't watch my favorite nieces and play hide and go seek and dress up?"

"Can we paint your nails again Uncle Ryder?" Marcy asks, effectively revoking my man card.

Hadley's laugh fills the room.

"Who is that girl?" Macy asks.

I smile when I find Hadley in the door frame watching us. "That's Hadley," I tell them.

Marcy pulls on my shirt so I can lean down and whispers in my ear, "Is that your girlfriend?"

I turn my head to whisper back but loud enough so Hadley can hear. "I wish she was my girlfriend."

"EWW!" The girls erupt into laughter and run to their rooms.

Walking over to Hadley, I lower my face to hers. Her breathing accelerates with each inch I get closer. "Have I told you how beautiful you look today?"

She shakes her head no and I kiss just under her ear. "You look beautiful today."

I feel her cheeks widen before she says, "And I'm sure you will too after you get your nails painted."

After three hours, which consisted of a lunch, a round of Uno and a pedicure for Hadley, we're all laid out on the couch stuffing our mouths with popcorn. The girls are laying on the loveseat cuddled in their sleeping bag while Hadley lies in my lap, blissfully sleeping. I pull the ponytail out of her hair and run my fingers through it. With her eyes closed, I'm reminded of so many times when she would fall asleep in my arms. God, I love this girl. Even now years later I still do, and it's so tough to love her not knowing what happened so long ago to make her leave. She has said she loved me too but there had to be something else, something that happened to make her want to run away from her life.

For a long time I thought my dad had something to do with it. It wasn't until he admitted to screwing with Hadley's dad but denied anything to do with her disappearance that I realized he didn't. A year after my dad passed away and another relationship with a girl at college failed, I went to her house again and her mom was the only one home. I told her I just wanted to make sure Hadley was happy and lied when I said I didn't want to know where she was. She assured me she was and I knew that I didn't need to worry about it anymore. When I started at the Elgin police I had to keep myself from using my resources to find her. I was going to let fate step in and it led me right back to her.

If I have any chance at real happiness in my life, not the fake kind that just carries you through, then I have to make her mine again.

Julia walks in the door as soon as the movie ends and the girls jump up excitedly. I look down finding Hadley still snoozing and wait for my sister to come into the living room.

"How could you possibly watch my children when you have a girl in your lap?" she asks hands on her hips.

"Shhh," I whisper and point down at Hadley. "She is sleeping and the girls were watching Big Hero 6 five feet away from me. They were fine."

She takes a seat across from me, looking tired. "I can see it," she says pointing at Hadley.

I stop mid-caress. "What's that?"

"I can see all the things that love requires."

I pick up another strand of Hadley's hair and twirl it around gently. "What are you talking about?"

"Comfort, jealousy, denial at the beginning. The uncontrollable desire to be near one another." Julia sighs. "I wish I had that."

Her voice is sad. It's hard to find a man let alone find one that would accept my nieces or pass my background check. "You will one day. But Hadley, she is battling the end of a relationship and with my boss no less."

Julia's eyes widen in shock. I haven't had a chance so I tell her about the events of the previous nights in between her fielding questions from the girls.

"It seems like this is a conflict of interest, Ryder. Is she worth it?"

I look back down into my lap, Hadley's eyes are open and her face has an unreadable expression. Since day one I've never hidden my feelings for Hadley. Not back in high school, not the night at the bar and I sure as shit am not going to hide them here. I never look away from her stare as I say, "She is worth every damn obstacle that life brings my way."

Chapter 18

Hadley

The drive over to my parent's house on Sunday morning is short and familiar. They have lived in the same house since I was just four years old. The neighborhood looks the same as when I grew up. Houses that need love and attention and others that got the long awaited makeover are all basically lying on top of one another. As I pull into the driveway, I think about my day with Ryder yesterday. I haven't felt so alive in so long and when he walked me to my door all I wanted was for his lips to be on mine again. I wanted to pull him inside and into my bedroom. He was a true gentleman and just walked me to my door. My mind is definitely at war with my body, although it wasn't my body thinking about every door he opened for me, every chair he pulled out or how he remembered things about me I had forgotten about. I smile as I walk into my childhood home.

I make myself all cozy and pour a glass of wine that I brought with me and watch my mother as she makes dinner.

My mother is stunning. Even in her late forties she looks as though she could be in her late twenties. Her medium length brown hair is pulled back into a low ponytail and her petite body is wrapped in a light pink apron. Her green eyes sparkle as she busies herself around the kitchen. I wish she would have passed down her love of cooking to me.

"Honey, can you grab the ground beef out of the fridge?" she asks while stirring her delicious spaghetti sauce.

My mouth waters at the smell, and I cannot wait to taste her lasagna.

"Sure," I tell her as I walk over to the fridge and pluck the thawed meat off the top shelf. After handing it to her, I lean against the counter with my glass of wine.

"So," she starts, taking her eyes off of the stove for a brief moment to look at me before turning back to her task. "What do I owe the pleasure of having my daughter for dinner tonight?"

I take a deep breath unsure of how this will go. She has the right to be suspicious. Since I officially moved out of the house after college, I don't come over enough but I need some advice. Growing up I never really voiced my opinions when it came to my parents or went against their wishes. That was until Ryder came into the picture and turned my world upside down–or right side up at the time.

"Braden and I broke up," I quickly say, ripping the Band-Aid off. I know how much she loved him.

The spoon drops onto the counter as she turns to me. "Thank God! That guy was a moron!" she exclaims.

Or maybe she didn't.

"What do you mean thank God?" I ask very confused.

She walks over to the fridge pulling out my bottle of wine and pours a glass for herself before she answers. "I never liked him, honey. He was no good for you but I'm curious as to what happened between the two of you. Things seemed like they were finally starting to get very serious."

"He was," I say aloud but really am just thinking it to myself.

Putting the ring on the table made me nervous. I was scared he was going to propose and my first instinct told me to say no. I was actually going to say no to him. After processing that a moment of clarity took over as I realized I no longer felt for him what I used to. I didn't want that ring. Neither one of us could trust the other anymore. I almost feel as though all the amazing things he had done for me after he felt threatened by Ryder wasn't something he wanted to do but something he felt like he had to do. I just don't know what had been real and what hadn't. I guess, according to his parting words, none of it had been.

My mom pushes more, and I tell her about our depleted relationship. When I mention Ryder's role in it, her body goes rigid. I was going to stop so she didn't feel uncomfortable anymore but I felt like I had to go on. I need the advice of my mother so I describe every moment up until yesterday.

She is silent for a minute as she leans her hands on the counter. "Do you still love him,

Hadley?"

I shrug, unsure how to respond. "I don't know, Mom. We were together for two years. I mean I still love him but I don't think I'm in love with him anymore."

She reaches over gently taking my upper arms into her hands. "Not Braden. Ryder. Do you still love Ryder?"

The question shocks me. I never told my mother I was in love with him. When I found out I was pregnant after I left I had to tell her a few things about our relationship. I didn't dare say we had been together all summer and into our senior year. I thought she assumed it was a one-time thing. If she only knew how many times he snuck into my window.

She shakes me slightly bringing me back to her question. "I'm not stupid, Hadley. I wasn't then and I'm not now. Do. You. Still. Love. Ryder?" She accentuates every word making my knees go weak with each one.

"I...I don't know. I think I would say the same. That I love him but I'm not in love with him. It's like a first love kind of thing," I say honestly. Even after all these years the anguish I felt that day still hurts and blocks out the intense feelings Ryder made me feel. The past couple of weeks I've seen glimpses of it.

Swiping my finger under my eye I look to my mother. Her eyes are filling with tears as well. "I know you loved him, Had. I know what I did to Ryder's father was wrong and I know that your dad and I made that boy to look like the child of the devil but it was our fault. All Ryder's father did was love me unconditionally but I couldn't help where my heart led me. Where is your heart leading you?"

I think about that and answer her truthfully, "The only thing I know is that it's leading me away from Braden. I don't belong with him."

That's the first time I've said it out loud and it feels freeing. I haven't missed him. I wasn't as co-dependent on him as I thought I was or was pretending to be. There just isn't any chemistry anymore between the two of us. I had more spark with Ryder caressing my hair on his sister's couch yesterday than I did the last time I had sex with Braden.

"So, what do you want to ask exactly?" She interrupts my thoughts. "I know you didn't just want to tell me you and Braden broke up. I'm sure you could have done a fine job of telling me that over the phone." The pan sizzles as she adds the ground beef to it.

I collect my thoughts trying to figure out how to put what I want to ask into words. "Is it okay? Is it okay to leave such a long relationship and not be sad about it?"

She sets the stove on low and brings me over to the dining room table. I sit across from her as she takes my hands in hers.

"Do you think you aren't sad because your heart found what it was missing all along?"

My mother is not only beautiful but she is smart and makes you think about things in a way you didn't before.

"Hey, sweetie," my dad greets me as he walks in from the garage. "I didn't expect you to join us tonight."

He leans over kissing my temple and walks to the sink to wash his hands. I look at my mom and she shakes her head ending our conversation. As understanding as my mom is about the whole situation my dad is another story.

"Yea, well I was just telling Mom that Braden and I broke up."

He stops drying his hands and glances my way, most likely to assess my mood. "I'm sorry. Do you want to talk about it?"

I shake my head no and he nods before walking back out into the garage. My dad is over six feet tall and has dark brown hair, brown eyes and a heart of gold, but I would never talk to him about my relationships. He doesn't even know about the baby.

Dinner is wonderful and quiet so I have time to contemplate my mom's question. I don't know if I'm not heartbroken over the end of my relationship with Braden because my heart belonged to Ryder all along. How can that be after what he said about me to his friends? I know we were in high school and it hurt then but things change and we're grownups now. Right?

"So, why did you two kids break up?" my dad asks between bites. He's eating it faster than I am. No one bakes a mean lasagna like Mrs. Chase.

My mother's fork clings on the table and I look to her for how to proceed. She answers for me and I'm stunned by what comes out of her mouth. "She's in love with someone else."

I stare at her, wide-eyed, angry, scared and

confused. "Mom."

"Someone else?" My dad interrupts. "Who? I thought things were good. Braden was here six weeks ago asking for your hand in marriage."

This doesn't surprise me. "It's no one, Dad." I brush it off hoping to drop the subject.

My mother doesn't take the hint.

"Ryder Blake," she speaks confidently looking dead into his eyes but she is stoic as she waits for his response. She has to know this won't go well.

"I'm not in love with..." I start but my father's hand comes up to stop me. I feel like I'm seventeen again and scared to death of what he would say.

"Ryder Blake?" His tone is heated. "Ryan's boy?"

Nodding her head yes, my mom reaches over and grabs a napkin to wipe off her hands. "Yes. The boy who came to our house after Hadley left to live with my sister."

I jump as his hands slam down on the table. "What the hell is going on? One minute you're about to get proposed to and the next..." he turns his attention to me, "you're with that asshole's son!?"

"She loves him," my mother speaks calmly. My insides start to cramp with nervousness.

"Mom," I warn.

"No, Hadley. If anyone should understand it would be your father. I couldn't help who I loved as much as he couldn't." She looks at him. "I know you didn't want to go after your best friend's girlfriend but you did and look what we have. We might not have a lot of money but we have each other and we have a beautiful daughter who despite all the bullshit Braden just put her through she is sitting here smiling because of that boy."

He instantly calms down as he looks at my mother lovingly. "You're right. I'm sorry. That man made me miserable when he was alive but I wouldn't trade your mother for anything."

That seemed too easy.

"But how can you be in love with him. Were you seeing him when you and Braden were together?" he asks.

"I never cheated on Braden but I wasn't honest with him." I begin to tell him the story of the past few months with a little help from my mom. When we're finished with the meal and the talk I add, "And I'm not in love with Ryder. I just have some feelings stirring around inside that might be making a reappearance."

My dad stands up as do I and brings me in for a hug. "I admit," he says in my ear. "I'm not a fan of that family but I support you in whatever choice you make."

I pull him closer and squeeze feeling a weight lifted off my shoulder. I didn't come here to tell my dramatic story that has unfolded the past few months but I'm glad it's out there.

"I need to get going. I have to work in the morning."

They both hug me. When my mom pulls back she rubs her hands over my forehead. "You okay, sweetie? You feel warm."

"I think so. Kinda tired. I'll go straight to bed

when I get home."

She nods and I walk to my car. Once inside I check my phone and see a missed call from Ryder. I hit send and the ringing fills the Bluetooth in my car.

"Why hello, Spark," he answers and I instantly smile.

"Hello there," I say as I back out of the driveway and onto the street.

"I've missed your voice today," Ryder says and I can hear clanging in the background.

"What's the matter? No one to keep you in line today?"

"Nope," he accentuates the pop of the "p" sound. "I've been kind of bad. You should come spank me."

This causes me to have a full blown belly laugh. "You wish, Ryder."

"I love that laugh, Hadley." He groans. "But seriously. I have the paddle."

Heat rises in my cheeks and all over my body. I imagine myself bent over his bed and him paddling me and it surprises me.

His voice comes over low and sensual over the speakers. "You're thinking about it, aren't you? Thinking about spanking me, or even better me spanking you."

"We're friends, Ryder. Remember?"

"I do, however, friends don't give sexy bedroom eyes to other friends when they are dropping them off at their house," he says. "Did you want me to come in last night?"

I sigh because I did in fact want him to come in. "I have to go. I'll call you tomorrow."

"Okay," he relents. "Promise?"

"Yes." I laugh just as a piercing pain shoots through my stomach.

Maybe I'm not feeling well.

"Night, Hadley."

"Goodnight, Ryder," I say hitting the end button and turning the car off after pulling into my parking spot.

I run into the house and make it to the bathroom in time to see my lasagna again.

Chapter 19

Ryder

As I walk the long hallway to the locker room of the police department on Monday morning I catch a few stares of my co-workers. Most of them come from the admin staff but I'm not looking forward to seeing my fellow officers. Even though I didn't know that Hadley was James' girlfriend it sure doesn't help that I cornered her next to the DJ booth after I did find out.

"Shit, man. Sarge's girlfriend!" Nate yells as soon as I enter the room. There are three other guys in there pretending to ignore us. "I didn't think you had it in you."

I throw my bag down on the bench and start to untie my shoes. I get more pissed as my laces snag. "I didn't know she was his girlfriend, Nate. Shut the hell up."

"Alright, man, but I don't blame you. She is a hot piece."

I raise my eyes to meet his giving him a glare that could strike him dead. "I said to shut your fucking mouth, Nate. The next time you talk about her like that I will kick your ass."

Just when the last word leaves my mouth, the door opens again and James walks in. His vicious stare finds me, and I don't dare to turn my back on him this time. I did that Saturday night and got sucker punched. He won't get so lucky today. The locker room grows eerily quiet as everyone goes back to changing for our morning shift.

I take more time than I usually do and as I lean over to pull down the bottom of my pants he shoves me up against the lockers, his arm going to my neck, holding me there.

"Sarge, man." Nate appears next to the two of us. "Let him go. He said he didn't know that she was yours."

His arm puts more pressure on me and I can feel the tightness in my throat. I could push him off of me but I'm letting him have his moment. I know how it feels to lose Hadley and I almost feel for him.

"She told me everything, Blake. Everything! I wasn't going to go down without a fight." He pushes off of my neck and walks towards the door.

I try to keep myself from saying what I'm thinking.

But it doesn't work.

"From what I've heard you stopped fighting a long time ago, Braden." I spit his name out and he whips around, his nose flaring like a bull. "Plus," I add rubbing my jaw where he punched me Friday night. "You don't have much fight in you."

He launches towards me but is immediately held back by the other men in the room. I just stand there while he struggles against them. He swings but each time it misses me.

I cross my arms over my chest, showing that he doesn't affect me. They let him go after he stops struggling. "Watch your back, Ryder." He warns pointing a finger to my face before turning around and stalking out of the room.

"I'm not sure poking the bear was a great idea, Blake," Nate comments as we get into our cruiser.

"Well, I'll be sure to bring my hunting rifle next time," I joke.

~~

A few hours later and two calls to Hadley that go unanswered, Nate and I are responding to a domestic disturbance in an apartment complex. It's in one of the run down areas of the town where we get the most calls from.

Walking up the steps we can already hear commotion coming from inside the apartment. Nate bangs on the door three times.

"Buffalo Grove Police!" he calls out putting his hand on his gun. "Open the door."

Things inside the apartment calm down and just as he is about to knock again the door flies open and a large white male comes barreling out knocking me into the wall. I get my bearings and point to the suspect. "You go after him!" I tell Nate before making my way inside.

Inside the apartment, on the floor, is a woman. She has short blonde hair, blue eyes surrounded by streaks of red with a busted lip and ripped shirt. "Is anyone else in the house, ma'am?" I ask.

She shakes her head no and as I kneel down beside her I hear a gun shot from the parking lot. I jump up, drawing my weapon, and run out the door. My feet scramble down the stairs and I take in the scene looking to find where the shots were fired. I hear Nate yelling from the east end of the lot and head that way. When I arrive, I find him lying on the ground one hand over his arm. Blood oozing from beneath his fingertips.

"You okay, man?" I ask while grabbing my radio.

"Fuck it hurts!" he yells. "But it's just a flesh wound. I'll be fine. Go get him."

I look around for the suspect as I press the button to ask for back up. "This is Officer Blake requesting back..."

Bang!

Bang!

~~

Beep. Beep. Beep.

The machine goes off every few seconds as I sit and watch as Nate gets the full check up. He seems unaffected by what happened but I'm a bit freaked out. The suspect missed hitting me in the head by mere inches. I could feel the bullets as they zoomed by. I chased after him on foot but ended up losing him. The entire department is still looking for the suspect.

It took a lot of convincing for the victim to press charges and file a restraining order. She gave us his name and information but by the time we arrived at his residence he was no longer there. We put an officer outside her apartment until we can find the fucker that busted her up. I will never get why a man would want to hurt a woman. Does it make them feel superior because let me tell you that I would bow down at Hadley's feet if she would let me. I couldn't imagine hitting her let alone just raising my hand at her. You see a lot of that in my line of work–men who don't know the worth of their women and women who forget it themselves.

Nate coughs and then cringes. Guilt racks my body as I watch him. I was the one who told him to go after the guy. It could have been a hell of a lot worse if when he got shot his gun went flying. The suspect could have turned back and finished. Instead he decided to run but not before taking a shot, literally, at me.

I got really lucky that he was a shit shooter. Once we got her statement and I gave mine I drove the hospital to meet up with the ambulance that took Nate. I called Hadley's phone nonstop. She was all I could think about. I just wanted to hold her in my arms and have her tell me it was okay. In all my time as an officer I have never been shot at. It seems dumb to say that my life flashed before my eyes. It didn't. But my future did. I saw myself old and gray with the love of my life next to me and I just knew I needed to be okay for her. After the first and second missed shot, I thought for sure he wouldn't stop until he hit me too. Thankfully, he did.

"Oh my God, baby! Are you okay?" Cathy, Nate's wife, cries as she runs into the room. She startles him awake and he smiles. "They called me but your mom wouldn't let me drive over here alone. I'm so glad you're okay."

He opens his arms and she falls into them,

sobbing. "I'm okay, Cath. I promise. I'm fine. This is all for show," he tells her pointing to all the machines while attempting to calm her down.

I take that as my cue to leave and pull my phone out of my pocket for round three of "Where in the world is Hadley?" I've played this game before and I'm not interested in a repeat.

Still no answer. Maybe I scared her off on Saturday night while we were at my sister's house. I meant every word. She is worth giving everything up for. Right now I don't care what her reasons for leaving were for. I just know that she is here now and I won't let her go again.

I try her number one more time. I bring my wrist up, glancing at my watch, and see its past four in the afternoon. I try her work line for the third time and get nothing. An uneasy feeling overwhelms me and use my final resource before looking like a stalker and go to Hadley's apartment. I dial up Jace.

"Hey, man," he answers after the second ring. I can hear weights being slammed down in the background of the gym he owns.

"Hey! I hate to ask and I know you're busy at work but can I get Noelle's number from you? I can't get a hold of Hadley and I'm starting to get worried," I tell him practically begging for his help. I know he is trying to move on from Noelle choosing Trent over him. From what I've heard the co-owner of his gym, Valerie, would love to help him along. AJ said she has wanted him for years.

"Sure." He offers and tells me he will text it to me so I hang up and wait for what feels like an hour before the text comes in. I don't hesitate to call her.

"Noelle Grant of Events Unlimited, how can I help you?" Her pleasant voice comes through the receiver.

"Hi, Noelle. This is Ryder Blake. I'm looking for Hadley." I channel my inner third grader and cross my fingers that she doesn't hang up on me.

Silence.

"Hello?"

"Yea." She laughs. "I'm here. I was just letting you sweat it out for a minute."

I roll my eyes. I've heard stories about crazy Noelle and how she doesn't play nice sometimes. I resort to begging. "Please, Noelle. I know you don't know me that well but I'm not looking to hurt her. I just want to make sure she is okay. I haven't heard from her all day and I'm starting to get concerned."

"Come to the Starbucks on Lake Cook. I'll give you the key to her house." She covers the phone up as she speaks to someone else.

I wait until she finishes talking to them before asking, "Why would I need the key to her house?"

"Because she is sick, douche twat," she says it like I should know and almost makes me second guess if I should have. "I was going to check on her in a bit but I just got roped into another client meeting. It's a win win situation. You get to clean up her puke and I don't."

I feel bad. I wish I would have known she wasn't feeling well. I talked to her last night and she sounded fine. "How is that a win for me?"

"You get to clean up her puke and I don't," she repeats like I'm stupid.

I laugh as I hang up and walk back into Nate's room. His wife has crawled up onto the bed with him and has fallen asleep.

"The doctor said I'll be out of here soon. Go home," he tells me.

"Nate, I'm so..." I start but he cuts me off.

"I swear if you apologize I'm going to find a new partner. Don't pussy out on me now."

We say our goodbyes and I leave to get the key from Noelle.

~~

I saw Noelle in the bar that one night a few months back but since it's been a while I forgot how stunning she is, though she has nothing on Hadley. She is sitting in a booth next to a large window looking out towards the parking lot. Her toned legs peek out of a dark green dress and she's wearing black boots. The golden locks of her hair are piled on top of her head and her undivided attention is on a man dressed in a white polo shirt. I swear if he flexes the shirt will rip. A hat is covering his dark brown hair and they are so close that they border on kissing distance.

"Is this your client meeting?" I jokingly ask as I approach the table.

She turns a vicious stare towards me, and I stumble. "As a matter of fact it is. This is Trent Decker, who owns Decker Construction and he's hired me to plan his weekend for him. It consists of me tying his sexy ass to the bed and fucking him senseless. I'm doing this pro bono of course. I'd hate to be called a prostitute." She smirks.

Trent chuckles and extends his hand towards

me. “Trent Decker, Noelle’s fiancé.”

“I heard.” I laugh. “I’m Ryder Blake, Noelle’s current tongue lashing victim.”

His handshake is firm. “Nice to meet you.”

“Likewise,” I comment letting go.

“Okay, ladies, is the sleepover done?” she asks holding out her hand with a key in it. “Here is the key. She probably has the flu so make sure you get a mask and a lot of Lysol before you head over there.”

I take it from her. “Thank you so much.”

“Thank YOU. Now I won’t have to restock my cabinets in Airborne. Tell her to make sure that shit is gone before she comes back to work.”

I wave and leave them to their meeting. Walking back to my car, I think about Noelle and Trent. Sure Jace got hurt, and he is my friend, but you could see from a distance that they are meant to be. I wonder if people would see the same thing if they observed Hadley and me. Would they see a couple who could never make it work or would they see the soul mates that I feel like we are. I don’t care. I just want to get to Hadley.

I'm going to die.

This has to be the end. I can feel it.

Soon I will see the bright light and I'll have no choice but to follow it and hope that I get into Heaven's doors.

My head is pounding. My ears hurt and my eyes won't stop watering. I've gone through two boxes of Kleenex and due to the constant vomiting I've had to change my clothes three times. The last time I didn't bother putting new ones on.

So here I lie in my bed, panties only, on top of my covers, with my head hanging over the side so that if I puke again I'll be sure to hit the bucket I placed down on the floor.

I can hear my phone ringing in the distance though I swear its right next to me. My arms are too heavy to reach out and grab it. I can barely push back the hair that is stuck to my face.

I glance over at the clock finding the bright

light of it offensive and see it's just after four o'clock. My phone rings again but all it does is lull me back to sleep.

The closing of my door startles me awake but I can't muster the energy to grab the gun in my nightstand or even just lift my head to see who it is. Running through the day I figure Noelle has come to check on me since I left a message early this morning that I was dying and would like her to clear my Google searches. Who looks up zombie porn images anyways?

A cold compress hits my forehead and it's euphoric, instantly easing my headache. Warm hands rub up and down my back but they are too large to be Noe's.

"Hadley," Ryder's sweet tone calls out. "What can I do for you?"

"Bucket…" I moan out feeling another wave of nausea.

Ryder sounds confused. "Bucket?"

Before I can answer I lean over further and empty the nonexistent contents of my stomach.

His hands drag along and pull my hair away from my mouth before he continues to rub my back. "It's okay. Get it out."

"Go home, Ryder. I don't want you to see this," I warn him, attempting to push him away from me when the vomiting subsides.

He ignores me, taking the bucket away. I hear his footsteps lead into my bathroom, the flushing of the toilet and the running of the water in the bathtub tells me he is cleaning up after me.

I bet I look sexy now.

The bed dips behind me and the last thing I remember before I fall back asleep is the soft caress of my hair beneath his touch.

~~

"Hadley," his voice softly calls out again. I look up, finding it's now nine o'clock at night. Noticing I can actually move I turn over finding Ryder sitting on the edge of the bed. His dark blue eyes look concerned, and his hair is matted down on one side.

"You look sleepy." My voice croaks.

He smiles. "I made you a bath. Come on."

I allow him to help me up and practically carry me to the awaiting bath. "Turn around," I tell him before I pull my panties down.

He eyes me. "Seriously, Spark. If I let you go then you're going to fall and I told you before, your naked body is engrained into the back of my eyelids."

I hesitate and groan before giving in and sliding my panties off of me. He gently holds my hand and helps me into the warm water. I sink down, laying my head on the edge of the tub.

"Too hot?" he asks from beside me.

"No." I shake my hazy head. "It's perfect. Thank you. How did you get into my house?"

He laughs. "Noelle gave me a key."

My body relaxes more as I feel him bring water up and over my shoulders and collarbone. "Aren't you worried I'm going to give you whatever bug I have?"

"You mean the flu? No. I had my flu shot. Did you?"

I open my eyes finding his. "No," I whisper. I can't say much more because the stare he is giving me is that of a caretaker. Even sick I thought he would use this as an advantage to get closer to me. To touch me but all I see is someone who is concerned and wants to take care of me. "Thank you," I say but it doesn't feel like enough.

Braden never took care of me when I was sick. He was always worried that I might contaminate him. So, all those times I just wanted to be held when I didn't feel well I had to cuddle up with my pillow and make do on my own.

Ryder smiles. "Of course."

When the bath starts to get cold he helps me out and into some warm pajamas. As I lay in my bed I hear him messing around in the kitchen and when he walks back in he has a bottle of water, some crackers and the charger for my cell phone.

He places the items down on the nightstand and plugs my phone in. "Call me if you need anything, okay?"

Leaning down, he brushes a kiss underneath my ear. As he turns to walk away I call out his name, "Ryder. Will you stay?"

He pauses. "Are you sure? I can sleep on the couch and you can just yell if you need anything."

"Yes. I'm sure," I reply. "But I'd like you to just hold me if that is okay."

He nods and says, "Anything you want," as he crawls behind me and pulls me to him.

~~

My body is stiff, and I feel weak as I wake up the next morning after an x rated dream. I take a quick inventory finding the nausea is gone and the headache is dull but I feel warm. Feverish. It must have to do with the over six foot man, who was the star in said dream, wrapped around my body. His hard muscles pull me against him, and his fingertips are hovering just under my belly button causing my hormones to go into overdrive. I shift and freeze as his morning wood makes its presence known. I can feel his breathing on my neck and it starts to become longer. Deeper. Heavier. His hands move, dropping lower, caressing the skin above barrier of my panties. I want to grab them and push them between my folds. His erection hardens, if that's even possible, and my body lights up starting in my toes and shooting straight up to my chest. My hands reach down, feeling brazen and more turned on than I've been in a long time, and lie on top of his putting pressure on them. Directing them past the elastic of my thong and lower.

"Hadley," he whispers, taking a nip out of my shoulder. "How are you feeling?"

"I'd feel better if your fingers were inside me." It has to be the flu. It's made me crazy because there is no other way I would've said that otherwise. Or maybe it was the dream but I'm desperate for his touch.

He takes the lobe of my ear between his teeth and sucks. "Don't say it if you don't mean it." His voice comes out raw and primal, sending shivers down my spine.

I reach back behind me, snaking my free hand

into his boxers and gripping his dick tightly. I drag my fingers up and down his length. "I mean it, Ryder. I need this right now."

A satisfied groan escapes his lips as he pushes himself up and down in my hands. His fingers go to work rubbing through the juices that his nearness has created. I haven't been this wet in a long time.

"God, Hadley. I missed this," he says pushing two fingers inside me. I buck at the invasion and squirm as he scissors them within me hitting every nerve ending they can. My pace on his cock quickens as does the tempo of his fingers.

We're panting, writhing beneath each other's hand, and I quickly feel myself come to the brink. "Ryder..." I whisper.

"I can feel you, Hadley. I can feel your walls clenching around my fingers," he says picking up the pace. "I know your body like the back of my hand. Come for me, Hadley."

His words send me over the edge and my hand grips his dick harder as I ride out my wave. He stiffens underneath me and breathes out my name before he lifts up my shirt and his warm liquid spills onto my back.

I fall onto my stomach so none of it seeps onto the sheets. Ryder doesn't move for a moment before saying, "That looks fucking sexy."

"Ryder!" I yell over my shoulder.

The bed springs up and a minute later he is rubbing my back with a warm towel. After I'm cleaned up I reach over and grab my water bottle and one of the crackers. I sit against the headrest and watch Ryder as he walks back in from the bathroom.

I lift the food and drink up. “Thank you for this.”

He reaches over me, grabbing a cracker of his own. “I was so worried about you yesterday. I tried to call you a dozen times and nothing. I finally called Jace for Noelle’s number since no one was answering at your work and she told me you called out and were sick.”

“I’m sorry. I could barely even lift my head to see who it was.”

“Or put on anything other than panties. Do you know how hard it was, or I was when I walked in and saw your ass hanging out in the air? I had to remember you were sick before I violated you,” he says.

“That would have been a nice way to wake me up, though I did puke once you did.”

He shakes his head to, I assume, get the mental image out of his head. “I have to get to work but do you want me to do anything before I leave. I hate to go when you aren’t feeling better.”

I finish chewing and swallow the cracker. “I’m doing a lot better than yesterday.”

He sighs and looks away from me. “Yea. Me too.”

The way he says it concerns me. “Did something happen? Was it Braden?” I cringe when his name leaves my lips.

He shakes his head no. “My partner and I got shot at. He got hit and I didn’t but I feel like it’s my fault.”

My stomach drops and not from the flu. In my two years with Braden I was always worried about something like that happening. When he was on nights I would barely be able to sleep knowing that the harshest crimes happen during the nighttime hours. Knowing that Ryder actually got shot at makes me feel nauseous all over again.

"Is he going to be okay?" I ask rubbing his forearm up and down.

"Yea, it's just a flesh wound to his left arm. He didn't even have to stay overnight. I just hate that we didn't catch the guy."

"Are you scared to go to work today?" I ask only because he looks nervous.

"No." He laughs. "But I'm pretty sure that your boyfriend will be riding along with me today."

I almost forgot they work together, almost. "He's not my boyfriend, Ryder."

"Well." He pulls me closer. "The spot is vacant. Is this something I could fill?"

I laugh. "Well, I know you want to but right now I think we need to just see where things go. Be friends."

He nods and then kisses me on the cheek before getting up. "Well, I don't know if your friend Noelle ever put her fingers inside you but please give me a call if she ever plans to. I'd like to be there...or videotape."

I smile as I watch him collect all his things. He kisses me on the cheek again and reminds me to call or text him if I need anything. As the door shuts behind him I fall back onto my bed and look up at the ceiling.

What the hell am I doing?

I don't want Braden.

I don't know if I want more with Ryder but what we did this morning felt so comfortable and sexy as hell.

I need to take my time. Make sure everything that needs to be said is said. He needs to explain why he said what he did about me under those bleachers. He needs to know why I left and he needs to know about our baby.

Chapter 21

Ryder

My hand on Hadley's lower back feels natural, like it belongs there, as I lead her into Jace's house. It's been a few days since she had the flu and besides being a little weak she seems to be recovering just fine. Thankfully, I didn't get it.

"Well, look who the fuck it is!" AJ calls from his place on the couch.

I shake my head. "Do you ever get up off your lazy ass?"

"Never." He jumps up eyeing Hadley next to me. "But for this fine specimen of a woman I would."

He reaches his hand out and when Hadley lets him take it he places a kiss on her fingers. "The name's AJ, and you must be Hadley."

Her cheeks flush. "I am."

I shove his shoulder. "Get your hands off, AJ. This one is mine."

Hadley looks up at me with a smirk. "You look fucking hot when you're jealous," she says repeating the words I said to her at my sister's house.

"Well," I lean in and whisper so only she can hear. "Feel free to make me jealous anytime you want."

She shivers, and I take pride in knowing that I gave her them. She hasn't mentioned our manual stimulation from Tuesday morning but I feel like she is being more receptive to me. Whereas before she would take her time answering my texts or send my call to voicemail, now it seems like she is the one initiating. For the first time since I've found her again she called me last night "just to talk."

We sat on the phone for an hour talking about our day. I told her about Nate returning to work but never mentioned Braden giving me desk duty all week since the domestic disturbance call on Monday. He and I just coexist at work and I'm thankful that we don't have to interact as much. She told me she secured her second solo event. I'm proud of her and I really hope that she is happy doing what she is doing. I could feel her face light up over the phone when she said Noelle told her she believed and trusted in her.

As everyone else gets to Jace's house I introduce Hadley. When Wendy walks in I feel Hadley tense up and I ease her by grabbing her hand. This time around, even though we are "friends", I want her to know that I won't hide her again. When we become official again, and we will, I will make sure that everyone knows she is mine.

Wendy smiles at her and introduces herself. If there was tension between the two of them you wouldn't know it. When Valerie is the last to arrive we all put our jackets on and head out the door again.

"You sure you're up to doing this? I don't want you to get sick again," I ask as we pile into AJ's truck.

She nods. "I'm sure. If I start to feel bad I'll just take a break."

I pull the glove off of my left hand and the one off her right and clasp them together. "Friends don't hold hands this much, Ryder," she says looking down at them.

"Yes, but friends who want to be more than friends do," I respond, settling into my seat for the long drive to the tubing hill. Every time she tries to pull away I grip her tighter. I think she is doing it on purpose because each time she giggles a little bit. It's a beautiful sound. After a few weeks of down and out Hadley, I feel like she is starting to loosen up a bit more.

When we arrive at the hill, it is filled with people. It looks almost too crowded, but that doesn't deter us. We all love to go tubing together and this is our favorite spot. Piling out of the truck our first stop is the rental shack where we can rent double and single sledding tubes. I rent one for Hadley and me. While waiting for the rest to get theirs, I take in Hadley's smiling face.

Her grin spreads from one cheek to the other as her eyes light up looking at the hill before us. She's wearing a pink Columbia jacket and a white hat that holds down the strands of dark hair that flows over her shoulders. I can't help but fall for her even more every time I see her. It feels like she was the missing piece all along. I know I hurt when she left but I thought I was getting by. Getting through it. I guess I was wrong. I'm yet again a changed man with her in my life.

"What are you looking at?" she asks.

I didn't realize she had turned my way. I lift my hand, brushing a gloved finger over the exposed skin on her face. "My missing piece."

Her head falls into my hand, and I linger my thumb over her lips. She doesn't make a motion to move so I lean in and gently place my lips on hers. The spark that ignites jolts me, and I deepen the kiss never breaking the barrier of her mouth.

"Come on you crazy kids," Jace calls over my shoulder. I pull away from Hadley and find her pupils dilated. Her chest heaving up and down.

"What was that?" she whispers.

I shrug before picking up both of our tubes. "A friendly kiss."

~~

The climb up the hill is steep and long. Wendy, AJ, Valerie and Jace all follow us. The girls complain but Hadley is keeping up like a champ. When we reach the top, I set the tubes down and look out towards the north. The sky is clear, and the wind is minimal. It's a beautiful day to race down the hill covered in snow.

"Who wants to go first?" Wendy asks from besides us.

Without hesitation, both AJ and Jace take their spots ready to race like they always do. They make everything a competition. I don't know how they haven't killed each other yet. They shoot off down the mountain and Wendy and Valerie take their vacant spots. We watch as Jace hits the bottom line first and then the girls take off.

I set my tube down and sit on it, waiting for Hadley to do the same. When she doesn't I look over and find her staring down the hill.

"What's wrong, Had?"

She shakes whatever thought was in her head and says, "This hill is much higher than the one by my house. I'm scared."

The vulnerability she exudes is sexy but confusing. This is the girl who wanted to parasail and zip line. I know last week we didn't actually skydive but I feel like the adventurous Hadley was still there.

I reach out towards her as a line forms behind us. "Come here."

She does as I say and I grab onto her, causing her to fall into my lap. "Ryder!"

"We'll do it together," I whisper into her ear.

She relents and sits between my legs. "Thank you."

"I'm the one who should be thanking you." I push back her hair and kiss her neck.

She hums. "Why's that?"

"Because," I start to push off the ground, "anytime I get to have my body flush with yours, material between us or not, I am thankful for it."

The wind starts nipping at our uncovered skin as we fly down the hill. Hadley's elated screams fill the air and all I can do is smile. She starts to laugh and puts her arms up in the air.

"Do you feel free, Hadley?" I loudly ask into the winter chill.

"Yes!" she hollers. "It's amazing."

At the bottom of the hill she jumps off the tube, barely containing her excitement. "Again!" She points to the stairway leading back up, where the rest of our group has started to ascend.

"Yes, ma'am." I agree, standing and picking up the tube.

She walks over and wraps her arms around my torso looking up. "Ma'am huh? Sounds sexy." Her body shifts when she leans up and places a chaste kiss on my lips.

I slowly pull away. "What was that?"

"A friendly kiss." She winks and lets go of me, taking off towards the hill.

I'm not sure but I think I fall in love with her more and more with each passing day and today is no exception.

Three more treks up the snow hill and back down on the same tube I'm wound up tight. Her smile and her carefree attitude have me reeling and those friendly kisses aren't going to tide me over much longer. I need more.

The café that sits alongside the rental shack is spacious. The ceiling is two stories high, and the west wall of it is made up entirely of glass so you can watch snow tubers and boarders fly down the hill. We choose a table next to the fireplace and the guys head over to the cashier to get some hot drinks. I order both Hadley and I hot chocolate and then turn to watch the girls all chatting with one another. They are all smiling and I pray that Hadley accepts Wendy. I may have slept with her, something I still need to tell Hadley, but Wendy is in love with AJ. We stopped our rendezvous a long time ago once I realized the man she was lusting after was my best friend. He knows about our trysts but I can see he might want her too. Jace, on the other hand, is completely blind when it comes to Valerie. Even though they constantly see each other at JV Fitness, the gym they own together, I don't think he even has a clue.

I watch as Hadley throws her head back at something Wendy says and it makes me smile. Maybe there is hope though she never gave the vibe that it would be a problem.

Jace's hand comes down hard on my shoulder. "You buy the ring yet?"

"No." I shake my head, never taking my eyes off of her. She must sense it because she finds me and blushes. "But I swear if she ever mentions the word marriage to me I'll run to the nearest jewelry store."

"Holy shit," AJ chimes in. "He was joking. You two aren't even dating yet. Didn't she friend zone your ass?"

I turn to grab our drinks before muttering, "Not for long, my friend."

When I arrive back at the table I'm met with a fit of giggles. "What's so funny, ladies?"

Hadley can barely breathe she is laughing so

hard. “Valerie’s face after she just called Noelle a ‘dumb slut who didn’t know what she had with Jace’ and Wendy informed her that she was my friend and boss.” She snorts and they all erupt in another fit of laughter.

I set Hadley’s drink in front of her. “I fail to see how that’s funny,” I state confused. Girls are insane.

“It’s funny because...nevermind.” Hadley waves it off and takes a sip of her hot chocolate. “Mmm.” She moans. “Caramel.”

I sit beside her. “I told you, Spark. I remember everything.”

If I wasn’t looking dead at her I wouldn’t have seen how she faltered for a moment mid-sip. Wendy stands up and excuses herself to help the guys bring the rest of the drinks.

Valerie rests her elbows on the table. She’s a pretty girl. Blonde hair, pretty eyes and desperately in love with Jace. I don’t know why he doesn’t pull his head out of his ass. “So,” she asks Hadley. “Why does he call you Spark?”

Without hesitation Hadley responds, “Because he always knew how to set my body on fire with just the briefest of touches.”

“Damn,” Valerie says. “That’s kinda hot.”

“Excuse us.” I jump up, grabbing Hadley’s hand and pull her along behind me. I’m close to caveman status because I’m just short of throwing her over my shoulder and carrying her.

“Ryder,” she calls out as we round the corner. “You’re taller than me. My legs don’t move that fast.”

I whip around and lift her up behind her thighs. Her legs immediately wrap around me and I push her up against the wall in the darkened hallway. Our faces are inches apart. "You're teasing me, Hadley, and I've had enough."

Her breath is hot and comes out erratically. "I'm not doing anything," she whispers.

I lean in brushing my lips along her jawline making her grip around my neck tighten. "The friendly kisses, the winks, the stares and the fact that I can still feel your hands wrapped around my dick are making me come apart."

"What happens when you come apart, Ryder?"

"This," I warn before slamming my lips to hers. The kiss is needy and she opens her lips to allow my tongue to slip in. It feels like heaven, almost better than sex. Her tongue collides with mine and I push my growing erection in between her jean clad thighs. She moans into my mouth pushing me to deepen the kiss. We move in sync, our bodies remembering each other from long ago. I rub myself on her again earning me another heated moan. She breaks the kiss, her head falling back onto the wall, and calls out my name. "Ryder, you have to stop," she begs.

"Why?" I ask peppering kisses down her neck and continue to hit her sweet spot.

"I'm going to come from you dry humping me like a goddamn high schooler."

I smile and bite her lip. "Under or above clothes, Spark. I don't care as long as I can still set your body on fire."

I nip at her earlobe pushing myself relentlessly

against her, and it's enough to make her come undone. She grabs onto the hair at the nape of my neck and pulls. I cover her moans with my mouth and slip my tongue back in. When her body comes down from her orgasm, I lower her feet to the ground. Bliss is written all over her face.

"Oh my God," she pants clasping at her chest. "What was that?"

"Oh, you know. Just a friendly orgasm," I say. Shock flashes across her face and I lean down taking another kiss from her.

When Ryder and I walk back to the table all eyes are on us. My cheeks grow hot as I sit in my seat and pick up my cup, taking a sip. His touch is still burning my skin in a trail of fire. I feel embarrassed that I came by just him rubbing himself against me but it felt amazing. I love me some friendly orgasms.

I choke on my hot chocolate at that last thought.

"I'm sorry," Ryder whispers so only I can hear him. "I didn't realize your gag reflex was so sensitive."

"Oh, it's not," I say casually as I bring my cup to my mouth again. "I've been known to take in much more than that."

I don't look but I can feel his stare still on me. I inwardly high five myself for rendering him speechless. He groans and then looks to the rest of the group.

We all fall into comfortable conversation and the boys decide to play air hockey. Valerie joins them leaving me with Wendy. We've been getting along great so far but have yet to be left alone. I guess there is no time like the present.

"Hadley," she calls my name pulling me away from watching them play across the room.

I turn. "Yes."

"I'm his friend," she states.

She is beautiful. Her body is svelte and her blonde hair lies perfectly straight. Even underneath all of the winter gear you can still see the nice natural breasts she has. Her perfectly white smile hits her cute dimples and her eyes are a deep puppy dog brown and crystal clear.

I know Ryder says I'm beautiful but I still feel jealous. "Did you sleep together?"

"Yes," she answers immediately. "Twice. But that was all before you saw him again in November at the other sledding hill. When you stood up and I saw his eyes I knew you were *the* Hadley. The way he talked about you to me was the same way he was looking at you. Still does."

"He talked about me?" My heart soars. I didn't know I was a topic of their conversations.

"All the time." She leans in to emphasis her answer. "I probably know more about you then you know about yourself."

"Then why would he sleep with you?"

She lifts her shoulders in a shrug. "Did you think about Ryder while you were with your boyfriend?"

I reflect on that. There were quite a few times where Ryder ran through my mind while I was dating Braden. “That’s different.”

“How? Would it be better if we had been dating?”

I look away. Maybe she is right.

“We were just two people in love with other people, and those two others were sleeping with who they wanted to. We were just vulnerable and needed someone.”

“Do you still need him?” I question, turning my attention back to her to gauge her answer. “In that way I mean?”

“No. I see the way he looks at you and talks about you now and I want for him to be happy. My needs are met elsewhere while I wait.” She looks over at AJ.

“I’m sorry.”

“I’m not. One day he will wake up and realize I’ve been in front of him all along. Maybe you need to realize that too but when you do I swear if you hurt him again I will personally hunt you down.”

“He hurt me first,” I spit out like a two year old.

“Does he know how?”

I shake my head no.

“Lack of communication is the culprit in the majority of misunderstandings. Maybe if you talk to him then he can explain or can ease your mind.”

I nod. “Maybe. I’m just not ready to dig into the past just yet. Things still hurt and I know once I tell him everything there is a chance he might not want me anyways."

She quirks an eyebrow at me. "Why would he..."

"Ladies, are you ready to go?" AJ asks and I watch as Wendy's body comes alive with his proximity. I understand how she feels because as soon as Ryder is in front of me mine does too.

I stand up and loop my arm around his. "Ready?" he asks.

"I am." I smile.

~~

We make it back to Jace's in record time and we immediately climb back into Ryder's car. We stopped and had dinner so it's late and I'm still trying to recuperate from my bout with the flu.

Snow falls as he pulls into my parking lot. Putting the car in park he opens the door motioning for me to wait and runs around the car to open mine. "Thank you, sir." I curtsy making him chuckle.

He kisses the top of my head. "You're too cute."

I place my hand over my heart acting heartbroken. "Just cute? I'd rather be sexy."

His large hands grip my hips and he pushes me up against his car. "Hadley." He growls, dipping his head into the curve of my shoulder and nipping at the flesh. "You are nothing short of sexy."

I whimper as he nips get harder and his hand snakes up my body gripping my hair at the nape of my neck. "Oh, God," I call out into the darkened parking lot.

His grasp tightens, and he pulls my head back giving him unhindered access to my mouth. His lips hover over mine, his stare intense. “I want to come upstairs, Hadley, but I don’t think that is the best idea.”

I frown and he kisses the side of my mouth gently though not making it easier to let him go home right now. “Why not?” I breathe out.

“Because,” he says pulling away slightly. “I see Braden’s car over there and the light in your living room is on.”

I tense up waiting for him to yell, throw a tantrum or demand that he go upstairs and deal with him but all he does is pull me in tight for a hug. “I had a good time today.”

Thinking about all the fun we had I smile up at him. “Me too.”

He releases me and asks that I call once Braden leaves.

As soon as I turn the knob to my apartment door, I hear Ryder’s car pull away and I walk into the dimly lit room. Only the lamps on the end tables are on. Braden is hunched over on the couch, his elbows resting on his knees and his head in his hand. He looks unshowered. I don’t know why he is here but I don’t dare to move or even speak first.

“That was rough,” he finally says and looks up at me. His facial hair is grown out a little bit, the dark color in contrast to his shaggy blond hair.

I cross the room and sit on the chair opposite of the couch feeling at ease enough to do so. “What was?”

He points to the window and yells, “That!

Seeing his mother fucking hands on you, Hadley!"

I quickly stand, suddenly feeling very uncomfortable and grab my phone out of my jacket pocket for safety. "Settle down, Braden. Why the hell are you even here?"

He bolts from the couch and stalks towards me, backing me up against the door. My defense training kicks in and I'm ready to knee him in the balls, but his shoulders slump and slams his hand against the wall.

My body settles once he turns around and walks to the couch to pick up a bag I hadn't seen. "I came to pick my stuff up and talk to you but after what I just saw I have no desire to be in the same room with you anymore. You barely waited a week before you dropped your panties for him, you slut!"

"Get out!" I scream. His words, though caused by pain, truly hurt. I've never been called that name before. "Get the fuck out and never come back here again!"

He starts for the door, knocking my lamp over in his wake, but before he leaves he slams what looks to be my key on the table. "Don't call me when this blows up in your face, Hadley. I could have given you a great life. I was the one who taught you how to trust again after he obliterated you. ME! Good luck with your life." And with his exit the door slams rattling the paintings on the walls.

I fall to the floor and bring my knees into my chest and start to sob.

He's right. When he found me I was lost and still broken. He brought me out of the depths of my hurt and anguish. I struggled for five years after I left Ryder under those bleachers to get my life in order. Braden did help me heal, but that doesn't give him the right to own me or to hurt me. I deserve better than that.

I need a fresh start, a clean cut, and even though Ryder is from my past, I believe he might be a key to my future. I can feel it anytime he is in the room. That pull to him. The one that used to bring out the real Hadley. I want to be her again and Ryder is succeeding in that. But I have secrets. Whether this works out or we just remain friends, he needs to know everything. He deserves to and if I'm ever going to get over the heartbreak he caused me then I have to find out why he disrespected me and our relationship the way he did. His words from that night ring through my head. 'Been there, done that.'

It's still tough for me to believe that he said what he did. Even years later, I still remember it like it was yesterday.

Ryder places gentle kisses on my neck as he fumbles with the clasp on my bra. We're in the trainer room just before his football game. I volunteered to be a student trainer so I can be on the sidelines and help out with the team. It gives me more time to ogle Ryder while he plays. They needed the first-aid kits restocked and so we offered. We definitely didn't pass up the opportunity for secret alone time. Just as he gives up his bra unclasping mission and decides to pull my right cup down the door slowly starts to open. I push off of him and pretend to look for the Band-Aids while Ryder flips on the lights.

"What are you two doing in here?" A too perfect voice asks.

I turn around finding Bridgette Tate, Ryder's ex-girlfriend and queen of the cheerleader bitches.

"Just looking for supplies, Bridg. What the hell do you want?" Ryder asks annoyed.

Ever since they broke up last year, she's always finding a way to be close to him. I wish I could tell her to stay away, and that he is mine, but right now we can't expose our four month long relationship. But soon enough the world will know that Ryder and I are in love.

"Nothing. I saw you walk in here but I didn't know she was with you. I just wanted to remind you to call me later, not that you need to be reminded." She winks at him as she puts her hip out, placing a hand on it.

Bitch.

"I won't." He sighs, turning to me and blows an inconspicuous kiss my way before grabbing some supplies and leaving.

I reach up on the shelf grabbing a few more things so it doesn't look suspicious, dropping all of them on the floor when I find Bridgette still standing there.

"You know it won't last." She sneers.

I bend down to pick up the dropped items. "I don't know what you're talking about."

She kicks a roll of gauze just out of my reach. "He's just using you."

The door slams shut behind her. I finally collect everything and walk back through the hallway and towards the field thinking about her words.

After Ryder started pursuing me I wondered if he had ulterior motives. This summer he proved me wrong by constantly going out of his way to show his affection, but the nagging feeling is always there. We spent the summer together experiencing things that we never had before and we fell in love. The night before school started, I finally gave myself to him for the first time. My first time. It was sweet and gentle and he made sure to take good care of me.

I shake her harsh thoughts out of my head and walk up on Ryder and Todd underneath the bleachers before game time, stopping just far away enough so I can listen.

"I'm sure, man," Ryder says to Todd.

My heart tightens at how sexy his voice is. I want to finish what we started a few minutes ago.

"I just saw both of you go into the training room. Nothing is going on?" Todd's eyebrows raise in question.

"She's nothing but trash. Been there, done that. You can have her," he comments as they walk away out of earshot.

"Told ya," Bridgette whispers, shouldering past me.

My phone rings in my hand but I ignore it and pull myself up off the floor shaking the memory out of my head. I flip all the locks on the door before stripping myself of my jacket, hat, gloves and boots, dumping them beside the doormat.

My text pings as I walk into my bedroom and I drop it on my nightstand. Once I rid myself of my clothes I climb into the hot shower. When I've scrubbed my body and shampooed my hair, I finally allow tears to fall. They fall for the loss of my two year relationship. They fall for the harsh words Braden said to me. They fall in confusion over my feelings for a man who caused me to put a brick wall around my heart. They fall because I know I have to tell Ryder what happened and he might hate me for it and they fall because the memory still stings like a mother fucker.

Cold air fills the shower and I'm startled when the curtain opens slightly. Ryder's voice instantly calms me down. "Hadley?"

I wipe away the tears though the water cascading down on me hides them but there is no mistaking the bloodshot of my eyes.

Covering my breasts with my hands I turn around. "I'm done. I'm coming out."

"Okay."

When I'm out and dried off, I wrap a towel around me and find Ryder sitting on my bed. He pats the spot next to him. "Come here."

I comply and allow him to wrap his arms around my body and draw me into him. My wet hair falls onto his shoulder. If it bothers him he doesn't tell me.

"I'd ask you how you got in here but I figure that you still have Noe's key," I say while I pick at my nail beds.

His shoulders bounce with laughter. "I do but I only did it because I was worried. I saw him leave and you didn't answer your phone."

I tell him about the confrontation and have to practically hold him down so he wouldn't go find Braden. Ryder calms down but I'm sure he is probably plotting something for Monday morning.

I get dressed in some shorts and a tank top and crawl into bed. "Do you want me to stay or go?" he asks giving me the option.

My flashback tells me he needs to leave but my ever growing feelings for him tell me I want him to stay.

"Stay please, but I just want to be held," I tell him.

Standing up he tugs his pants down and pulls his shirt off. It's the first time I've been able to look at him unashamed in a very long time. His six pack ripples down to a patch of happy trail that disappears underneath his boxers. My mouth starts to salivate knowing just how amazing he can make me feel.

Ryder slides into the bed behind me. "Spark. You have to stop staring at me like that. I'm trying to be a gentleman."

I wiggle back into him to get comfortable. "What if I don't like it gentle?" I ask trying to sound innocent and inwardly giggling.

I can feel him grow hard against my back. "Go to bed, Had."

My mind is still reeling and I'm having a hard time falling asleep. I'm not sure if right now is a good time but I decided to try anyways. "Ryder, we need to talk."

"I know." He kisses the back of my head. "Tomorrow."

He starts humming and tension immediately releases from my body. It's soothing and calm and just what I need right now. Ryder's humming stops after a few minutes and his breathing deepens. Just as I'm about to fall asleep he utters four words that will keep me awake for the rest of the night. "I love you, Spark."

Chapter 23

Ryder

It's not the best place to have this conversation but both Hadley and I are on our lunch breaks and she said she needed to get some things off her chest. So, here I am at Market Square Restaurant waiting for her to arrive. I look around, the place buzzing, and try to calm my nerves. I'm trying to figure out what she wants to tell me and after finding out from Wendy that she told Hadley about our trysts I'm nervous she won't want to continue whatever it is that we're doing.

I love doing whatever it is that we're doing.

I smile to myself and think about the other day. I'm making progress breaking down her walls while simultaneously building her up.

"Can I get you anything while you're waiting," the overly friendly server asks me. When I tell her no she hurriedly moves to the next table.

As I scan the room I see someone I haven't seen in years and inwardly cringe.

Nothing much has changed about her. You can tell from the way she sits that she is as pretentious as she was in high school.

Her curly blonde hair is a bit tamer and I don't know a lot about fashion but her shirt costs more than anything on my body. Including the cash in my wallet.

Yea, I grew up with a lot of money, but it was my parent's money and if I'm being honest with myself it embarrassed me more than anything. My parents liked to flaunt it whereas Julia and I pretended like we didn't get fifty thousand dollar cars for our sixteenth birthday. We drove Chevy's and Dodge's just to fit in. To this day we both won't take a penny from them unless the power is about to be turned off. We seem to make it on our own, even if Julia struggles sometimes. Usually any money my mom sends to her she automatically puts into the girls' accounts. Where we tried to hide our money, Emie did everything she could to flaunt it, just as she is right now.

Her blue eyes finally look up and recognition registers. Her facial features turn angry as she excuses herself from someone I can only describe as a beefcake and stalks her way over with purpose. When she nears the table I have to tilt my head back so that I can meet her stare.

Her hand comes out and leans on the back of the booth behind me, her fingers just inches away from my shoulder. She puffs out her chest, making her boobs look bigger than they are, and clicks her tongue.

"Ryder Blake." She licks her lipstick clad lips. "I haven't seen you in a while, but I heard you were in town."

I quirk and eyebrow at her. "You have, huh? From who?"

She takes it upon herself to slide into the seat across from me and I'm instantly annoyed. "Why Hadley, of course. Seems like you've been sniffing around her lately and I don't like it."

I shake my head looking to the door and silently praying that Hadley walks. When I find the door empty I turn my attention back to Emie.

"Oh yea, well I guess I like her scent. Can you leave? I'm waiting on someone." I point to her table not so subtly excusing her.

"Ryder." Her hands graze over the top of mine. "Why are you still hung up on her?"

Pulling my hands away I give her a look that should drop her dead where she sits. "Don't touch me again."

Not taking the hint she continues, "I just don't understand what your draw to her was in high school. I think her leaving you was the best thing she could have done."

"Are you serious right now?" I ask astonished.

"Why wouldn't I be?" she asks sweetly though I know better. This is the girl who lied to me about knowing where Hadley was and then told her I was sleeping around after she left.

"You have a lot of nerve, Emie. I came to you and spilled my guts begging for information where she went." I raise my voice. "You told me you didn't know and I recently found out that was a fucking lie."

I try to calm myself down but it's not working. "And," I continue. "Does your best friend know that you tried to sleep with me and I turned you down?"

Her face straightens out. Long gone is the tigress that walked over here a minute ago. "Fuck you, Ryder."

"I thought we established this in high school, Emie. I've already said no thank you." I insult her and continue, "I don't get why you lied to her."

She looks out the window and then back to me. "What did I lie about?"

I look at her like she is stupid. How could she not know what she did? Hadley said she told Emie all about us.

I take a sip of my water and can see my hand shaking. I'm trying to get over what happened back then. Trying to allow Hadley more time to tell me why she left but having Emie here in my face is bringing back those old wounds. When I see Hadley I think of all the amazing times we had together but when I look at Emie all I see is the heartbreak that I suffered. To think maybe things would have been different had Emie told her the truth, that I was looking for her and I could barely look at another girl or even that she cornered me and tried to have her way with me. But then I think that if she hadn't left none of that would have mattered.

"You lied to Hadley about what I was doing after she left," I whisper yell so I don't draw too much attention to us.

Her eyes widen in shock. She doesn't say anything so I continue, "Yea, she told me what you said. I haven't told her the real story just yet but don't fucking push me, Emie. I won't hesitate."

She stands up abruptly. "You can't threaten me. And who do you think she is going to believe, Ryder, you or me?"

Now we have the attention of the other patrons.

I don't look up but I hope I get my point across. "I don't know, Emie, but I will tell her eventually. I won't have secrets between Hadley and me."

"Oh, really." She sneers leaning in but her voice is still annoyingly high. I'd like to shove a pencil in my ear so I'd never have to hear her voice again.

"Yea, really. I plan on pursuing her until she is mine and making sure she knows what really happened is part of it. No more lies."

"Well." She straightens up. "Make sure you ask her about your baby she aborted right after she left. I'm sure clearing up that little lie will help in your pursuit."

My breathing stops and I feel my stomach coil. I feel sick.

A baby?

My baby?

Abortion?

"Oh my God!" I hear the betrayal in Hadley's voice come from behind Emie.

Emie whips around. "Hadley." She breathes out, embarrassed.

Hadley looks at me, tears welling in her eyes,

before she turns and runs out the door.

"Is everything okay here?" the manager comes over to ask.

I ignore him pushing back Emie and following after Hadley. I make it past the second set of doors and look left and right finding her just as she gets to her car. Before she can slam her door shut. I block it with my hand.

"Let me go, Ryder!" she yells tugging harder on the door.

I throw it open. "No!" I scream leaning down onto my knees so I'm eye level with her. She won't even look at me.

"Look at me," I command but she doesn't listen. She just puts the keys in the ignition and turns her car on. I can feel a warm blast of air float out into the cold. "Look at me now!"

When she finally listens, and she turns her body towards me, I find a broken woman. Tears stream down her face and all I want to do is wipe them away.

"Hadley, talk to me," I beg after.

Looking down she whispers, "I was pregnant. I wanted to tell you, Ryder, but Emie told me you moved on and I..." Her sobs get loud and I close her door.

I can see her look around to see if I'm leaving. I don't. I walk to the passenger side and pull the door open and climb in. Reaching out I bring Hadley's shaking body into mine.

"It's okay, Had. It's okay. You did what you had to do in your situation." I try to comfort her but I'm not sure I'm speaking the truth. I don't know if it was okay to leave me out of the decision making process. I feel gutted right now.

She drags herself away from me. "No."

"No? No what?" I ask.

"I didn't have an abortion, Ryder." She cries. "I lost the baby. I lost our baby. I'm so sorry. I was going to tell you."

Relief takes over me. For a brief moment I doubted Hadley. I doubted that she ever really loved me and if she terminated my child than she didn't have the faith in us that I did. She left me, yes, but even if what I did–and I still don't know what–was so terrible I believe she would have kept that baby and let me love it too. We would have a made it work.

"Don't apologize." I grab both of her hands into mine. "God, Hadley. I'm so sorry I wasn't there for you. I'm sorry that whatever it is I did or you think I did caused you to have to go through that alone."

Her green eyes, filled with dread and apology, look me dead in the face and I know that there is more. "I need to know, Ryder, what was all of it for?"

My brows furrow with confusion. "All of what for?"

She lets go of one of my hands to wipe a stray tear. "Us, in high school. Did you ever love me or did you really think I was trash?"

"Hadley," I chastise. "How could you ever think that? I was willing to give it all up for you. I was about to tell my parents to fuck off before you hightailed it out of there. I was devastated. Why would you even say that?"

"That night," she starts. "After we left the training room."

I nod, remembering. It was the last time I had seen her. I don't even remember seeing her on the field that night but that wasn't uncommon.

"I remember."

"I heard what you said to Todd Mitchell," is all she says and then looks at me like I should know what the hell she is talking about.

"You have to be more specific, Spark," I tell her as I reach over and push her hair behind her ears and wipe a thumb down her cheek. "What did you hear?"

I don't even remember talking to Todd too much that night. I just recall looking for her afterwards and then figuring she had to go straight home. It wasn't until the next day I realized something was wrong.

Hadley pulls the other hand away from me. Her next words coming out harsh through her sobs. "She's nothing but trash. Been there, done that. You can have her."

"Had, what are you..." I start to say but then it all becomes very clear.

"Hey, Ryder!" Todd calls out as I walk towards him, supplies in hand, a smile plastered on my face and my fingers still burning from Hadley's skin. I can't wait until tomorrow after I talk to my parents and tell them about her. Then I can tell everyone that Hadley Chase is mine.

"What's up, man?" I ask, handing him some supplies.

He stutters for a moment, looking nervous. "Well, I was wondering if you were still seeing Bridgette Tate. I was thinking of asking her to homecoming."

I laugh. "You sure about that, man? She is kinda nuts."

"Yea. We've been talking on the phone the past few weeks and I wanted to make sure you were okay with it." He laughs, brushing off the insult but feel like I need to warn him. Bridgette is conniving and gets around–a lot.

I pat him on the shoulder. "I'm sure, man."

"I just saw both of you going into the training room. Nothing is going on?" Todd's eyebrows raise in question.

I shake my head no and steer him towards the field. "She's nothing but trash. Been there, done that. You can have her."

When I come to from my memory Hadley has moved all the way over to her side of the car and now has her arms crossed over her chest.

"Let me just talk you down from that ledge you've perched yourself up on."

She huffs so I reach over and pull her chin my way.

"That night, the night after we snuck away in the training room, Todd was asking if he could take Bridgette Tate to homecoming. I was giving him a warning," I tell her straight into her eyes so she can see I'm not bullshitting her. "I loved you and I would have never disrespected you like that."

That was it all along. That tiny moment in time where words that were said were taken out of context. Three sentences changed my entire world in a heartbeat and here I am seven years later just learning about it. Flashes of all the heartache, anguish, sadness, depression, burying myself in other women when it should have been Hadley all along. If she would have just talked to me about it, confronted me, hell, hit me. I would have gladly taken it so that I wouldn't have lost all this time with her.

"Oh my God," she whispers, drawing her chin out of my fingers, and then repeats it. "Oh my God."

"What?"

"All this time. All this time I thought you were talking about me and you were talking about Bridgette." Her voice raises an octave. "I left you. I lost our baby. I spent my college years nursing a heartbreak that was nonexistent." Then she turns to me. "I left you. Oh, God, Ryder. How do I even start to ask for your forgiveness? I'm so sorry."

I reach over, grasp her under her arms and pull her on top of me. Her legs spread and fall on either side of me. Taking her face into my hands, I pull her mouth just inches from mine. Her eyes are still filled with tears. I lift my lips and kiss her nose. "We start over."

Her body relaxes. "How can you even say that? Shouldn't you hate me?"

I kiss the corner of her mouth and snake one of my hands to her hips. "I don't hate you. I never have. We were young and naïve. Do I wish you would have talked to me about it? Yes, but you can't change what happened in the past. All we can do is start over. We won't let all that happened hinder what I think is happening between the two of us. I want to keep exploring what I think could be even better than it was before but no more running."

She nods, initiating a chaste kiss. "No more running."

I smile. "Let's have a friendly kiss to seal the deal."

Her mouth crashes to mine and I forget where we are and where I'm supposed to be. I don't care. The wrath of Sgt. Dickhead will be well worth it after I worship this beautiful mouth of hers.

Chapter 24

Hadley

I throw open the glass door leading back into the restaurant looking for my so called best friend. I don't know what she was doing here or why she told Ryder I aborted my baby. Never once did that thought even cross my mind and she knows how utterly devastated I was when I miscarried.

I had thought about calling Ryder numerous times after I found out I was pregnant. Despite Emie telling me he was being a manwhore, which I now, after our chat in the car, found out that wasn't true at all, I still knew I owed it to Ryder to tell him about the baby. I drove to my parent's house a week later. I knew I had to tell them too and after confessing to my mother that Friday night I went to sleep. Sometime in the middle of the night I woke up to blood all over me and the bed. My mom took me to the emergency room where they couldn't find a heartbeat and that I was miscarrying. After they ran some tests they asked me to come back a few weeks later for a check up to make sure everything looked okay.

I was devastated. The idea of being a mother grew on me in the two weeks since I had found out and I knew that once I told Ryder he would have been there for me one hundred percent, even if at the time I thought he saw me as trash.

I never went to see him or Emie that weekend. I stayed in bed and on Sunday evening my mother drove me back to my aunt's house. I tried to believe that it happened for a reason. That there was something wrong with the baby and God wanted to call them home before they even took their first breath. I did a lot of soul searching. I put my focus into my art, my school and getting my life back in order.

I never wanted to go through that again and so in college I avoided all the drunken one night stands that all my friends were having. That way I was protected both mentally and physically.

I look around the dining area and come up empty. She must have left when Ryder and I were in the car.

I walk back outside deciding on a drive thru since I didn't have time to eat before I head back to the office.

"You know I did what was best for you," I hear her voice from beside my car.

Anger rises and I feel my face heat up. I can't even look at her right now. "You lead me to believe he had moved on when you knew how much I loved him. Don't you think that I should decide what's best for me or not."

"Hadley."

I finally glare her way. "No. You knew I needed

him after I found out about the baby and yet you still decided to give me bullshit information. You're supposed to be my best friend, Emie."

"I am!" she yells throwing her hands up. "Don't you think it hurt me to do that?"

I scoff. "Ha! Do what exactly? Try to seduce the guy I was in love with?"

She moves closer to me but I step away. I feel like I don't know her anymore, like I never did.

"I was trying to keep you from the heartbreak that came at the end. It was never going to work out. You were both from opposite sides of the track." She tries to reason.

"So, I was poor and he was rich. Who cares? You're wealthy too, Em. You were still my best friend, unless that was a fucking lie too."

She shakes her head. "Don't say that."

"Why did you tell him I got an abortion, Emie? We're trying to work back to where we used to be and you tried to sabotage it. You've been doing that since the day you found out we had been together. Are you jealous?"

"Why would I be jealous of you?" she questions then slams her hand over her mouth.

"Well." I open the door to my car. "I guess you don't have any reason to be. But your little scheme didn't work. We both know everything now and the only thing that has changed is now you are out of the equation. Might make for a better outcome."

"You're right," she says stopping me in my tracks.

I glare at her. "About?"

She sighs. "I was jealous. I knew, Hadley. I caught you two a few times." She shakes her head. "When you would ditch plans with me I would drive to your house and watch him climb in your window. I knew and I was jealous because I wanted him. So, when you left I used it to my advantage. I only have high school immaturity to blame."

"And what excuse do you have for your lies today, Emie?" I climb in my car, blasting the heater, and slam the door. I try not to drive over her toes as I reverse out of the parking spot. I leave her there staring as I drive away.

~~

"I don't know if I can ever forgive her, Noe," I explain as I shove a French fry in my mouth.

I've thought about my predicament with Emie and realize she is nothing but the same toxin I need to rid my life of.

"She's a twat waffle." She leans back in her chair. "She fed you bullshit lines about Ryder in high school and then she takes the most devastating part of your life and twists it to run him away from you."

Sighing, I grab my phone. "I know but at least he believed me."

"He was probably staring at your tits when you told him what really happened," she says trying to lighten the mood. I laugh. "Men will believe anything you say if they can stare at your rack."

What makes Noelle so funny is that she can say all this with a straight face and be dead serious about it. Like she truly believes if she pulls her shirt up that any guy will agree with her.

Well, maybe she's right.

I laugh again. "I just hate that I spent all these years feeling heartbroken about something he said about his ex girlfriend."

"You believe him?" she sincerely asks.

I think for a second. "I do."

She points one of her pretty French tipped manicured nails at me. "That's how you know, Had. That's how you know you will last. You can be in love, you can find him sexy as well but until you can believe what they say without question then you know it's for real."

"Huh," is all I say.

"You can't have a healthy relationship without trust. I could leave Trent in a room with a hundred naked woman and trust that he won't mess with any of them and believe he would tell me if they tried anything."

"Trent would never cheat on you." I point out.

"Oh, I know." She smiles. "Why would he go for hamburger when he's got steak waiting at home."

I chuckle at her confidence. But she's right. Besides her OCD tendencies, she really is the whole package.

"You know," she says tapping her pen to her lips. "You should invite Ryder over for dinner and make him some steak."

"I can't cook." I deadpan. "You know this. I burn water."

She stands up and leans over her desk. "Let me

be clearer. Get Ryder some steak. Dress it up in some sexy lingerie, spread it on the bed and let him feast, Hadley. Steak!"

Realization hits and a slow smile creeps up on my face as an image of Ryder ravaging me on my bed passes through my thoughts.

Then I start thinking of all the things that would be involved. "I don't have lingerie, and I haven't shaved my legs. Plus, how do you initiate? I have never been the initiator."

My nerves start to take over and I panic. I don't know how to be confident like Noelle.

"Go! Leave. Take the rest of the day off." She sits back down, picking up her desk phone. "Soon because Trent will be here in twenty minutes and no one is due back in the office for another hour."

"Are you pushing me out the door so you can have sex with Trent...again?" I laugh as I collect my stuff. I might not be leaving to go prepare the steak but I sure as hell am not going to hang around for another show.

"I'd say no but then I would be lying. Plus this gets us both laid."

If I thought they were bad now I can't imagine how it's going to be when they get married. I'm not sure I want to be around for that.

I leave her to her business call and pull my cell phone from my purse dialing up Ryder.

He answers on the first ring and I can hear commotion in the background.

"I'm sorry. I wasn't thinking. You sound busy. Just give me a call when you get a minute." I say ready to hit the end button.

"Had, I wouldn't have answered if I couldn't talk. Plus, I'd always make time for you. It's nice to hear your voice."

I'm sure he can hear my smile in my response. "You just saw me a few hours ago."

"I know." He sighs. "But we were working through something and it's nice to hear the pep in your step."

"Pep in my step? You sound like an old lady."

"I'm not old and I'm not a lady." His voice rumbling from his chest. "I'm all man, baby."

I laugh. He never calls me baby. "Well, I was thinking that since we had kind of a tense afternoon that we could meet again tonight."

"Wow!" he exclaims. "Two times in one day, Hads? You might wear me out."

I blush. His playful flirting is turning me on. Well anything he has been doing lately is turning me on.

"You would think with all that working out you do that you could handle it." I flirt back. "I guess not. Maybe I should date someone else with better endurance."

Silence comes from the other end of the phone and I wonder if maybe he took it as an insult.

"So, we're dating then?" Ryder asks sounding optimistic yet nervous.

I look out my windshield at the flurries falling from the sky and think once again about being a snowflake. A few months ago, I felt like the ones that fell to the ground conformed to the others, but Ryder makes me feel like the ones that float in the sky never touch the ground. He makes me feel like I'll always be unique, and that I can be myself.

I smile as I answer. "Yes. I think we are."

I'm having Ryder pick up takeout while I ready the "steak." I forgo the lingerie and settle for a cute lavender bra and panty set over my newly waxed and shaved body. I'm not expecting anything but if it does happen I want to be prepared. I take another look in the mirror and adjust my ponytail before smoothing my makeup over my face. Reaching into my closet I pull out a pair of skinny jeans and a purple V-neck sweater.

I walk out into the living room just in time for a knock at the door. Like a teenage girl I skip down the hallway and open it before he has the chance to knock again. His smile seems to brighten the room as he holds up two plastic bags of Chinese.

"What? You didn't want to use your key?" I joke and step aside so he can come in.

He kisses me on the lips quickly before setting the food on the table. When he turns around to take off his coat I have to contain my drool. This is the first time I've been able to look at him since I found the words he said under the bleachers weren't meant for me. I would let that nasty misunderstanding fester but not tonight. Tonight I am enjoying his freshly showered body, and how his hair looks like he tugged on it just before he got here. The way his arms stretch out after taking off his jacket, his black thermal shirt and his jeans fit his hips and thighs but are loose down to the bottom where they lie on top of black boots. He's raw, primal sexiness and I don't think I'll have a problem initiating. When I meet his eyes, I can feel the carnal lust behind them. They strike me where I stand.

"Don't stare at me like that, Spark. I just might have to show you how much endurance I really have," he warns.

I intentionally bite my lip knowing how crazy he can get. I wrap my arms around his torso. "That's not what I remember from when we were teenagers. I was pushing it getting you to go for anything past round one."

He grabs my arms from around his waist and pulls them around his neck. Reaching down he pulls me up by my thighs bringing his mouth over mine. "I'm not a teenager anymore, Hadley." He growls. "I'm all man and as soon as you stop denying me I'll show you just how much man I am."

I run my tongue across my lips and let my words come out clear. "I'm not denying you anymore, Ryder."

His lips collide with mine, and he carries me to my bedroom, stopping at the foot of my bed and dropping me to my feet. His palms cup my face, and he leans in nipping at my bottom lip.

"You're so beautiful," he whispers moving his lips along my jawbone and up to my ear.

My head falls back granting him the access he is asking for. I drag my hands up his body and slowly glide the tips of my fingers up along the sides of his abdomen, not hesitating to lift his shirt over his head. Taking my earlobe between his teeth, goose bumps prickle my skin all the way down to my toes. I'm so turned on I can barely think straight.

So I don't.

He pulls my sweater up and over my head, and I reach back and unclasp my bra, letting the soft material fall to the floor.

"I want to worship you, Hadley." He breathes his words onto my skin. "I want to take my time with you. Show each and every part of your body how much I missed it."

My knees feel weak with his words. Just the few touches he's given have shown me how much my body misses his. How comfortable I am with him. I trust him with my body.

Bending down on his knees he reaches for the button on my jeans and carefully unclasps them. He pushes the denim down leaving them bundled up around my ankles. Just as slowly, he lowers my panties that I put on only a half hour earlier. He lifts one foot and then the other untangling me of my clothes. When I think he's going to lay his mouth between my legs he stands.

Looking down at my body he draws a finger from my neck all the way down to my belly button, stopping just above where I was hoping he would go. "Perfect." He compliments. "Lay down."

I do as I'm told and scoot myself all the way to the headboard, my body flat on my back, my knees bent. Ryder leans down and takes his boots off then teasingly lowers his jeans never breaking eye contact. It's erotic to watch him undress.

Leaning on the bed he grabs my left foot and

kisses the top of it, his other hand caresses my leg. He peppers kisses up my ankle, to my calf and then bites my thigh. I jump.

"I'm a little rougher now, Spark, but you'll like it. I promise," he speaks, the tone is menacing.

He turns and gives the same attention to my other leg but this time I'm waiting for the bite. When it doesn't come I relax and he pulls my pussy to his face.

"Do you know how fucking sexy this is down here?" he asks blowing hot breath across before pushing his tongue out and lazily licking up through my folds. I jerk but his arms are now wrapped around my thighs and are holding me down. "Don't move, Hadley," he commands kissing my inner thigh and taking little pieces of skin between his teeth.

It doesn't hurt. It's fucking hot.

"I won't."

"Good girl."

His mouth is back on me but this time he licks with purpose. Hardening his tongue and rubbing it on me so hard the friction could start a fire. I call out his name and he puts more force behind it. I'm writhing, jerking and wanting him to end the torture but wanting him to keep his mouth there all night.

He leans back far enough to talk. "Come on my face, Spark." And then his fingers push inside me and his mouth clamps down on my clit, sucking like a vacuum cleaner.

"Oh, God," I scream as an orgasm crashes down on me. "Oh, shit."

When my body bows off the bed he allows it and my hands fist the sheets. I realize how loud I'm being but I can't help it. This is the most intense orgasm I've ever had and it doesn't end. I continue to rub myself into him, not caring if I break his damn nose. I plant my feet down, shoving myself away from his mouth. I can't take it, it feels too sensitive.

"Holy shit." I pant out trying to catch my breath. He's still down on his knees eyeing me like a piece of steak.

Ah, I get it.

Ryder climbs up the bed towards me and kisses me, gripping my ponytail and tugging. His grasp tightens, and it causes my nipples to do the same. The part of my body that was sensitive just a minute ago is now begging for more.

"Do you want more?" he asks like he's reading my mind.

I turn the tables and bite his lip, hard. "Does that answer your question?"

A sensual smirk crosses his face and he leans back, grabbing my feet and tugging me until I'm on my back again. "Why yes it does."

My hands grab her wrists and tug them up to the headboard. When securely in place I lower my head to her right breast taking a tight nipple into my mouth. They are just like I remember. The perfect size. I move my hand to the other breast and pinch it as I clamp down on the one my mouth is on. It earns me an erotic moan making my cock twitch in anticipation.

I love that she likes my aggressiveness because I'm about to show her how a good woman should be worshiped and fucked.

Holding her hands down isn't going to allow me to do the things I want to so I let them go and they immediately find my hair. She pulls tight and her glistening pussy rubs along my torso.

"Patience, Hadley. You need to be patient." I tsk at her.

She lifts my head up and her green eyes have turned dark, heated. "I have been. I don't want to be patient anymore. I'm fucking begging you to get inside me. Please!"

"Well," I tell her, standing up and dropping my boxers down on the ground. "Since you said please."

I reach down, pulling a condom out of my wallet and slipping it on all while she watches me with heated anticipation. Hadley sits up, her weight resting on her elbows. I kneel on the bed and lean down to kiss her sweet lips. She intoxicates me with her sweet taste. She takes it deeper grabbing my neck and slipping her tongue in my mouth, bringing us down to the sheets.

My fingers reach down, gripping her hips tightly, and she squirms beneath me. My sheathed cock throbs at her entrance and I grab it, using it to rub up and down her folds, spreading her juices, driving her wild. I let go of myself and slip a finger in, earning me another moan from her lips, and curl my fingers up, hitting that familiar spot that used to make her beg me for more. Her body bows off the bed forcing my fingers in deeper.

"You're so tight, Hadley." I hover my words over her skin. "And wet. Dammit, you're fucking soaked."

Her small fingers reach between us, grasping my rock hard dick. "It's because I'm ready for you. Please."

I push myself up and down through her fingers while rapidly fucking her with my own, stretching her to make sure she can handle my girth.

I love how this feels. My body remembers everything–her skin is comforting and her touches familiar. I can't believe we spent so many years apart and she dated that douche. How could he ever have let her get away?

"Do you want me to make love to you, Hadley?" I ask pulling away from her slightly, looking into lust filled green eyes. "Or do you want me to fuck you because fuck if I don't want to slam into you right now."

She stops all motion, her hand still wrapped around my latex clad cock, and looks to me with resolve. "I'm too wound up for you to go slow. Slam into me and make me come again."

Her words cause me to lose the last bit of control I have. I pull my fingers from her sticking them into my mouth and slowly dragging them out. "So fucking sweet." I moan as her eyes go wide at the action.

Before she can say anything I line my dick up with her pussy and shove myself in to the hilt, launching her up the bed. She screams out in pleasure. My hands grip underneath her thighs and I send out a warning. "Put your hands against the headboard."

"Why?" she asks confused.

"Because..." I start pumping slowly. "I don't want you to hit your head when I start fucking moving."

She complies, placing the palms of her hand on the wood. It makes her tits stick out further. Without warning I start slamming into her relentlessly. The screams of passion begin again and her breasts start bouncing up and down. It's fucking mesmerizing.

"Damn, I missed this," I say as my eyes meet

hers. I can see she is loving every second of this, yes, but something else looms between the two of us.

She clenches tightly around me and the feel of it catches me so off guard that I have to slow my pace before I finish too soon. I don't care if she has had an orgasm already. She will come with me inside her before I do.

My name comes out barely a whisper. "Ryder..."

"I know, Spark. God I know." I can feel what we used to have creep up back into me. All the amazing times we had getting to know one another, growing up more that year than any other and doing it together.

Owning her. Taking her virginity and claiming her as mine. She was mine. She is mine. I'll make sure she knows.

I pick my pace back up, slapping my hips against her–the green of her eyes disappearing as they dilate, never leaving mine. They seem as though they see through me, and they do. She knows me. Even years later she knows me. And as much as I want to own her, she already owns me. Always has. She has my heart and all of this fuels my drive to claim her once again. Show her that there can be no one else.

The silence of the night is filled with our rushed breaths and the slapping of our skin together.

Hadley's hands drop from the headboard and she grabs onto the bed sheets and holds on for dear life.

"Ryder," she calls my name again, the knuckles on her hands turning white.

I watch her hold her breath and her head whip from side to side, her chest coming up with each push into her.

"I've never seen something so beautiful as you right before you come," I tell her. Her eyes flash to mine and her teeth secure her bottom lip as she starts to whimper.

"Scream, Spark," I command. "Yell so the fucking neighbors can hear my name fall from that mouth."

She lets out another heated moan. "Harder, Ryder. I need it harder," she begs.

I lift her legs and throw them over my shoulder, before plunging back into her.

"Yes!" she screams as her pussy tightens.

"Tell me how much you want this," I say wanting to hear how bad she craves me.

Her breathing is ragged, and I spread her legs wider, resting them in the crease of my elbows. I look down watching as my cock, slickened with her arousal, pushes in and pulls out in a rapid pace.

"So bad for so long. Fuck." She swears and it launches me into a state of utter loss of control. I lean further into her body, letting her legs fall to the bed and bite her collarbone as my fingers pinch her nipples hard. She yells out but it's in pleasured pain.

"Did that feel good, Hadley." I taunt, pinching the other one just as hard. "Do you like it rough."

"Yes, yes, yes," she repeats as I continue to nip

at her.

My pace is punishing, my touch hard, and my teeth marking every inch I can reach.

"Shit. Harder!" she screams out and I feel her tighten around me. "Oh my God!"

"That's it, Hadley. Come." My pace quickens and she goes quiet as she loses her breath. "Come all over me."

I reach down, pinching her clit right as she comes, her ass bows off the bed. "FUCK!" she screams as loud as she can. "RYDER! Oh, God."

She starts milking my cock with her orgasm and I can't hold it any longer. I come, buried deep inside, harder than I've ever come before, and claim Hadley as my own–again.

I fucking own her now whether she wants me to or not.

~~

I open my eyes relishing in the warmness of Hadley's slumbering body next to mine. The early morning sunrise shines through the window above her headboard. The one she used to hold on to for dear life last night.

Moving from my back to my side, I pull her into me and nestle my face in the crevice between her neck and shoulder. It's my favorite part.

She lets out a content sigh and adjusts herself deeper into my arms.

I brush my lips against her neck, spreading kisses up and down, waking her up gently. "I have to get going to work, hun."

She starts giggling and shimmies her ass against my morning wood.

“What’s so funny?” I ask while turning her onto her back. Her green eyes shine in the morning light.

Lifting her head, she chastely kisses me. “You called me hun and...” she shimmies again. “You’re poking me.”

“Well,” I kiss her back, “if you don’t like that I called you hun then we can stick with Spark and I’m sorry that I’m poking you,” I tell her as I crawl out of bed. “I can’t help but be rock hard waking up next to you.”

I leave her in bed, while she watches my naked ass as I go and walk into her bathroom to take a shower. Once I have a towel and the water is warm I slip in and wash myself.

I use her girl shampoo and start to wash my body with her Caress body soap. Memories of last night creep back in and I couldn’t wipe the stupid grin off my face if I wanted to. Her body was fucking sexy bowing off the bed at my touch and watching her come again with me inside her after all these years had set me off. When we crawled back into bed after cleaning up, I couldn’t help but have hope for us. After seven years without her and months of wondering if, now that I know where she is, we could ever try again I finally started to gain back the hope I lost so many years ago.

“Ryder?” I hear her call into the steam.

“Almost done if you need to jump in.” I scrub the last of the soap over my neck and set it down and begin to rise myself.

I'm startled as her voice comes from right beside me. "I do but that's not why I'm in here."

I turn, finding her inches behind me. Her arms wrap around me from behind grasping onto my still hard cock. "Hadley," I whisper. "God that feels..."

My words trail off as her other hand grabs me just under my balls and gently cups them. Her thumb rubs the sensitive area just underneath.

Her lips find my shoulder blades. "Good, Ryder? Were you going to say good?"

My head falls forward as my hands brace themselves on the wall in front of me, letting the water cascade down my back. She glides her hand up and down my shaft fast as her other hand pulls slowly on my balls.

My body starts to tense up, waiting for release but she let's go. I moan, frustrated, and whip around finding her lip snagged between her teeth. I reach up, pulling it free. "If you're looking to help me with my problem, just know you are making it worse."

A seductive smile reaches her eyes and she looks down and drops down to her knees. "No," she says gripping my cock in her hands again. "I'm not trying to make it worse. I'm just evening the score. It seems I owe you an orgasm."

Before I can protest, not that I would, she takes me into her mouth. Her tongue flat, allowing it to slip with ease. Her eyes, looking straight up at me, are hungry. She takes it as deep as she can, using her hand to reach the parts she can't all while torturing with the gentle tug of my balls. It's not long before I'm gripping the back of her head and setting the pace. I watch her as she watches me. The look of my cock disappearing into her mouth is erotic and with a few final thrusts I come in her mouth, slowing the pace so that she has time to swallow it all down.

Pulling slowly out of her, she wipes her bottom lip and stands up. I quickly turn off the shower and pick her up, not caring about the water that splashes onto the tile of the bathroom floor. Careful not to slip I make it to the carpet of the bedroom and throw her on the bed.

She squeals. “What are you doing?”

I push her legs open and secure my mouth to her clit. Her feet try to push her body up off the bed but I hold her down. I’m not letting her get away. Not again.

Chapter 26

Hadley

I'm happy.

That's all I can say about how my life has gone the past six weeks. Though Ryder and I haven't slept together again since the "second first time", we still continue to get to know one another all over again.

We've caught up on pretty much everything that we've missed out on the past seven years. We haven't spoken any more about what separated us in the first place, but we've talked about the miscarriage a little bit. He feels terrible for not being there for me but if I wouldn't have run away then maybe he would have. I feel guilty at times for that. He's also told me stories about Emie and her devious ways and her quest to get in his pants. Before last month, I wouldn't have believed him but hearing her with my own ears at the vicious things she told him I don't put it past her.

Besides all the drama, Ryder and I are going strong. He says Braden is not bothering him at work too much, and I've been busy planning another wedding. After the Christmas party, Noelle has given me more responsibility, and I'm actually starting to come into my own with my job.

Sure, I'd love to work in a job where I can paint all day but right now I'm content with where I am. My work life is going well and my personal life is too. Ryder and I are dating but have yet to have the "are we exclusive" conversation. I'm not seeing anyone and I'm sure he isn't but I know that talk has to come soon. I just feel as though we are taking things slow and finding ourselves again.

It's Saturday, a week before Valentine's Day and I'm standing outside of my apartment, on the curb, waiting for Ryder to pick me up. He comes into the parking lot and I can't help but skip to his car. He jumps out, running over to my side and opens the door, before pulling me in for a deep kiss. My toes curl and all I want to do is take him back upstairs.

The "no sex" thing isn't something one of us just decided on. We just have been trying to focus on ourselves and not the physical part of us.

I sit down in the passenger seat, adjusting my light coat for the unseasonal warmer weather, and I pull my seatbelt on.

When he gets in, he pats my knee and pulls out onto the street.

"Did you have a good morning?" I ask pulling the sun visor mirror down and applying some chapstick.

His fingers glide along my cheek. "It's much better now."

He drives towards the city and I look around confused. "I thought we were going to indoor skydiving?"

Ryder and I have been regulars there. We go every weekend and I'm starting to become a pro at it. I managed my first flip in the air last weekend. He keeps mentioning that he wants to take me skydiving from the actual sky in the spring and is using this to ease my mind a bit. I want to be tough and say "let's do it" but just thinking about it makes me sick.

His fingers reach over and lace with mine. "Not today, Spark. I have a surprise."

I don't ask any more questions knowing that he won't answer them anyways and enjoy the calm ride to downtown Chicago with our hands intertwined.

When he turns down a one way street I take in the environment. The buildings are close together and rise up ten stories, which isn't much for the skyline.

His car pulls to an open space on the curb and my confusion deepens. He steps out, walking around the car to my side and opens the door, helping me out.

I lean my head back looking up as far as I can and am jolted when he tugs on my hand.

"Where are we?" I question once we step inside a building.

He turns around to face me just short of the first set of steps and lifts his fingers to secure my face–the deep ocean color of his eyes burn deep into mine. "I love you, Hadley. I never stopped, and

I hope one day to hear those words said back to me when you're ready. But right now, I want to show you how much I know you. How happy I can make you and what life would be like with me."

"Ryder..."

"No." He stops me. "Listen. I want to show you what it's like to be free and how you can do that with me beside you."

Without another word, he drops his hands and grabs a hold of me taking the steps up ten flights. His words sink in. That was the second time I've heard him say he loves me in as many months. My feelings for him have hit me like a freight train the past couple of weeks. I love him but I'm scared. Scared to fully let him back in even though everything I ever thought I knew about us was wrong. It's hard to unguard your heart so quickly after finding out it didn't need to be in the first place. I watch as he takes step after step and smile. I think I could love us again.

By the time we get there I'm almost out of breath.

The door swings open and I'm met with the February sunshine on top of the building's roof. He motions for me to walk through the doorway first and I take steps onto the concrete. It's empty but the view is stunning. In the distance, I can see the Chicago skyline towering over the rest of the city. Lake Michigan behind it a crystal blue. It's an amazing view.

"This is beautiful," I tell him.

His arms wrap around me from behind and he whispers in my ear, "Not as beautiful as you."

I bring my hands up and lay them over his. "I love my surprise."

He turns my body slowly one hundred eighty degrees to a bare brick wall. "No," he says kissing my ear. "This is your surprise."

I turn in his arms looking at him face to face. "I don't understand."

Nodding towards the wall he smiles wide. "A sea of blue in the middle of the concrete jungle."

I gasp turning back to the wall. No. Not a wall. A canvas. "I get to paint this?"

His lips find the crease between my neck and shoulder. "Yes. It's all yours for one year. Paint whatever you want but I think an ocean would be beautiful."

A sea of blue in the middle of the concrete jungle I think to myself and remember the night I told him I wanted to do this.

"Your skin is soft," Ryder says caressing my arm as we lay on top of BG Hill, the high school make out spot. We've found a secluded place along the golf course.

On a clear night we can see the city lights all the way from here.

"I did shower today," I joke, turning in his arms to face him. "The city is beautiful."

His lips find mine. "Not as beautiful as you."

I laugh, shoving at his chest. "You always say that."

He falls flat on his back taking me with him so

I end up straddling his hips.

"You know what I want to do someday?" I ask knowing that he doesn't know the answer.

My hair is pushed back behind my ears with the gentlest of touches. "Hmm."

I look out back over to the city. "I'd love to paint the ocean on the side of a building."

When he doesn't say anything I glance back at him. He's looking at me lovingly. "Why's that?" he finally says.

"All of those buildings and concrete. I'd love to paint a sea of blue in the middle of a concrete jungle." I still, waiting for his response.

I know he tries to understand my passion for art and has been doing well in class over the past two weeks but for some reason it makes me nervous to tell him that.

"I think it would be amazing," he comments looking sincere.

I smile. "Really?"

"Of course. Anything you do is amazing."

My heart is beating rapidly underneath the hand that's on my chest. "You did this for me?"

He pulls me into him. "I'd do anything for you if it makes you happy."

"Ryder," I start but pause momentarily, my emotions taking over. My heart is filled right now–beating only for him. He did this for me because he knows me. Ryder knew it would make me happy. So, I tell him how I honestly feel. "I think I'm falling in love with you again."

Our foreheads touch and his eyes drift lower. His words coming out a whisper, "I don't want you to think it, Hadley. I want you to know it. I want you to tell me when you do."

I'm desperate to tell him that's how I feel but I have to be sure that when I do I'm positive. There is no room for getting hurt again. So I do the only thing I can to show how I feel. I tell him what I'm sure of. "I know that I want you," I say right before claiming his lips.

He doesn't hesitate to deepen the kiss, and I know that there is no mistaking what I want. Sliding my hands over his jacket, he allows me to push it all the way down off his shoulders. His hands find my hips, and he doesn't hesitate to unbutton my jeans. I don't care that we're outside. I don't care that it's only forty degrees. All I care about is having him inside me. I need to feel that physical connection.

He pushes me up against the wall, my wall, and drops down to his knees to slide my zipper down and my pants follow. I step out of them and reach for his jeans doing the same but taking his boxers down with them. His rough hands grip me underneath my thighs, and he lifts me up, pinning me against the harsh brick, my legs instantly wrapping around his waist. A finger delves into my panties from underneath and he pushes them aside easily slipping inside me.

I'm filled to the brim with Ryder at this moment, and I feel as though all is right in the world. My skin vibrates with each slow thrust into me.

"How'd we go a month without doing this again?" He growls quietly in my ear pushing harder inside me.

I moan. "I don't know."

His lips crash to mine and his tongue lashes me with heat and desire. His slow movements have turned erratic like he can't get enough of me. I know I can't get enough of him. I hold onto his shoulders with all my strength as he pounds into me, my ass scraping against the rough surface.

The sound of a door opening and closing startles me and Ryder slows his pace but doesn't stop. "They can't see us, Spark, and if they could I wouldn't fucking stop."

My head falls back, hitting the wall behind me, and I allow him to continue giving me the pleasure my body craves from him. I wouldn't care if they saw us either. I feel the buildup start at my toes and allow myself to relax and let it wash all over me.

"I can feel you tightening, Had. Are you going to come?" He pulls away and I look as he stares deep into my eyes–my soul.

I bite my lip to keep from screaming out and nod. Leaning in, his teeth clamp down on my bottom lip and pull so that it frees it from my grasp. "I want to hear you, Hadley. Don't hold back."

His words fuel me and I whimper. His pounding is relentless now and all I can feel is the start of an intense orgasm. I constrict around his hard as steel dick and a wave of ecstasy rolls over me. I lose control, digging my fingernails into his t-shirt clad back, positive I'm drawing blood.

"Fuck," he yells as he gets harder inside me

and stills allowing himself to come.

His head falls to my shoulders, our breathing rapidly calming. I finally lift my head to glance around the rooftop finding that no one is around.

Maybe we scared them off.

Ever so slowly he pulls out of me and lowers me to the ground. “How did that feel, Spark?”

The sun shines brightly on my face. “Free,” I tell him, smiling.

He smiles back. “That’s how I always want to make you feel.”

When we are finally decent we turn around to face my wall again. “Hadley, I have to tell you something.”

Dread consumes me. After the blissful moment we just had I feel like he is about to shatter my world. I face him, bracing myself for a blow. “I don’t like those words.”

He pulls his hands down over his face and when they drop to his side he says, “I didn’t use a condom.”

I just stare at him as he waits for my response.

When I don’t answer he continues. “I lost myself and I’m sorry.”

I step up to him, grabbing him behind his neck and pull his mouth to mine. “It’s okay. I’m on the pill.”

His words blow over my lips. “It was irresponsible regardless. I should have been more careful.”

This is a side of Ryder I have never seen

before. The side that isn't confident and cocky.

"It's fine." I promise, kissing him. "I take it daily at the same time. It's ninety nine percent effective."

He sighs. "What about the other one percent?"

"Well," I step back from him, grabbing onto both of his hands, "let's not worry about it unless we have to."

I start to walk to the door but he pulls back on me. When I turn I find his expression serious yet sad. "I may be naïve to how it all works but I do know that I don't want you to go through what you did back in high school without us being on solid ground. I know we still have a lot of work to do."

I think about it for a moment as he pulls me in for a hug. His words are caring. He wants us to be strong before we have to deal with such a major situation like that. "I understand," I tell him. "Relationships aren't easy and we don't need anything big happening to put us under stress."

I can feel his head shake above me. "That's not it, Hadley. I wouldn't mind if you got pregnant but I would hate if we had to go through something like that again. I don't ever want to see you hurt. Never again."

At this moment I realize that I know. He wants nothing more in this world than to make me happy. It's always been that way. If I were to erase the day under the bleachers and think about how he treated me I would have seen it before. Ryder lives to make me happy and he doesn't want me hurt. I feel the same for him. I know now that I love him.

Chapter 27

Hadley

Valentine's Day has never meant that much to me in the past. By the time it rolled around during Braden's and my relationship we had already been dating for a while and had been on plenty of normal, casual ones. But today is different. Today I'm going on my first official date with Ryder.

Sure we've been out, gone places, and done things with other people but this is the first time he asked me out on an official date and I'm over the moon with excitement.

Since he gave me my wall last week, which I have yet to paint, I've been walking on cloud nine. There have been a couple of times where I have wanted to tell him that I love him over the phone or when we have lunch together but I've been waiting for this day, Valentine's Day, to tell him.

I've been stressing all week about what to wear and Noelle decided to take me to Macy's to pick something extra special out. It's not really in my budget but I pulled some extra cash out of my savings account to splurge a little bit.

As we walk through the women's section I grab things that I think might look good on me or things that I think Ryder would like.

"Don't look at the price tags, Hadley." Noe chastises when I take a glance at a soft pink dress that would fall just above my knees. I automatically put it down when I find it costs more than what I make in a week.

"I can't help it." I sigh, picking up another dress trying not to look. "I've always been conscious of what I'm spending."

She smiles devilishly as she grabs an emerald green colored number and shows it to me.

My mouth drops open at how stunning it is. It is much shorter than the pink dress I was just looking at and has a deep neckline that plunges so far down I'm sure I will be showing ample cleavage. The material scrunches at the waist on one side and flows freely down.

"I think this would look amazing with your eye color, Had. You have to try it on." She throws the dress into my hands.

Holding it up to my body I pull here and there making sure I don't take it into the dressing room and find it doesn't fit. When I'm sure it will, I lay it over my arm and continue my search.

"Ugh." Noelle moans. I look over and find her hunched over.

I quickly make it to her side and bend down. "Are you okay?"

Shaking her head side to side she waves me off.

"Yea, just not feeling well lately. I'm hoping this isn't a stomach bug coming on."

After a moment she stands up. "You sure you're okay?" I ask.

"Yes." She stares at me annoyed. "Can you try the damn dress on?"

I laugh off her abrasiveness and look around for a dressing room. Finding one in the back corner I let the lady know I have one item to try on. I hope it fits because I don't feel like looking for more. I already know the bra and panty set I'll wear underneath and imagine him using his teeth to pull them off. I've been craving him inside me all week.

She hands me my number and Noelle says she needs to use the restroom for the third time today, so I walk towards one of the many open rooms.

Immediately I hear commotion coming from the first one on the right. I blush as I listen to the female who is obviously talking to a male. "I've missed this." She breathes out, desperation in her voice, and I start to feel like I'm intruding on a private moment. I jump back when the door flies open and a red faced Ryder steps out. His shirt wrinkled and lipstick on the side of his face.

When he sees me his eyes grow wide with surprise. We both look as the girl comes out from the room and I instantly feel sick as Wendy steps out wiping the smears of lipstick off of her mouth. I drop the dress in my hand and start running trying to keep the tears at bay. I can hear him screaming my name but I run as fast as I can. When I find a bathroom on the bottom level I go into the handicap stall and slam the door shut, locking it behind me.

I listen, hoping Ryder doesn't come in and find me but when a few minutes pass and he never enters I slump down onto the floor and let the tears fall.

I can feel my phone ringing in my purse but I refuse to look. I don't want to talk to him.

How could he do this to me? And with Wendy of all people.

I feel sick to my stomach as I recall all the times that he's told me they hung out. It's like a knife is twisting in my gut and I can't breathe.

Then everything that has happened over the past couple of months starts to flash before me. The persistence. Ryder trying to win me back. The party. The indoor skydiving. My fucking wall he bought me.

Why would he do all that? I can feel my heart shattering all over again but this time it's much easier to break because I guess it was never really mended.

As I sit on the bathroom floor in a department store I realize what the hell I'm doing. I'm crying over someone who never really cared about me.

No.

Fuck this.

I'm a strong person and I refuse to let hurt define me. Not anymore.

Fuck him.

Fuck Wendy.

I'm free now and I won't let this bring me down.

I pull myself together and take my phone out of my purse. I see eighteen missed calls from Ryder as well as five texts from him. I delete them all without looking and hit the missed call from Noelle and dial her up.

"Where the hell are you?" she yells into the phone. "I need to go home. I threw up and I feel like shit."

I wipe a renegade tear from my eye and fix the smudged mascara in the mirror. "I'm ready to go. I'll meet you at the car."

With my shoulders straight and my head held high I walk back into the store and make my way to the exit not giving a shit if Ryder sees me.

When I walk outside into the crisp air I find Noelle waiting at my car, shivering. "Hurry the fuck up, bitch. I'm cold and I feel like shit."

I jog over unlocking her door and sliding into my side. When the heat is turned on she pivots in her seat to face me. "I'm assuming the dress didn't fit?"

All thoughts of being strong disintegrate with that one question and the tears start to stream down my face once again. Noelle pulls me into her and I relay what happened. Besides her few choice words for Ryder she just comforts me and tells me everything is going to be okay.

"I was going to tell him I loved him today!" I yell hitting the steering wheel.

She rubs my arm up and down gently. "You love him, huh?"

I look at her square in the face. "No. I fucking hate him, Noelle. I hate him."

After I got home, I showered and crawled into bed. I've spent the entire night avoiding Ryder's calls and texts and hiding in my room reading while he bangs on the door. He hasn't once tried to use the key he never gave back to Noelle but even if he did the chain on the door will deter him.

When midnight hits he seems to give up and I attempt to fall asleep.

A few days later, hundreds of declined calls from Ryder and just as many unread texts, I am on my way to Erin's house for her daughter's first birthday party. I was invited by Noelle so I could get out of my house. Working from home Thursday and Friday I was able to avoid any run-ins with Ryder and today I need to see something besides the four walls inside my house.

I don't know why going to a one year olds birthday party is a great idea right now but it seems to be taking my mind off of my situation. Besides us all celebrating Savannah's birthday both Erin and Noelle told everyone they were pregnant. Well Erin told everyone for Noe as well. She hadn't even told Trent yet.

I smile as I watch Trent and Walker's excitement over having new babies in the house and I feel a brief moment of sadness wondering if I will ever have that. I'm trying to remain strong despite the roller coaster that is my life but it's becoming increasingly hard.

When I can't take all the happy couples anymore I decide to get some fresh air outside.

I instantly regret it when I find Ryder leaning up against my car outside.

"I knew you had to come out eventually," he says, his arms crossed over one another. "I'm just glad I didn't have to wait too long."

Any other time I would think he looked sexy but right now all I can see is red. Just like the lipstick he had on him the other day.

"Leave, Ryder," I turn to the house, "and don't come back."

My words come out harsh but all I feel is a pull to him. A draw so strong that even in my deepest sadness and anger, I still want to be near him. My heart is elated that he is here but my head is angry.

In a flash he is on me, grabbing my wrists in his hands.

"What you saw..." He growls and even though I'm pissed, his aggression is turning me on. "It wasn't at all what you think. I was trying to be nice and help her shop while I was trying to pick something out for you and she attacked me. She's having a hard time with AJ. I threw a couple of nice words her way and she tried to get me to give her something I wasn't willing to give her."

I laugh mockingly. "Sure, Ryder. You couldn't push her off of you?"

His forehead falls to mine. "I did. That's what you saw. She pushed herself on me and I pushed her away. I got ambushed!"

"Yea, just like Bridgette in high school, huh?" I spit out. "I bet I misunderstood that too! That wasn't what it looked like either"

"You disappeared, Hadley! You didn't give me a chance to explain. To tell you it wasn't what you thought," Ryder says, his lips so close they brush against mine with his words.

"Bullshit, Ryder. You promised you would never hurt me. I was seventeen for Christ's sake!" I yell back. "I loved you!"

Without warning his lips are on mine as he pushes me into the garage door. I writhe against him letting all the hurt I feel supply my strength but it's no match for his.

I give in, letting my hormones take over. My body craves his, and I can feel his craving mine. This kiss is explosive, and it tells me everything I needed to know.

He's here.

He's fighting for me.

He's telling the truth.

I know he is.

We're startled when we hear someone approach.

Both of us look over and find Trent, Noelle's husband, watching us.

"I'm so sorry," he says. "I thought someone got hurt. Looks like you're just fine."

He leaves us there, breathless, and I find Ryder's eyes.

I shove off of him. "I have to go," I say and run to my car, leaving a stunned Ryder in the driveway.

I believe him. I know I believe him but I just need to clear my head.

Chapter 28

Hadley

It's finally five o'clock on Monday and after a long day I can finally go home. This past weekend has drained me and after leaving Ryder at Walker and Erin's house I feel too embarrassed to call him back.

I saw it in his eyes. It's what I would have seen if I stayed to confront him back in high school. Genuine honesty and the upmost love for me and I probably blew it. I've been racking my brain unsure how to go about fixing this.

My gaze watches my feet take each step, bringing me closer to my car parked on the street.

"Hadley," a seemingly familiar voice calls my name and I lift my head up surprised at who I find.

Wendy.

I pull my keys out of my purse. "Go away, Wendy."

She steps in my way, blocking me from the driver's side door. "No."

My eyes lift to hers and she falters for a brief moment at the threatening stare I give her. "Move."

Both hands come up in surrender. "One minute. Just one minute and I will leave you alone. I promise."

I sigh, looking up to the heavens for peace and the patience not to slap this woman. When I take three calming breaths I lower my head. "You have one minute."

"AJ has a girlfriend or at least I think he does," she starts quickly, rushing out every word. "A pretty one at that and it's tearing me up. It was Valentine's Day and I was feeling sorry for myself and I just did the wrong thing."

I snort. "No fucking kidding."

"You have to know how sorry I am." She pleads. "And Ryder pushed me away. It was stupid and inconsiderate. I didn't care about anyone else's feelings, only my own. I had to make this right, though. I had to come here and tell you so you would believe him."

She stops talking for a moment, allowing me to think about her words.

"I already believe him, Wendy, I didn't need you to come and seek me out." I cross my hands over my chest. "Now move please."

"He won't talk to me anymore, Hadley. I don't blame him but before I met Ryder I was flying through life, sleeping my way around and I had no friends. He's all I had until he introduced me to AJ, Jace, and Valerie. I felt like maybe I didn't have to be lonely anymore. Now he won't talk to me. I've lost them all."

I shake my head side to side in disgust. “Is that why you’re here? So I can fix things for you?”

Her eyes fill with tears that threaten to fall down her cheeks at any moment. “No, of course not. I came because I know how much he loves you and I know you love him too. I needed to fix this.”

The tears fall and I can’t help but feel bad for her. “Do yourself a favor, Wendy. Get off of your ass and tell AJ how you feel before it’s too late.”

She nods and turns to walk away but I grab her and pull her in for a hug. “Thank you,” she mumbles into my shoulder.

“No problem but just so you know,” I step away from her, “don’t you ever touch my man again or I’ll make sure you won’t be able to use your hands for weeks.”

She nods quickly. “Never again. I promise.”

I watch as Wendy walks down the sidewalk but call her back before she is out of earshot. “Wendy! You need to tell AJ.”

She smiles and continues to walk away.

~~

I speed down the street ready to get home and take a nice long hot bath but my thoughts drift. I don’t know how I’m going to go crawling back on my hands and knees to Ryder. The image has my body tingling.

I must have been too distracted because as I get through the last red light I find flashing ones behind me. I hit the steering wheel, upset that I’m about to get a ticket and pull over into a neighborhood.

When I've parked, I lean over and grab my insurance cards out of the glove compartment and wait for the officer to come to my now open window.

It takes a few minutes before he is leaning down asking for my license. I hand it over and wait, tapping my thighs nervously. He hasn't told me why he pulled me over but I know I couldn't have been going that much over the speed limit.

"Ma'am," he calls into the window. "I'm going to need your keys."

Confused I turn the car off, pull them out of the ignition, doing as he says, and place them into his waiting hand.

He jingles them in his hands before saying. "She's all yours."

My body fuels with rage as I hear the next words come from that all too familiar voice. "Thanks, man. I'll take her from here."

I jump out of the car, ready to give the officer a piece of my mind for pulling me over just for Ryder's benefit but I'm met with a chest of steel. His hands come out to steady me.

"Where you going, Spark?" His menacing voice shoots shockwaves through my body as his grip tightens around my arms.

My back hits the car as I pull out of his grasp. "You have some nerve doing what you just did."

The blue of his eyes darkens to black and in an instant I'm spun around and my hands are trapped behind my back. Cold, hard, steel circles my wrists as he places handcuffs around them.

“Now these aren’t my police issued handcuffs but they do the job. So don’t struggle too much,” he warns and it’s so fucking hot.

The past couple of months have been nothing but loving to hate him and right now I would love to bow down on my knees.

I am most certainly not thinking with my head right now.

~~

I’m gently placed onto Ryder’s bed, my hands still secured behind me.

“I would have taken you to your house but I like home field advantage,” he tells me as he places his watch down onto his dresser. His slow, methodical walk back towards me sending shivers down my spine. “Now, let’s start.”

Feeling around I try to find a latch that will free me. “Isn’t this kidnapping, Ryder?”

He stands in front of me, his jean covered pelvis just six inches from my face, and he looks down, grabbing my chin up towards him. “I’m tired of you running, Hadley. You’re not leaving until I’ve convinced you that my heart only beats for you and then once I’ve done that I’m going to fuck you until I’ve fully satisfied your body.” His fingers lower to my cleavage. “I can tell, even mad, how turned on I’m making you.”

He’s right. My tight nipples poking through my shirt are giving me away.

“You want to be free, correct?” he asks me, leaning down to kiss the side of my mouth.

I can only shake my head yes because I’m

afraid to talk.

He leans down on the carpet, settling himself between my legs, allowing the hem of my skirt to push up and the moisture in my panties to accelerate.

"Stand up," he commands and without hesitation I comply.

My knees go weak as his mouth is now mere inches from my core. There are just two layers of material preventing them from colliding.

His eyes pierce mine as he stands up slowly and wraps his arms around me to fidget with the cuffs. One of my hands breaks free but he grasps both of my wrists firmly before I have a chance to move them. With a slow menacing growl he says, "Don't fight me, Had."

In an instant he brings my hands in front of me and quickly cuffs them once again.

"Put your hands around my neck," Ryder commands and when I do he lifts me up by my thighs and carries me up the bed until I'm laying flat on my back. He reaches into the nightstand and pulls out a second set of handcuffs and before I realize what he is going to do he clasps them onto the middle of the ones around my hands and secures them to his wrought iron headboard.

I yell out in shock, tugging as hard as I can to free myself but it's no use.

"Unlock these now, Ryder," I warn but he just laughs as he slides back down my body, stopping between my legs.

I try to kick but his hands hold my thighs down. "Don't move, Spark." He growls. "I already have your arms tied up. Don't make me secure your legs too."

If I wasn't wet already I'm dripping now. I'm debating on if I want to move or not because the thought of him tying the rest of me down has me completely keyed up.

My eyes fall to his and a knowing smirk is plastered on his face. "I'm only going to say this once," he whispers, his heated breath piercing through the thin material of my skirt and panties. "Wendy means nothing. You mean everything."

His head dips down and he kisses me just above my pubic bone. "Everything." He repeats and his hands push my skirt up over my waist.

I'm left feeling exposed and vulnerable. He can do anything he wants but I know if I ask him to stop he would. I just can't bring myself to do it. I want his mouth on my bare skin.

"Ryder," I call out.

"I can hear it in your voice, Hadley. You want me but I need to make sure you believe me." His eyes look to me, pleading. "There is a fine line between lust and love–but an even finer line between love and trust. I need you to trust me. It's only ever been you."

His lips place slow, gentle, sensual kisses on my hips and tears prick at the sides of my eyes. Noelle's words creep back in. *"You can be in love, you can find him sexy as well but until you can believe what they say without question then you know it's for real."*

When I don't answer he says, "I'll make Wendy explain it to you." He pleads, not knowing she already has, his head falling to my stomach. "Hadley, I know what it looked like but please believe me when I say that I didn't want any of that. I never have. She has known from the first day that I've been in love with you. I'll do whatever it takes to make you realize how much."

I take a deep breath–ready to take the plunge. "I believe you," I clearly say and because I don't think I can ever live without him again I add. "And I love you too."

In a flash, his head lifts up and his body comes to rest as it hovers above me. "You believe me?"

I chuckle bringing my knees up and around his hips. "I just said I love you and you ask me that?"

His pelvis grinds in between my legs and I can feel how much he wants me. "I've known you loved me for much longer than you have, Hadley. I don't think you ever stopped but I need you to trust me. If you trust me I know we will work. This can work."

"I trust you." I wiggle beneath him. "Now please kiss me," I request.

He lips draw closer just before claiming mine. I try to reach down but my hands are still handcuffed to the rails. I can feel him smile when he realizes what I'm trying to do.

"I'm not releasing you, Hadley." He leans back on his haunches. "Not yet."

His firm hands grip my shirt and he pulls it apart, sending buttons scattering all over the floor. The cold air hits my skin and it prickles making my nipples so hard they could cut glass. Ryder smiles at the damage he's done and goes in for the clasp on the front of my bra. His eyes linger once my breasts break free. "So perfect," he comments, taking one in each hand and pinching the tight bud, hard. "I want to fuck these perfect tits, Hadley."

My breathing hitches and an image of him gliding his dick between my breasts has me writhing. "I'm obviously at your disposal," I tell him.

He stands up off of me and steps down to the side of the bed, pulling his shirt off and slowly pulling at the belt around his waist. "You're right. You are, aren't you? But I'll save those tits for another day."

I lick my lips and nod as he pulls his jeans and boxers down, springing his erection free. My legs involuntarily fall open, spreading me out for him. Walking around to the end of the bed he leans down, grabbing the top of my panties and pulls down, ridding me of them. Taking longer than usual, I watch as he just stares between my legs.

"I can see how fucking turned on you are, Hadley. I could probably pound into you right now and would slip right in with how slick you are."

I moan wanting him to just push into me and fuck me relentlessly. "Do it." I plead, my wrists pinching against the metal.

He reaches over, grabbing a pillow and places it beneath my ass so that when he is on his knees I'm at the perfect angle to...

"Oh, fuck!" I scream as he shoves himself into me and grabs onto my skirt for purchase. His pace quickens once he has the balance and within seconds I can feel myself bracing for an intense orgasm.

When I look up, Ryder's eyes are on mine, a drop of sweat falling down his temple and onto his cheek. "Say it again, Hadley."

For a second I'm confused, but then I realize exactly what he wants. "I love you, Ryder. I love you." I repeat over and over until I let the pleasure take over my body, and I scream his name out in release.

He leans forward, biting my nipple until he can no longer take it. He pumps into me three more times. "I'm going to pull out." He pants.

I egg him on, clenching my inner walls, and he loses it, pulling his cock out of me and coming all over my pussy. I can feel how hot his come is as he spreads it through my folds with his dick.

"That is fucking sexy," he comments while looking where we were just connected.

I pull on my restraints. "Can you take these off now? I think you've made your point.

"Hmm," he says eyeing his mark on me. "I don't think I have. In fact, I think I may need a few more hours to make sure you never run away from me again."

It's the big day. I can't believe it's finally here. I've been waiting over a year since Ryder asked me and my nerves are out of control.

I look at myself in the mirror one more time to make sure that my makeup hasn't run with all the happy tears I have cried today. I look outside the car and butterflies take off all over again.

I'm excited.

I'm happy.

But most of all I'm nervous.

My door swings open and my sexy boyfriend's hand reaches out to mine. "Let's go, Had. We don't want to keep them waiting," Ryder says with a megawatt smile on his face.

He takes my shaking hands into his and I'm instantly at ease. All I needed was his touch.

I climb out and look up at the sign.

"Spark of Arts" can be seen in big red letters

with a paintbrush and palate on the corner.

I shake my head in disbelief. "I can't believe I'm opening my own business today."

Ryder twirls me around and pushes me against the car. My knees go weak. "I can. I always knew you could do it."

He kisses me, a deep long kiss, and if it wasn't for us opening in an hour I would take him back to our place, or take him back inside, and ravish him.

Ryder and I moved in together last spring after he left the Buffalo Grove police department in search of any other one that didn't involve my ex. He was lucky enough to find room at the Wheeling PD. I packed up all my stuff out of my tiny apartment and brought it to Ryder's house. It not only has brought us closer together but since we were always sleeping at one or the other's house every night it just made sense. Plus it helped me save up enough money to buy this place.

He was the one who came up with the idea of opening my own art studio. Once he put the idea in my head I was on a roll with what it could entail and today is the grand opening.

I'm not only going to be living my dream and painting every day but I will be teaching others to do it too. Out of this little space I will finger paint with kids, do wine and paint nights with women and also rent out space to other artists.

To say I'm excited is an understatement. I couldn't have done it without Ryder.

"I love you so much," I tell him as I turn the key and unlock the door.

"I love you too," he says kissing my bare

shoulder.

I walk in and my eyes go wide as I take in the huge painting that wasn't there last night when I did my final walk through. My hands fly to my chest taking in the beauty before me.

In bold, vibrant colors looks to be a teenage boy and a teenage girl kissing on a blanket underneath a dozen booming fireworks. They both resemble us, the boy with dark hair and the girl with long flowing brown hair. They're wearing the same clothes Ryder and I wore the night we kissed at the family fest. Next to them is a burning fire and a picture of spin art with initials "RB & HB Forever."

"HB?" I question looking back to him. "My initials are HC."

My eyes never leave his as he grabs my hand from my chest and lowers himself down on one knee.

Oh my God.

"I'm hoping to change that." He reaches into his pocket, pulling out a black box. "Hadley, since the day I laid eyes on you in high school you are all I've ever thought about. Your drive to live life, the way you love and trust me unconditionally allows me to be who I am with no question. I long to keep you for the rest of my life. I want to wake up to your smile every day. I want to have crazy, amazing children with you and watch them bring our grandchildren over to our house so we can spoil them rotten."

My breath hitches as the tears start to fall desperately to the floor.

"I want to watch you paint naked and burn the house down when you try to cook. I want to be your first, your last and your eternity. Will you please do me the honor of becoming my wife?"

"Yes!" I scream not hesitating for a moment and pull him up to his feet. I jump into his arms and he swings me around until he grows dizzy and falls to the tile.

As I straddle him, he opens the black box and takes out the ring. I lose my breath, stunned at its beauty. He slips it on, and it fits perfectly. I admire the round cut diamond on top of a white gold band with smaller diamonds all the way around the band.

"It's beautiful," I tell him, admiring it from afar and then leaning in to kiss him.

He pushes my hair aside and behind my ears. "You're beautiful, Spark. The ring pales in comparison."

I lean back, blushing at the compliment and stand up. He follows and turns me around, circling his hands around my waist and we stare at his painting.

"Did you really paint this?" I ask hoping I don't offend him.

I feel his body move with his silent laugh. "Yes, but I had a lot of help."

A few hours later the studio is filled with all of those I love. My mom is in the corner hugging Ryder's mom. After Ryder and I officially got together they started doing monthly lunch dates. I smile at their interaction. They seem to have become the best of friends.

When I find Ryder, he is trapped against a wall. I watch as my dad towers over him and pokes a few fingers in his chest. Ryder says something to him and my dad smiles, bringing him in for a hug.

Ryder walks over to me and I can't help but chuckle. "What was that about?"

"Nothing." He shrugs nervously, making me laugh even harder. "Just some good old fashioned threatening."

"Hadley, this place is amazing!" Noelle says, interrupting us, while holding her daughter Charlotte in her hands. The baby has green and purple paint all over her and Noelle. "Charlotte is having a great time!"

I smile at how much Noelle has changed. Long gone are the days of washing everything down the minute it gets dirty. She gets right there in the mud along with both Charlotte and Jason. That doesn't mean other aspects of her life aren't in perfect order.

"Thank you." I accept the compliment.

"Of course, but I'll miss you at the office." She brings me in for a three way hug and pulls quickly away. "Now to take the little ones to Mama Decker's house so Daddy and I can practice making another one of these cute things."

I roll my eyes. Those two still act like teenagers.

"I'm so proud of you," Ryder says wrapping his arms back around me and places his chin on my shoulder.

We look out into the large crowd filling the small space and I can't help but start to tear up.

"We did this."

My life is finally coming together. I'm with a man I love, engaged to be married, living my dream of painting each and every day. He took me skydiving, cliff diving and parasailing last summer and I'm officially addicted to the rush. There is nothing else I could possibly want.

I feel free.

"So," my mother starts. "When are you giving us some grandbabies?"

I look at her astonished as she stands there with Ryder's mom. "Mom!"

When the studio closes after a very successful day I take a few minutes to admire the stunning ring on my left hand while standing in front of his painting.

"Come on." Ryder pulls me from my gazing towards the back room.

I follow but run into the back of him as he abruptly stops.

"This is my favorite wall." He looks up at the brick wall that runs along the side facing the street. It gives the place a unique touch.

"Why?" I ask.

Lifting me up by my thighs he turns to push me against it. "Because I dream of fucking you hard against it."

"Just like the day you bought my wall on the rooftop?"

I went back a few weeks later and painted my

sea of blue in a concrete jungle. After Ryder saw it, he put a down payment on it for the next five years.

He smirks at my memory of that day and I give him a bored look.

His eyebrows scrunch. "You didn't like it?"

I bite down on my lip and seduce him with the lust in my eyes. "A little."

"Well, you only need a little spark to start a forest fire," Ryder says just before taking my lips and claiming his fiancée's body–repeatedly.

The End

You can find me on Facebook at
www.facebook.com/authoramymarie
www.tsu.co/authoramymarie
www.twitter.com/authoramymarie
Instagram: AuthorAmyMarie
Or
Email me at AuthorAmyMarie@yahoo.com

Acknowledgements

I always like to thank my husband and my children first. So many hours sacrificed for me to do something I never imagined I could do. You're love and support has given me the courage to put my heart out there for the world to see. Thank you so much. I love you.

Of course all of this wouldn't be possible without my best friend Valerie. You will always get an acknowledgement in my books because you get not only the good celebrations but also you help me through the struggles and I've struggled with a lot since I started writing book three. Thank you for being there and helping me through it all. You truly are the best friend a girl could ask for…even hundreds of miles away.

To the Twat Waffles. You know who you are and you know what you have done. Thank you for making me laugh when I was stressed out and loving my books. I heart you…hard. Really hard. Like up against the wall hard.

To Amy's AmyAzing Pimpettes. I'm so thankful for my little team that could. It's awesome to have 24 little PIMPS that don't slap me around and ask for their money. I wish to one day meet you all in person because you all make my life easier.

Wendy Shatwell. You've brought organization to my

chaotic life and for that I owe you a huge thank you. You don't hesitate when I need something and I still say you look like a sexy twenty-nine year old. Cannot wait to meet you next year.

Sara Eirew. I have told you so many times over the past couple of months that you are a blessing. You picked me up when I was down and made the new covers amazing. Thank you so much for you understanding and your patience. I don't know what I would have done without you.

Angel...as usual you tolerated my many many requests and I love you for it. Your work is beautiful. Thank you so much for putting up with me!

Kathy Krick...You. Make. Me. Look. Good. Without you I don't know if anyone would understand my ramblings. I'm so lucky to have been referred to you. Three books down and many many many more to go! Can't wait to give you a big hug in person some day!

Made in the USA
Columbia, SC
11 March 2025

54923663R00167